THE DECEPTION

BY
STEVEN J. WRIGHT

THE DECEPTION

By Steven J. Wright

Copyright © 2013 Steven J. Wright

Cover Design: Erica Weise

ISBN-13: 978-0989148689
ISBN-10: 0989148688

To the Creator of the Heavens and the Earth
The Alpha and the Omega
The King of Kings
The Lord of Lords

Dedicated to my son, Devon

Special thanks to those who helped make this book possible by reviewing it, offering suggestions, and giving advice:

(In alphabetical order)
Zack Browning
Doris Cothron
Melissa Holland
Dan Tankersley (co-author of "The Rain" & "The Tower")
Judy Tankersley
Amy Wright
Ann Wright
Rene Yancy (author of "A Secret Hope")

TABLE OF CONTENTS

In the Lord I take refuge;

how can you say to my soul,

"Flee like a bird to your mountain,

for behold, the wicked bend the bow;

they have fitted their arrow to the string

to shoot in the dark at the upright in heart;

if the foundations are destroyed,

what can the righteous do?"

Psalms 11:1-3 (ESV)

PROLOGUE

"VERY GOOD," proclaimed God, the creator of the heavens and the earth.

The six days of creation had come to a triumphant closure as God sat upon His throne and admired His creative work. On the newly formed earth below Him, a large continent teemed with the various kinds of animals He had created, each with its own unique characteristics. A vast blue ocean surrounded the land full of beautiful plants bearing fruit for all living things to eat. In the middle of the massive continent sat the Garden of Eden, a perfectly created paradise furnished with everything needed to sustain life. A mighty river flowed out from Eden, and from there it divided into four smaller rivers that meandered throughout the virgin landscape. God's greatest creation, Man and Woman, explored the garden, gazing at the beauty of the creation and living in peace with each other and the animals. As He rested in Heaven, God smiled at His work while a chorus of angels sang praises to their king. God's rest was soon interrupted by a nearby muttering voice.

"He thinks He is so great," said Lucifer, one of God's most beautiful angels.

Hearing Lucifer's comment, an angel named Othaniel turned to him and asked, "What do you mean? Of course God is great! It's His very essence."

"I could do it. I could make everything God made, but it would be much better. He wants all of the world to worship

1

Him and admire His creative power, but wait until you see what I can do," Lucifer boasted in a louder voice. Other angels heard him speaking and they formed a small crowd around him.

"If you did everything God has done and made it even better, I would serve you," said one of the angels in the crowd.

"I would do the same," said another.

"If you become greater than God, then I will serve you instead," said yet another angel.

Lucifer smiled as more angels gathered around and expressed their admiration and potential servitude to him. "You see God's throne? I will remove God from His throne and then I will be the one who sits there."

"Do it, Lucifer! Show us you power!" an angel shouted.

"I will go beyond the throne! I will rule over the earth and the entire universe! I will be like the Most High God, and everyone will worship me!" proclaimed Lucifer as the growing number of angels cheered him on.

One third of Heaven's angels had now gathered around Lucifer as he continued making his prideful remarks. They were encouraging him and even calling him "god." The other angels in heaven—those who had overheard the dangerous talk coming from Lucifer—backed away from the crowd, knowing that their King would not tolerate such pride and arrogance.

Having overheard all of Lucifer's proclamations and seeing the crowd of angels gather around him, God boiled with anger. The light emitting from His glory grew dim as dark, ominous clouds formed. Thunder shook and lightning struck as God got off His throne and approached the rebellious angel. Those who had been rallying around Lucifer stood behind him and shielded themselves from God. They shuddered in fear knowing they had done wrong, but having placed so much trust in the angel Lucifer, they had a glimmer of hope that he would save them from God's wrath. Lucifer stood firm and defiantly stared at his creator.

"I created you as one of the most beautiful angels," God declared in a booming voice. "I adorned you with the most precious of stones and gave you a position of authority, but you have let yourself become drunk with pride."

"All of the angels in Heaven once worshipped you," Lucifer said, staring intently at God. "But look; now I have this multitude prepared to serve me. Elevate my position to be equal to you. Give me a throne next to you so that I may also rule over your creation! I can be as powerful as you are and do everything you do! Can't you see how beautiful and great I am? Now make me greater!"

The angels behind Lucifer started to praise him for his beauty and power. They had now placed all of their trust in him, causing his ego to overflow.

"Because of your utter defiance, you have lost your place here," God said as he raised his hand. The angels who had not gathered around Lucifer shielded their faces with their wings to hide themselves from the coming wrath of God. With a thunderous rumble sounding from all around, a bright, thick lightning bolt shot out from God's hand. It encircled Lucifer and the angels with him and in a flash, the rebellious group was shot down to the earth in a violent bolt of lightning, forever losing their eternal residency in Heaven.

The angels along with their new found leader landed on the earth in a state of shock and confusion.

"What do we do now, master?" Othaniel asked Lucifer.

Lucifer looked up into the sky. Part of him wished he could go back to live in Heaven, but he knew that would never be allowed again. Lucifer had made a grave mistake and would never regain his favor with God. Looking around at the bewildered multitude that had fallen with him, he replied, "We don't need the King anymore. I am your new king, and this is our new home here on Earth."

"Will we never go back to Heaven?" an angel asked.

"Who would ever want to go back to that place and be around God? He thinks He is so great for making the universe, the earth, the animals, the plants…but we will show Him. Follow me! We will get back at God by destroying His most favorite creation—humans!"

"But," Othaniel interrupted. "How will we destroy them? Humans are made in God's image."

Lucifer laughed. "It's simple. We will deceive them through hollow philosophies and unfulfilling religions. Humans will want to worship God because of His creation, but we will spread throughout the world and deceive them through lies and half-truths. We will convince them that they were not God's special creation but instead an accidental formation from the earth. Then, when they are convinced that the lies are true, they will stop worshipping God and serve me! Come, we must destroy the very foundation of God!"

After proclaiming his plan of action, Lucifer led the angels into the world, making their first stop at the Garden of Eden, the earthly paradise.

CHAPTER ONE

"CREATION OR EVOLUTION? It really doesn't matter," read the bold and colorful text on the large projection screen at the front of the church. The digital revolution allowed for news and announcements to be displayed in graphic images thereby catering to the majority of people who had grown to learn things through visual aids rather than hearing or reading. Pastor Bill Watson took advantage of modern technology to announce each morning's sermon topic as well as to accentuate the highlights during his sermons.

Using the new high-definition cameras, Bill's image was cast onto all three projection screens as he approached the stage and started to discuss the announcements. Each word and graphic flashed upon the screens in an array of colors. His friendly voice coming through the surround sound in the auditorium was the universal cue, at least at The Experience Church, for everyone to find their seats and prepare for the morning worship service.

"Remember," Bill reminded as he began to make the final announcement, "this week we will start construction on the new multi-purpose building. I know you will all be very impressed with it, especially our youth. Everything about it will be hi-tech—digital surround sound, wireless networking, two projection screens on each wall, three new high-definition cameras, stage lights—I look forward to seeing how many people this new addition will bring in to our church. We are destined to have exponential growth!" Several in the congregation applauded.

"Are there any other announcements?" he asked, a common phrase repeated each week to signify that the worship service was about to start.

"I've got one!" Kate shouted excitedly as she stood up.

"What are you doing! I told you not to say anything!" Jeff snapped in a hushed voice.

Kate looked down toward Jeff and gave him a playfully devious smile, similar to the one she gave him when she threw a surprise thirtieth birthday party for him at his favorite restaurant. Jeff never liked to be surprised. Usually, he could foil his wife's attempts before her plans came to fruition. This, however, was one of those surprises he didn't catch in time.

"Well, don't keep us hanging," Bill said with a laugh. "What's the good news, Mrs. Duncan?"

By now every head in the church turned around to face Kate. Jeff's heart pounded in his chest as his face reddened. Always a humble person, he never wanted to draw attention to himself, especially if it pertained to his accomplishments. Sure, he had had many successes in life thanks to his strong determination and encouraging mother, but he wanted to avoid letting others know about them. He never wanted to feel superior to others. Jeff had met many people who were wealthier and more educated than him, and they all had a 'high and mighty' arrogance about them that was none too appealing. He made every effort to shy away from getting attention, but now, with every eye looking in his direction, this would be the day that the entire congregation would know Jeff Duncan.

"We got the good news on Friday that my Dr. Jeff was hired full-time as a biology professor at Grogan University!" Kate announced, looking back down at her husband as she beamed a proud smile.

Now even more embarrassed, Jeff didn't know what to do. Everyone turned their attention away from Kate and focused their eyes on him. They erupted in applause, and some of those sitting nearby said "congratulations" to him among various other accolades. *Everyone is looking at me. Do they want me to give a speech or something?* Jeff put his Bible on the empty seat next to him and stood up. He waved his hand and gave an awkward smile while trying to hide the embarrassment from being singled out among a group of over five hundred people in attendance this morning. Pastor Bill smiled at Jeff as he also applauded for him. His clap reverberated through the speakers, making the sound even louder. *Of all days, why did we have to sit in the very middle of the sanctuary in full view of everyone?* The congregation's applause gradually died down as everyone turned back around to focus their attention on the pastor.

After Jeff and Kate sat down, she wrapped both arms around him and squeezed. He forced a smile so that it wouldn't look like he harbored any anger toward her. Deep down he wasn't mad, but she did embarrass him.

"I specifically asked you on the way to church this morning not to say anything about my new job," Jeff whispered to Kate as she continued hugging him.

"I'm proud of you, honey! This is a great accomplishment," Kate replied as she let loose her grip. She remembered he had told her not to say anything, but sometimes Kate couldn't contain herself. "You've been without work since you graduated last spring. Those student loans aren't going to pay themselves off, you know." She patted him on the leg. Jeff's beet red face started to regain its usual color. "The church has been praying for you to get a job, and now you have one. It's only fair to let them know the good news and that their prayers have been answered."

"I guess you're right, but I'm the most humble person I know," Jeff said tongue-in-cheek. His way of letting Kate know he wasn't mad at her had always been to make a sly joke, but she didn't catch the pun this time.

7

"I'd like to welcome everyone to The Experience Church," Pastor Bill said. "Feel free to worship however you see fit. This is a church of freedom and individuality. Follow your spirit wherever it leads you as you experience God!"

The twelve-member praise band entered stage left and picked up their instruments. Stage lights lit up and flashed a sequence of colors as the guitarist started to strum with an upbeat tempo. Bill exited the stage to join his wife on the front row. In one swift movement, everyone in the congregation stood up in preparation for the worship service. A loud bass line pounded through the speakers adorning the wall, and the drummer beat the kick drum to match up with the fast tempo of the guitarist. Jeff didn't mind the music, but this part of the service often lasted for an hour or longer. The worship service had the atmosphere of a rock concert as the music played at an almost deafening decibel and the stages lights flashed about. No one else seemed to mind it though, but usually after the half-hour mark Jeff would start glancing at his watch and hoping that by chance the worship service would be abbreviated and they could start learning about God. To his dismay, the music always played on, and Jeff's mind would wander away into a world of daydreams.

Jeff had grown up in a rather conservative and formal church where people stood and sat down in unison. Loud rock music was unheard of in his former church that only had an organ and upright piano. The Experience had no similarities to the traditional church paradigm. During these long worship services, the congregation danced about as they sang the various praise songs. There was no order or structure, and this allowed the congregation to have a broad sense of freedom. A select group dubbed as the "spiritually evolved" had their own seating section near the front. Many wanted to have their coveted spiritual experiences that these elitists displayed. It was a proud title to be known as one of the "evolved," but just like social cliques, it took much time and effort for the "others" to be accepted into that group.

8

This special group had free range during the worship service and were often seen "praise jogging" laps around the auditorium during the songs. Jeff could not figure out how they could focus on the music and lyrics as they ran around the room trying to avoid collisions with others. On occasion a few of them would do acrobatics in the aisles as a form of worship. These weekly spectacles were unique and oftentimes distracting, but Jeff did not feel it was his place to tell people how to worship. *Are they worshipping God or themselves?* He sometimes made a game to see how many close-call collisions occurred among these free-spirits.

The band played on, performing several more songs at an upbeat tempo and then slowing down to a moderate speed. Jeff eagerly awaited the slower songs because he knew the worship service would soon be ending and he could sit down and rest his legs. The congregation appeared to be enjoying the long worship service, though. Many had gone to the front of the room near the stage and danced wildly, hoping to fit in and be accepted by the elite. They jumped about, swayed their arms high into the air, and occasionally, but accidently, hit people next to them. *This is just one fist fight short of a mosh pit.* Jeff stood with his hands clasped together as he silently mouthed the words displayed on the large projection screens. It was difficult to stay focused as his ever active mind continued to daydream.

When Jeff was growing up, he and his mother, Evelyn, had attended a small, non-denominational church called Everlasting Glory. This was one of those churches that basically had the same members—no one ever left the church except people like Jeff, who had to leave so he could pursue his college degree out of state. Most everyone who did leave for college or military service always found themselves back in their regular pew when they returned home. Membership rarely increased unless someone had a baby.

The congregation at Everlasting Glory watched Jeff grow from a young boy to a tall, handsome man, and they were all in attendance when Jeff and Kate held their wedding at the church three years ago. That was one of the few times Kate had been in a church as she had no religious background. Her parents didn't like church because they thought churches were full of hypocrites, and they didn't want young Kate exposed to people who were two-faced. Jeff's mother had told him that he should "find a good Christian girl" to marry. Kate was a good person even if she wasn't a Christian when they finally tied the knot. He didn't want to displease his mother, but sometimes love has a way of causing us to forget our roots.

After they married, Jeff wanted Kate by his side every Sunday at Everlasting Glory so she could learn about God. His desire was for his wife to join him one day in Heaven, and it was important for her to understand her need for a savior. Jeff himself knew most of the basics of the faith although he had many questions still unanswered.

The whole church setting was an uneasy experience for Kate. Her parents played a large role in causing her to form many misconceptions about church and its sharply dressed "pew fillers." Jeff knew about these things when they were dating, and he had hoped he would be able to change her negative perspectives. During their honeymoon phase, when the two young lovers were floating on the fluffy clouds of romantic bliss, Kate went to church with Jeff without any hesitation. She was glued to his side and eagerly excited to do anything with him. Kate sat and listened to the sermons, and she tried to sing the old hymns. However, as the honeymoon phase began to fade away, Jeff could sense that his bride no longer had the enthusiasm to come to church with him anymore. Kate had the skill of putting on a pleasant face when around other people at the church, but Jeff was quick to pick up on her charade. Something had changed. Her church attendance began to dwindle to the point that Sunday mornings became an argument between Jeff's asking Kate why she wasn't getting ready for church and Kate's giving ambiguous answers in reply.

As the slow music began, Jeff's mind wandered back to the argument he had had with Kate a few months after their wedding that finally led them away from Everlasting Glory and ultimately to The Experience:

"Why can't you give me a good reason for not going? You need to understand the Bible. It's important to me and it's important for your salvation," Jeff had told Kate one Sunday morning when she insisted on staying home.

"I don't even know what you mean, Jeff!" Kate angrily replied. "What is salvation? What does 'being saved' mean? Saved from what? Who or what is God? Jeff, I've been going to that church with you and listening to those monotone sermons for weeks, and I have no idea what the preacher is talking about! He doesn't even speak on my level. He uses all of those fifty-dollar words, and everyone seems to understand them, but I have no clue what he means. I have no religious background and feel completely left out from the crowd. None of it makes sense!"

They had never argued when dating, but Jeff and Kate had learned that marriage brought about many challenges, especially when there were disagreements over important issues. This was the first argument between the young couple after their wedding, and Kate had made a good point. She won that round. Kate didn't understand any of the things the preacher said, and after Jeff's failed attempt to give an answer to the questions she had, he came to the sudden realization that he didn't know much about his faith either. He just knew how to regurgitate what he had been told from the pulpit, Sunday School, and youth group all those years growing up, but he had never really taken the time to understand the foundational truths of what he had been taught. There were many theological concepts he did not understand although he did follow the simple "old-time religion" of repentance and faith in Jesus Christ.

After their argument that morning, they agreed to look for a more modern church where Kate would not only fit in with the crowd, but she (and Jeff) would have a fresh start at understanding their faith. They decided to skip church that morning and start looking that week for different churches to attend in their home city of Grayson, Tennessee. Jeff and Kate had breakfast that morning at their favorite mom-and-pop restaurant. As they waited in the lobby for an open table, a flyer on the nearby bulletin board caught Jeff's attention. It read:

"Are you bored of the same old church service? Are you tired of having to find the best suit or dress to wear each Sunday? Are you ready to put aside the old hymns and organs and praise God with modern music and a live band? Then come as you are to The Experience!"

Jeff showed the flyer to his wife, and to his surprise she agreed to give the church a try. On the following Sunday, they visited The Experience. Many people greeted them with genuine sincerity when they entered through the doors, and immediately Jeff and Kate felt as though they had come to the right place. The dress was casual—Jeff and Kate both felt awkward for wearing their Sunday best while everyone else wore jeans and sandals. The upbeat music performed by the band and the colorful sermon given by Pastor Bill that day gave more confirmation that they found the perfect church to meet their needs. Finally, it would no longer be a Sunday morning struggle for Jeff to get Kate to come to church with him.

The band finally stopped playing. Jeff glanced at his watch to see that forty-five minutes had passed. *That was quite a day dream.* The band members exited the stage and joined their families in the congregation. Those who were dancing in the aisles and near the stage turned back to their seats, and the stage lights transformed to a mixture of blue, red, and yellow lights. A spot light shined down at center stage.

Pastor Bill approached his lectern. "Open your Bibles with me to the first chapter of Genesis," he requested. "I want to talk to you this morning about the ongoing conflict between evolution and creation. It's causing some unnecessary separation in the church, so I'm going to show you this morning that there is a way we can make a compromise and put this problem behind us!"

"Amen!" shouted a man near the front. A few others shouted "amen" or "preach it" as though each person wanted to get their moment of attention. Everlasting Glory never had the "amen" type of congregation, but The Experience had a plethora of them. Sometimes Jeff would hear a person call out for no reason at all.

Bill Watson took over as senior pastor after Larry Watson, his father and the former senior pastor, was forced into retirement. Larry had been diagnosed with cancer of the esophagus. His health dwindled away, and just a few weeks after his untimely diagnosis, he lost his voice and could only whisper. Larry started the church over thirty years ago, back when a suit and tie were required. Larry never liked the idea of people dressing fancy just to come to church. He could never find a Biblical explanation for it, and he knew that many of those lost souls that he encountered during the week were not even able to afford nice clothes, much less food for their families.

Larry wanted his church to be different—something that would attract the rejects of society. Even Jesus spent time with the crooked tax collectors. Jesus also advocated for the poor and taught the early Christians to take care of them. Jesus' earthly ministry is what led Larry to give his church the name "The Experience." He wanted people to experience God's love first hand, and to also have a community of believers who joined together because of their faith, not because of their social status. He believed that church needed to be exciting in order to get people motivated to put Christ's teachings into practice. Larry opened up a daily lunch program at the church for the needy in the community. He also started a used clothing store where old clothes were donated and sold for a dime each. The church's community service programs and the modern style of worship and preaching are what sealed the deal for Jeff and Kate to know they were in the right place.

Although Larry had a passion for the destitute, his view on Biblical doctrine and theology was often brought into question. He had attended a very liberal seminary and earned a Masters of Divinity degree. Larry believed that having a liberal view of Christianity would bring more people to the Lord instead of a conservative "fundamentalist" view that could scare people away. Larry understood that the gospel message in and of itself offered hope, but it also confronted people about sin in their lives. Instead of offending people and making them uncomfortable each week, Larry presented the gospel in a way that made people feel good about who they were as children of God. There was some doctrinal truth in Larry's sermons, but for those who were new to the faith, they could not discern truth from heresy.

Some of his teachings were antithetical to the essential doctrines of the faith. Larry taught that repentance was not necessary for a person to enter into Heaven. He never preached on Hell, and he taught that all people on earth would eventually go to Heaven. He believed the Bible to be more metaphorical than literal, and the majority of the Old Testament was unreliable history. Although he preached from the Bible, he never held it in high regard and viewed much of it as erroneous and mistranslated.

Other pastors in the city of Grayson had confronted Larry about his liberal beliefs, some of which teetered on the brink of heresy, but Larry always had an answer to defend his theology. His answers were so quick and clever that those opposing him were unable to provide a reasonable response. He often appealed to the phrase, "that's just your interpretation" when other pastors confronted him about his questionable theology. These pastors were concerned that Larry's liberal view on sin and essential doctrines would create false converts. In the end, those who had been confronting Larry started losing members from their own congregation as they were drawn to The Experience through Larry's multiple methods of outreach.

Larry always wanted Bill to be a pastor and have a love for the Lord, and Bill excelled at following in his father's footsteps. Larry taught Bill everything he had learned in seminary. While most young children were playing sports or socializing with friends, Bill sat in his father's lap as he learned the Bible through his father's theology. Bill excelled in his understanding, and after attending seminary himself, he developed new ideas about God that even surprised Larry. After his diagnosis of cancer, Larry decided that Bill would be the perfect person to take his place. Bill, a forty-year-old spitting image of his seventy-year-old father, had always been active in the church, and everyone in the congregation already knew Bill would be the successor.

After his father's illness, which some of the other pastors had said was a judgment from God because Larry did not preach the truth, Bill took over the church. Continuing with the teachings he received from his father, Bill taught from a liberal understanding of scripture, and he also took the church to a new level of spirituality. He opened the church up to the long, experiential worship services that Jeff had now come to dread. Jeff's former pastor at Everlasting Glory always used Scripture when preaching his sermons, but Bill's preaching was based more on feelings and emotion rather than God's word. The topics were centered on elevating man, and just like his father Larry, Bill wanted to make people feel good about themselves. Doing so kept the attendance up and the offering plate full.

Bill's sermons typically lasted about fifteen minutes. The congregation had become accustomed to the short sermons, and it was guaranteed that if he went past his usual time limit, people started glancing down at their watches like ducks bobbing for food under the water's surface. The church had become more focused on the worship and having spiritual experiences instead of the sermons which, over time, had become so watered down that it was difficult to determine if Bill was preaching from the Bible or the latest self-help book. Bill could keep everyone's full attention, especially since he followed the "feel-good" theology of his father and satisfied the emotions of his congregation.

Bill continued with his morning sermon. "Now, you all know the story of creation. The Bible tells us that God created the earth, the animals, the plants, and the people all during the time span of one week. That's what the Bible tells us, at least, but this was written at a time when people were not as educated in science as they are today. The author of Genesis was more concerned with taking care of the sheep in his field than understanding where the sheep came from.

"There are some fundamentalists who take the creation account as literal history, but I think it's time we put these old, medieval teachings behind us and open up our minds to reality. Science says that life itself did not start in just one week, so why does the church keep hanging on to this old dogma? Doesn't that make us look like fools? My fellow Christians, I plead with you to listen to logic and reason. These scientists, just like Jeff, have more degrees than a thermometer. They study this stuff for a living, and I think the church should listen to what these scientists are saying.

"These fundamentalists claim that God made everything in six literal days, that the earth is only some 10,000 years old, and that evolution is completely false. Well, I have some questions for them: What about the dinosaurs? Haven't their fossils been dated to be millions of years old? What about the geologists who say the earth is billions of years old? There has to be a logical explanation to this! And thankfully, scientists have figured it out for us. While the Bible leaves us with many questions unanswered, science has come in and given us all the answers we need. Science says the universe came into existence from the Big Bang. Evolution shows that all life came from a common ancestor, and we humans descended from a common primate ancestor. Is there any problem with God using evolution to create everything? Maybe He did use evolution, or maybe life just happened on its own, and God intervened when man finally evolved. I can believe that and believe in Jesus at the same time. Who will join me?"

Bill casually walked off the stage as he began his closing statements. "Mere men wrote the Bible thousands of years ago. It's been translated over and over throughout the centuries, and we simply cannot know if everything it says is true. Some scholars say that Moses wrote Genesis, but he wasn't even born until centuries after the supposed creation week. How can we know Moses was correct? Where did he get his information? Most likely he adapted the creation story from pagan myths. See, all of the different nations back in Old Testament times had their various gods, and those nations had their own stories about creation. Moses probably didn't know how it all came to be, but by simply gathering bits and pieces of stories from the surrounding cultures and then throwing the Hebrew God into the picture, he was able to form a version the Israelites could easily understand. I can conclude, and I know you'll agree with me, that the story of creation is just that—a story. But just like the parables Jesus told, there is a lesson we can learn from the story. And that message is loud and clear—God is powerful and in control of our lives, regardless of His involvement in life's origins. We have to trust in Him and live a life that is pleasing to Him. Put your faith and trust in God. He watches us and protects us. And God has given each of us a brain, so it's time we begin to use it! Let's listen to the scientists and respect the work they do. Evolution in no way affects the message of the gospel. So let's put our myths and childhood beliefs aside and focus on following the Spirit of the Lord!"

After his closing statement, many people stood up and shouted "Amen!" Others clapped to show their approval. Kate joined in on the clapping, but Jeff sat perplexed as he tried to connect the sermon to the "God is powerful and in control" summarization. Others seemed to make the connection, but Jeff was left scratching his head. He had always been taught that the story of creation was an actual historical event. He had never studied the topic in depth but simply trusted what his Sunday School teachers told him.

Jeff studied extensively about evolution in school. He went to a secular university where evolution was always supported and never questioned. The other theories on origins, like intelligent design and Biblical creationism, were never opened to unbiased discussion. After several semesters of hearing the evidence for evolution, Jeff became convinced that the account of creation he was taught as a child was just a myth or moral story. But still, he had never heard a preacher refer to it as such. He had grown to respect Pastor Bill, and he usually agreed with the sermons he had heard from him ever since they started coming to this church over two years ago, but today was the first time he had ever heard any pastor cast doubt upon the reliability of the Bible. *If the pastor says it, then it must be true.*

The praise band came back to the stage and played a couple of closing songs. Afterwards, Jeff and Kate stood up to leave. Kate enjoyed socializing after church and was never in a hurry to go home like she had been at Everlasting Glory. She walked around the auditorium to meet her friends and acquaintances. Jeff, on the other hand, was more than ready to leave. He went to the lobby and waited by one of the church's coffee shops while his social butterfly made her rounds.

Greg Hudson, one of Jeff's few acquaintances, found Jeff alone and waiting impatiently. "Congratulations, Jeff! I didn't know you were a doctor," Greg said as he stretched out his hand.

"I'm not a doctor-doctor," Jeff explained with a sly smile. "I have a doctoral degree, which basically means I have been in school for the majority of my life and am now in debt until I retire."

Greg laughed. "Oh, I see. I barely finished high school myself. I couldn't imagine going to college. So, are you excited about your new job?"

"Yes, I am," Jeff said humbly. "I always wanted to be a teacher, and science has fascinated me ever since I was a child. This is just the type of career I wanted, and now I finally have my chance to do it."

"Today's sermon applied a lot to science," Greg commented. "Pastor Bill made some really good points. It's about time we hear a sermon that deals with the real questions we have. I've always wondered if evolution was true, and now I know for sure. Well, good luck in your new job!" Greg patted him on the back and then went outside as Kate came up behind Jeff and tried to scare him with a bear hug. He could never be scared easily, but he faked a shudder as though she caught him off guard.

"Are you ready to go?" Kate asked.

"Yes, it's time for our Sunday visit with you-know-who," Jeff replied with a smirk.

CHAPTER TWO

EVELYN CAUTIOUSLY approached the center of the living room. She stared curiously at the ceiling, turning her head slightly, and furrowing her brow as she listened to the strange conversation above her. An unidentified man and woman carried on an exciting dialogue for several minutes.

"This is ridiculous," Evelyn muttered to herself as she listened. "I need some peace and quiet in this house, and I'm not going to tolerate those people talking all the time. Ever since they moved in they haven't stopped yapping their mouths."

She went to her kitchen, grabbed a broom, and returned back to the living room. Using the end of the handle, she tapped several times on the sheet rock above her, causing small chips of paint to fall into her hair. "You people knock it off up there! Keep your mouths shut! I can't hear myself think anymore."

No response. The conversation above continued.

"You better listen to me!" Evelyn yelled. "I don't want you up there anymore. Get out and find another place to live!"

Her efforts had no effect.

Frustrated, Evelyn threw the broom down on the carpet and paced back and forth, muttering to herself. "I don't even know who they are. Maybe they were homeless and just needed a place to stay. Why they picked my house I'll never know." She glanced out the window as the noon sun cast its rays to the earth. Her treasured flower garden had wilted away as the unusually intense summer heat killed almost every type of seasonal vegetation. "It's awfully hot outside. I don't want to kick them out into the heat, but if they chose to live up there, they will at least need to get some fresh air and something to eat."

A loud knock sounded on the front door.

Evelyn turned to the door and before opening it, glanced up at the ceiling one more time. "I'll deal with you later," she muttered.

"Hi, Mom!" Jeff said as Evelyn opened the door. He wrapped his arms around his mother and gave her a hug.

"Come on in, Son," Evelyn exclaimed. Her bright blue eyes twinkled at the sight of her son as a warm smiled formed over her face. "Who is this you have with you?"

"My name is Kate. I'm Jeff's wi…friend," Kate said. Little by little, the people, places, and things of Evelyn Duncan's life faded away as the gray plaque caused by Alzheimer's disease took over her brain. Kate was fond of Evelyn and looked up to her as a mother figure. Her own mother died when she was a teenager, and after Kate and Jeff started dating, she was quickly drawn to Evelyn because she filled the void Kate's real mother had left. They formed a close relationship, and Evelyn even planned and organized Jeff and Kate's wedding ceremony. It was painful for Kate to feel forgotten by her own mother-in-law, but she understood this to be the nature of the disease and nothing more. She adapted to the routine of reintroducing herself to her Evelyn at each Sunday visit.

When Evelyn first forgot Kate's name, Kate made the mistake of reminding her that she was Jeff's wife. That innocent blunder resulted in Evelyn having a long and drawn out emotional breakdown. She could no longer remember Jeff's wedding, so the realization that he was married and Evelyn had no memory of that event made her come to the conclusion that Jeff had not invited her to the wedding. She cried for hours as she felt betrayed and forgotten. Had her memory been intact, she would have recalled that she attended the rehearsal, wedding, and reception. Kate never made that mistake again, and she concluded to always tell Evelyn that she was Jeff's friend, which, in reality, was the truth, because she had married her best friend.

As soon as they walked inside, Jeff couldn't help but gag at the familiar odor of his mother's home—garbage. Evelyn had started a habit of hoarding her garbage. She would not throw anything into the trash can but instead put all of her trash—old food, napkins, and mail— into plastic grocery sacks. She then tied the sack handles into an overhand knot and piled them in Jeff's old bedroom. He never understood why she kept the garbage, especially since she had always had a clean home. Living alone, she only accumulated a small amount of trash each week, but ever since this habit started, a few small bags of trash gradually grew into a large pile that basically turned Jeff's old bedroom into a landfill. The summer heat had amplified the smell, and Jeff could not tolerate it anymore.

"Mom, why are you keeping this garbage here?" he asked, although he knew questioning Evelyn these days would get her upset. He always had to use kid gloves when confronting her because the Alzheimer's had caused a drastic change to her personality. His once soft-spoken mother now had a violent temper. "It smells terrible. Doesn't it bother you?"

"I may need some of those things in the future so I'm not going to throw it away," Evelyn snapped. She wagged her finger at him. "You mind your own business, Jeffery. I know what I'm doing."

"But, Mom, it's unhealthy," he replied, trying to sound calm as Evelyn's temper flared. "You weren't always like this."

"So what?" she replied sarcastically. "People change all the time."

"You are breathing in this nasty smell and it can't be good for you, Mom. It's attracting flies and rodents. I'm going to throw it away."

"You will not!" Evelyn barked. "I don't come to your house and tell you how to live. I'll go through those bags when I get time."

Changing the conversation, Jeff asked "Who were you talking to before we came inside?"

Evelyn paused for a moment and then replied, "I wasn't talking to anyone."

"You were talking to someone, Mom. You said something about it being hot outside. Who were you talking to?"

"I told you I wasn't talking to anyone. Mind your own business!" Evelyn yelled. An angry scowl formed over her face, and the twinkle in her eye disappeared

I tried. Evelyn was both angry and embarrassed. Her harsh reactions had become her new defense mechanism. Deep down, Jeff believed Evelyn was aware of the health risks from her new found hoarding habit, but trying to change her now would be near impossible.

He sighed. "Is there anything you need us to do while we are here?" He asked, hoping that he hadn't gotten Evelyn too mad. Normally he and Kate would clean the house for her (the trash room was off limits, of course) and either prepare a meal or take her out to lunch.

"Let's see," Evelyn said as she turned around to look at her living room. The room was clean and free of clutter, but the malodorous trash coming from the spare bedroom gave the whole house an unsanitary feeling. "I don't think I need anything done today."

"Do you want to go have lunch?" Kate asked.

"No, I'm not very hungry. I think I'd rather lie down for a while. I've been busy lately."

Jeff laughed to himself. "What have you been doing?"

Evelyn immediately snapped back, "Mind your own business and stop asking so many questions!"

"Sorry!" Jeff replied as he threw his hands up like he was surrendering to the police. "No more questions."

"Just leave," Evelyn ordered. "You've gotten me all upset."

"I'm sorry, Mom. I didn't mean to upset you."

"Well, you did. Now go away."

Jeff turned to Kate and motioned for them to leave. He didn't take her harsh words personally because he, just like Kate, knew that Evelyn's hateful personality was a result of the disease. Evelyn was still the loving, caring, and nurturing person Jeff grew up with, but those wonderful traits had been masked by the debilitating dementia.

Wanting to do everything he could to take care of his mother, Jeff and Kate dedicated part of their Sunday afternoons to helping Evelyn. It was just a year ago when she was given the untimely diagnosis of Alzheimer's disease, and it came as a shock to the family. Jeff had heard of the disease affecting the elderly, but Evelyn was only sixty years old at the time. She had always been a very independent woman ever since Jeff's father abandoned the family. Evelyn prided herself in keeping her house clean as well as maintaining her own personal hygiene. She had always been mentally alert and cognizant of current events.

This all changed after the diagnosis was made. Jeff and Kate began to notice that Evelyn would misplace things in the home and blame others for stealing whatever was lost. Random items like the remote control or house shoes were often found hidden under a couch cushion or in the vegetable crisper. She would forget conversations she had and repeat herself verbatim several times. She also neglected her hygiene and her household, and that is when she started to hoard small bags of trash. All of these characteristics were strikingly opposite to Evelyn's normal behaviors, and although Jeff wanted to do everything in his power to take care of the woman who had provided for him, it had become an increasingly stressful obligation.

Evelyn would also ask about deceased relatives, such as her brother Thomas. When told that he had died years ago, Evelyn had an emotional breakdown. Jeff and Kate had to learn to speak to Evelyn on her level. She would ask the same questions over and over again, and if the answer was not something she wanted to hear, Jeff had to reply with an ambiguous answer such as "Thomas is at home" or "Thomas is doing fine." Of course, this only satisfied her until she asked the question again moments later.

"That was one of the shortest visits ever," Kate said as they walked back to the car. Usually they would spend at least an hour with Evelyn.

"Every day is different with her," Jeff said. "We just have to be patient, enjoy the good days, and tolerate the bad."

As they pulled out of the driveway, Kate asked, "You're not mad at me for announcing your job today at church, are you?" She was one of those people who needed constant reassuring that no one harbored any grudge toward her.

"I'm not mad," Jeff replied. "I just don't like people knowing stuff about me. I'm thankful for the job, but I don't want to look prideful. They might think I'm rich, and rich people get a bad reputation for being stuck-up."

"I understand, but I just couldn't contain myself," Kate replied. "You will be making a nice salary, but you've earned it after all those years of school."

"What did you think about the sermon?" Jeff asked her, wondering if she had the same confusion about it as he did.

"What I learned is that God is in control," Kate replied. "He is in control of His creation and He watches over us. How about you? What did you think about it?"

"Well," Jeff said, "I don't see how the pastor made that 'God is in control' summary after his rebuttal of the Genesis account of creation. It didn't connect at all. I grew up believing that the story of creation was true. This is the first time I've ever heard it taught in church as a myth. Pastor Bill had a good point. I've got a doctorate in biology, and they shove evolution down our throats during every class. By the time I graduated, I was a firm believer in evolution, but it has never occurred to me how the story of creation doesn't fit with evolution. I never really thought about it." *If the creation story isn't true, then what else isn't true?*

"Hmm," replied Kate. "If the pastor is a man of God, I think we should listen to him. And you said yourself that you already believe in evolution, so use what you learned today and apply that to what you already know about the Bible. All I know is we have to believe in Jesus." Kate was never one to get too involved in a deep theological discussion. Part of this was because she didn't like confrontation, but another reason being she still didn't have a firm grasp on her own faith, although she had learned some of the basics ever since they started going to The Experience.

The drive home from Evelyn's house was a pleasant ten mile trip. They lived on the east end of Grayson, and Jeff enjoyed the drive because he could watch the majestic Appalachian Mountains rising up into the sky. He grew up in Grayson, just outside of the Smokey Mountain National Park. He had many fond memories of spending the weekend hiking in the mountains or visiting the unique shops that were geared more for out-of-state tourists. Even as an adult he still acted like a child when he waded into the cold mountain rivers and hunted for skipping stones. Jeff felt fortunate to get a job at nearby Grogan University rather than having to move away from this beautiful landscape full of treasured memories.

After arriving home, Jeff had one thing on his mind—taking his ritual Sunday afternoon nap on the couch. Kate would go to the grocery, and the house would be quiet except for the whirring of the ceiling fan and the purring of Samson, Jeff's black and white tuxedo cat. Jeff had found the frail kitten in a parking lot at Barnett's Grocery back in the spring shortly after graduation. He assumed the little critter had been abandoned by some negligent person. Jeff always had a soft spot for animals, especially when they were neglected. Kate was none too thrilled when Jeff brought the kitten home, but she didn't think it would live very long because it was sick, so she allowed Jeff to keep his new friend. Jeff nursed it back to health, and because of the kitten's strength to live, he named it Samson based on the strong Biblical character from the Old Testament.

Jeff lay down on the couch and Samson jumped up on his chest. He gave a high-pitched "meow" to Jeff, which was the feline command for him to reach over and scratch his cat's head. Samson's purr sounded like a lawnmower, yet it was soothing and relaxing, and Jeff felt his eyes getting heavy.

"I'm off to the grocery," Kate said, arousing Jeff before he fell asleep. "I guess you'll be taking your nap?"

"It's my favorite pastime," he replied with a yawn. "Don't buy everything in the store—I haven't gotten a paycheck yet and our savings account is running on fumes."

"You say that every time," Kate said with a laugh. "I'll leave a few things behind."

Jeff often dreamed when he slept, and usually the dreams were vivid and full of memorable detail. With the ambience of the living room, comfortable couch, and Samson's purring, Jeff would be fast asleep and entering into a world of dreams.

Within five minutes, relaxation took over and Jeff began dreaming. He stood in a field full of knee-high weeds. In the middle of the field grew a large tree full of healthy branches and green leaves. Sections of thick roots near the base of the tree poked out from the ground. The system of roots extended several yards outward and into the earth. Jeff could easily see that the tree must have been a hundred years old, yet it was thriving and still growing strong.

Jeff walked up to the tree and put his hands on the bark. The tightly-knit wood surrounding the tree provided protection from the elements. He admired the tree's beauty and strength. A western wind began to blow, causing the weeds and branches to move about. Ominous storm clouds quickly filled the sky, and a rumbling thunder resounded in the heavens. The weeds moved back and forth as though they were dancing, and as they moved they grew taller.

Suddenly, weeds near the base of the tree leaned over and wrapped themselves around the roots. They seemed to have a mind of their own as they forcefully squeezed the roots. Their tight compression caused the roots to snap in half. Then, weeds that surrounded the tree wrapped themselves around its base. Thousands of weeds had a grasp of the tree's trunk, and they squeezed tightly just like they did with the roots. Small creases formed in the tree's bark as the weeds strangled it. Jeff stepped away as the weeds began tugging back and forth on the tree. Out of the sky, a bright bolt of lightning shot down and pierced the bottom of the trunk, shattering the strong footing. With the foundation destroyed, a loud, echoing crack sounded as the weeds pulled the tree to the ground. It landed with a crashing boom, causing the earth to shake.

The weeds let loose their grip. Jeff hurried over to the tree. He delicately placed his hands on it and caressed the bark. Tears formed in his eyes and he began to weep. While grieving, nearby weeds reached over and wrapped themselves around his legs. Quickly, he reached down and pulled each of the weeds out of the soil. As soon as he tore one weed off, another would latch on. Although it was a frightening struggle, Jeff managed to free himself and jump on top of the fallen tree to get away from the weeds reaching for him.

The weeds continued their attempts to grab Jeff. He scooted away from them by sliding back and forth along the length of the tree, but they kept coming for him no matter where he was positioned. The earth started to shake again, and something black caught Jeff's attention. To his left, a large, black hole formed in the soil. Peering into the hole, he saw bright yellow flames shooting up from far below. Immense heat tore through the opening, and Jeff shielded his face from the heat. Another hole formed to his right, and it too contained fire. Behind him on the other side of the tree, several more holes had already formed. The shaking of the ground caused the soil surrounding the holes to weaken and fall into the abyss. The holes continued to grow in diameter and spread toward the tree. Jeff yelled aloud, fearing he would fall into the fiery depths as the holes grew larger.

"Ahhh!"

Jeff jumped up from the couch. He checked his surroundings and, seeing that he was back at home, realized he had been dreaming. Samson remained curled up on the back of the couch, purring to the tune of his own dream and oblivious to Jeff's recent adventure. After coming to his senses, he smelled the enticing aroma of grilled meat. He looked at his watch. Five o'clock had already rolled around, and Kate was in the kitchen preparing supper. She walked into the living room.

"Are you okay? You were dreaming awfully loud," she said with a smile.

"I was?" Jeff asked. "What was I doing?"

"It sounded like you were crying, and then I heard you scream. What were you dreaming about?

"I don't know…something about a tree, weeds, and the earth caving in. It was weird, just like the majority of my other dreams." He paused, changing the subject. "What's for supper?"

"I picked up some sirloins at the grocery," Kate said and then quickly added, "They were on sale. I figured a good meal would be the best way to celebrate before you start your new job tomorrow. Now that you'll be earning a stable paycheck, we can actually afford something other than boxed macaroni and cheese."

After a delicious supper, Jeff retired to bed earlier than usual so he could get a good night's sleep and have a fresh start tomorrow. Although he usually had no trouble sleeping, he struggled because he could not get the strange dream out of his mind. He wanted to know the meaning of it, even though with past dreams he never sought any explanation. *There is no meaning, Jeff. Dreams don't carry secret messages. Go to sleep already!*

CHAPTER THREE

JEFF AWOKE at six o'clock on Monday morning, bright eyed and full of energy despite having recurring dreams about the tree. This was the big day he had been waiting for. All those years of studying, writing research papers, performing experiments, and sitting through lectures would now be put to good use.

Kate grunted when the repetitive buzzing of the alarm clock sounded, but Jeff was quick to switch off the obnoxious noise so it wouldn't awaken her. He jumped out of bed and went through his morning routine, and his first priority was to give Samson his morning treat. Every day, Samson insisted on having a treat first thing in the morning, and he would meow and walk in between Jeff's legs until his bipedal servant finally submitted to him. Jeff went into the kitchen as Samson followed his every move. He grabbed a box of cat treats and dropped a couple of the smelly morsels on the floor. Samson busied himself with the feline delicacy while Jeff poured some cereal.

After a quick breakfast, Jeff went to the bedroom to get dressed, all the while trying to avoid waking his wife up. He decided he'd make a good first impression at the university by wearing a navy suit with a power tie. Jeff kissed Kate goodbye. She was still asleep, or at least had her eyes closed, but she managed to groggily wish him good luck. Jeff left the house and joined the others on the highway as they all made their morning commute to work.

Grogan University was a thirty minute drive from home. The morning commute was boring and uneventful, but in the evening, just like the drive home from his mother's house, he was able to admire the beautiful Appalachian Mountains. This long commute would give him time in the morning to prepare for the day, and in the evening, time to clear his head. He enjoyed living in the suburbs located far away from the university where it was guaranteed to be free from college students away from home for the first time. Although Jeff lived in a dorm while pursuing his doctoral degree in Kentucky, he never lived the college life of partying and fraternities. He was well aware of what students did after class and on the weekends, and he never wanted any part in it. Besides, he never had the time to make any friends in college because he spent so much time studying. He had acquaintances when he did group projects with his classmates, but when the project ended, so did the brief relationship. College life had been a very lonely time for Jeff, but he made up for it by graduating in the top five percent of his class.

Jeff had been to Grogan University many times during the past month as he went through the rigorous interview process. He knew he was getting closer to the campus because of the abundance of fast food restaurants and coffee shops nearby, not to mention the many young adults taking a morning jog or bike ride. The classrooms sat on a large hillside, but the dorms were located at the bottom of the hill. A lot of students complained because they always had to walk uphill to get to class. Nothing could be done to alleviate the problem, but that didn't stop the students from complaining and having an occasional protest.

The Farris Science Hall housed Jeff's office along with every science class he would be assigned to teach. Jeff put his new faculty parking tag that he had received during employee orientation on his rearview mirror and pulled into the parking lot close to his office. He entered the Farris

31

Science Building and went to the faculty offices to meet with his new supervisor, Dr. Robert Farris. He had become acquainted with the layout of the faculty offices during orientation and remembered that Robert's office was the biggest room at the end of the hallway. He walked quietly toward Robert's office, poked his head through the door, and saw his new boss busily working at his computer.

"Good morning, Dr. Farris," Jeff said while he lightly knocked on the ajar door.

Robert sat at his computer replying to a long list of emails. He had been so focused on his typing that Jeff's voice startled him. "Oh, you scared me!" Robert said as he turned from his computer. He got up and walked to the door with his hand readied to greet Jeff. "Come on in," he said, shaking hands. "Have a seat."

Jeff had grown to like his new boss after having spoken with him so many times during the interviews. Robert Farris was a very intelligent person and had been the dean of the science department for over two decades. He had two doctoral degrees and was well known for his extensive knowledge and teaching ability. Jeff admired the multitude of diplomas and awards adorning the office walls. When Jeff met him during the first interview, he had to stifle a giggle because Robert fit the stereotype of a university professor. He wore a plaid overcoat with a loud bow-tie. His thick white hair and beard were strikingly similar to Colonel Sanders. Jeff had considered bringing him a bucket of Kentucky Fried Chicken and seeing if Robert would just hold the bucket up and give a big smile. However, Jeff, being a wise man, never did such a risky thing, but still, every time they had a conversation, Robert's appearance reminded Jeff of those eleven delicious herbs and spices. *Maybe he will play along after I make tenure.*

"So, this is your first day," Robert said with a big smile. "Are you excited?

"Yes, sir," Jeff replied confidently. "I've wanted to be a professor for so long and now the day has come!"

"I like your attitude. That's one of the reasons I hired you," Robert replied. "I'm sure you remember this is the in-service day for the faculty. We let all the professors come in on Mondays to prepare for the new semester; classes start on Tuesday. Also, tonight is our annual cocktail party for the faculty—a good time to meet and greet other colleagues."

"I look forward to it," Jeff said with a smile.

"Let me show you to your office. We won't have to go far—its right here next to mine."

Both of the men stood up and Robert led Jeff out of the room and to the office next to his. Robert cordially opened the door for Jeff, turned on the lights, and gestured for him to enter. Although the office was spacious, its size was only half that of the dean's office. A computer sat on his desk, and a new yearly planner along with a schedule of the science department classes lay in front of the computer. Two empty book shelves stood along the wall, and behind his desk, a narrow window allowed the morning sun to shine through.

"You should have everything you need in here already, but if not, our supply closet is by the receptionist's desk," Robert said. "You will see your schedule of classes there on the desk. Classes start tomorrow morning at eight o'clock." Jeff approached his desk and picked up his schedule to examine it.

"It's the same classes we agreed on during the final interview last week," Robert said. "Just the basics for now—intro to biology, intro to genetics, a lab…you may have to fill in for one of the other professors on occasion but that shouldn't happen too often. And, as I explained during the interview, you will be teaching some of the same classes to different groups of students. There are some students who have classes on Mondays, Wednesdays, and Fridays, and another group that has a longer class on Tuesdays and Thursdays. We try to offer the required classes several times each semester so as to accommodate their schedules."

"Yes, sir. Everything is on the schedule as we talked about," Jeff agreed. "I'd better start working on my lesson plan now." Jeff didn't mind being assigned only the introductory courses. He knew that with time, he would be able to teach the higher level classes.

As the day progressed and Jeff prepared his lectures, Robert occasionally introduced other faculty members to him. All of his colleagues held graduate-level degrees from prestigious universities, and they had many years of experience in academia. Jeff enjoyed meeting them but felt inferior because he was new and inexperienced. In addition, even though he was thirty years old, he was the youngest out of all faculty members, having only been out of school since he finished his dissertation in the spring a few months ago. Age didn't seem to be an issue to his colleagues, and Jeff's feeling of inadequacy subsided as each person he met warmly welcomed him to the university and treated him as a true member of the faculty.

Jeff felt good about his job. His co-workers were pleasant and his supervisor was easy to get along with. After several hours of work, Jeff finished preparing and editing all of his lectures for tomorrow's classes. He didn't want to get too in-depth and cause the students anxiety on their first day. Jeff never liked the first day of the semester when he was in college because the professors gave him a long list of assignments that had to be completed by the end of the term, and it was simply overwhelming. Jeff felt good about his lesson plan. He started to shut down his computer when Robert came back to his office.

"Before you go, I want to introduce you to one other colleague: Dr. Rhonda Matheson. She arrived later today, and I got tied up and failed to introduce her."

Robert motioned with his fingers for Jeff to come to the door. He then led him down the hallway to Dr. Matheson's office. She appeared busy as she typed on her computer and shuffled papers around.

"Dr. Matheson, allow me to introduce our newest member of the faculty: Dr. Jeff Duncan."

Dr. Matheson glanced up from her computer and offered a smile to Jeff. She stood up to greet him and Jeff met her halfway to shake hands. Her office was the same size as his, but her bookshelf contained an assortment of science textbooks, professional journals, and other papers; her walls were full of framed degrees and honorariums. Jeff hoped to eventually have that many things in his room. It would at least make him look more professional. He also saw that Dr. Matheson wore a small silver cross on her necklace. He hadn't seen any type of religious attire on the other people he met today.

"Nice to meet you, Dr. Matheson," said Jeff. "Are you ready for the new semester?"

"You can call me Rhonda," she replied with a brief smile. "I'm trying to get ready for tomorrow. I had to come in late this morning and now I'm playing catch up. That's the story of my life."

Jeff wasn't sure if Rhonda expected him to laugh or delve into her personal life. He avoided both options. "I've been preparing my lectures today also. I'm excited, but then again, this is my first teaching job and I don't fully know what to expect." Rhonda replied with another brief smile, showing that she was too busy to make small talk. "Don't let me keep you from your work. I'll see you in the morning."

"Okay, maybe I'll have more time tomorrow and we can talk. Good luck with your classes!" Rhonda said.

"Thank you, I'm going to need it."

Jeff and Robert left her office, and Robert said, "I have to get back to work. I'll see you in the morning."

"I used to dread the first day of school, but now I can't wait!" Jeff said with a laugh, hoping to show his excitement to have the job.

"Keep that enthusiasm going, Dr. Duncan," Robert replied. "We need it here."

Jeff smiled and turned to leave. He held his head up high, walking proudly and with elevated confidence. He had made a lot of progress on his first day, met all of his co-workers, and everything was ready for his first lecture in the morning.

CHAPTER FOUR

KATE GREETED Jeff at the door when he arrived home. "How did your first day go?"

"It was great!" Jeff replied with a big smile. "I got to meet my colleagues and prepare my lectures for tomorrow."

"So, you think you will like it?"

"Definitely. My dream job has finally arrived."

"I ordered pizza for supper," said Kate, knowing that would make her husband even happier.

"Could my day get any better?" Jeff asked rhetorically. He then hugged Kate and gave her a kiss. Over the few short years of their marriage, Jeff had come to learn the hard way that Kate needed simple acts of affection from him, so he did what he could to make her happy.

They ate their supper in the living room while they watched one of their favorite movies. Samson sat on the couch between them. The pleasant evening was suddenly interrupted by a phone call.

"I wonder who that could be. We rarely get phone calls at night," Kate remarked. She went into the kitchen to get the phone while Jeff paused the movie.

"Hello?" Kate asked.

Jeff listened, hoping he could figure out who was calling so late.

"Yes, he lives here....is something wrong?" Kate asked. There was silence for several seconds. Kate then exclaimed, "Oh, no! Is she okay?" She paused again for a few more seconds. "Yes, ma'am, we'll be right there!"

Kate hung the phone up and hurried back into the living room. "Jeff, that was the hospital calling. Your mother fell at home and was taken to the emergency room!"

He stared blankly at Kate in silence as he tried to digest her words. A wave of terror came over him as every worst-case scenario played in his mind. "Is she okay? Do they know how she fell? Did she break any bones?" he asked worriedly.

"The nurse said she is stable. They will be running some tests to see if there is any serious injury. We need to get down there and see her," Kate said anxiously. Kate did not function well when she worried. Jeff used to get amused by her disorganization when she was anxious, but this was no laughing matter.

"Okay, let's go," Jeff said. He turned the television off and put their plates into the refrigerator so Samson wouldn't be tempted to steal any pizza. Kate grabbed her purse and Jeff got his car keys. They hurried out the front door, got in the car, and sped to Grayson Regional Hospital.

"What do you think happened?" Jeff asked while passing the slower cars in his lane.

"Who knows," replied Kate. "I've been concerned about her for a while. This Alzheimer's disease has really progressed. Every week when we go see her she declines a little bit more."

"I know," Jeff replied with a sigh. "When I check on her, I can see how much her mind has been affected. She is losing more and more things. She's forgotten your name, and I dread the day she forgets mine."

"You've always been really close to your mom," Kate acknowledged. "It has to be hard for you to see her like this."

"I hope her hip isn't broken. She'll have to go to a nursing home, and I promised her she would never go to one of those places." Jeff paused for a moment. "I wish I had spent more time with her. Once or twice a week has not been enough. She has been getting worse, but I've been so preoccupied with finishing school and going to job interviews at the university."

"Don't start blaming yourself," Kate responded in her motherly tone. "It's not your fault she fell. You've helped a lot more than you realize. Most people would just abandon their parents to a nursing home and forget about them, but you stepped up to the plate and took an active role in caring for her."

"But still," Jeff replied, "I should have gone to see her more frequently. I'm a terrible son."

Kate knew that when Jeff started to talk bad about himself, he wouldn't stop no matter what she said to him. Kate remained quiet as she waited for Jeff to continue his spiral into self-pity, but he didn't make any further comments. Instead, he quietly focused on his driving.

Kate broke the silence. "I'm not trying to sound cliché, but let's try to be positive about this," she said in her "trying to help" voice. "If worse comes to worse, I'll stay with her at her house during the day, or we can move her in with us. I have no problem taking care of her. It's not like I have a job to go to."

"I've tried to get her to move in with us in the past, but she refused," Jeff said. "She always said she wanted to die in her home. The house is old—it will end up being the death of her when it collapses. Or, she will get sick from that nasty garbage she's been hoarding. Maybe this will be the chance to get her to move in with us now."

They arrived at the hospital and hastily walked to the emergency room. They came to a hectic nurses' station where medical staff were busying themselves with papers, talking to doctors, and responding to patients' bed calls. Jeff stood impatiently at the desk waiting on someone to help him. Finally, a nurse glanced up from a computer and made eye contact with him.

"Can I help you?" she asked in a tired voice.

"Uh, yes, um," Jeff fumbled, "the hospital called me tonight to say that my mother is here. She fell at home this evening."

"We have quite a few patients tonight, sir. What's her name?"

"Evelyn Duncan. She's sixty-one years old."

"Okay, she's in Room 12 down the hall," the nurse said as she pointed toward a long hallway. She then turned back to the computer and continued working. Jeff and Kate hurriedly walked through the hallway of patient rooms. Each room had a stenciled number on the outside, and curtains were drawn to allow for privacy. Jeff looked at each room number as he passed by. A few of the rooms had patients inside who could be heard moaning in pain. *I hope that's not her.* When they arrived at Room 12, Jeff grabbed the curtain and pulled it open to see Evelyn lying on the bed. She was dressed in a generic hospital gown, and two monitors made slow, repetitive beeps as they measured her vitals.

"Hey, Mom, what happened? Are you okay?" Jeff asked in a barrage of questions.

Evelyn didn't respond at first. Her left eye was encircled with a dark bruise, and her head was wrapped with a thick bandage. A red patch of blood stained the bandage where her forehead had been bleeding. Finally, she turned and stared at Jeff through her thick glasses. She opened her mouth as though she would respond, but no words came out.

"Mom, it's Jeff, your son. Are you hurting?"

"...Jeff?" Evelyn asked. "Where am I?"

"You're at the hospital. They said you fell at home."

"I don't remember anything," Evelyn said with a laugh. She pointed and asked, "Who is that?"

Jeff turned to his right where Kate stood. "Mom, that's Kate, your daughter-in-law."

"Daughter-in-law? When did you get married?"

Quickly changing the subject, Jeff interrupted, "Mom, why did you fall?"

"I just don't remember," she responded casually.

Jeff turned again to Kate. "Stay here with her. I'm going to find a nurse." He left the room and closed the curtain behind him. Nurses were not hard to find, but it was difficult locating an available nurse as they were all busy with other patients. He went back to the nurse's station. Again, he found them all preoccupied with someone else.

"Can anyone tell me what happened to Mom?" Jeff asked loudly.

"I'm sorry, sir," replied Donna, the nurse he had spoken with earlier. She walked over to the desk where he stood. "Are you asking about Ms. Duncan in Room 12? Is that your mother?"

"Yes, ma'am. I know you all are busy but I'm just trying to get some answers. I'm her son, Jeff Duncan. Can you tell me anything about her condition?"

Donna turned around to a shelf containing medical charts. She grabbed the one labeled "Duncan, Room 12" and turned back around. She opened the chart and thumbed through a few pages. "According to the records, all we have found so far is the bruised eye and a laceration on her forehead. She is complaining of pain in her head and right arm. The doctor has ordered an X-ray and MRI. Radiology will be doing those tests any time now, but we won't know anything else until those results come back. From what I can see, nothing looks broken, but I'm concerned about her mental status. She has been very confused ever since she arrived."

"Do you know what happened to her at home?" Jeff asked, hoping for some clues.

Donna turned back a few pages in the chart. "The paramedics said they found Ms. Duncan on the floor with a screwdriver next to her. There was a stool tipped over in the middle of the living room, and her head was bleeding. All we know is that she fell."

"I'll have to go to the home to see what happened," replied Jeff. "She was up to something."

Donna replied professionally, "Back to the confusion—has your mother ever been diagnosed with dementia?"

"A year ago she was diagnosed with Alzheimer's disease," Jeff replied sadly. "We've been dealing with her memory loss, personality change, and overall stubbornness. She's hoarding trash also and it's stinking up her house."

"She's awfully young to have Alzheimer's," Donna replied. "Who is her doctor?"

"Dr. Carl Norman. His office is here at the hospital."

"That's good to know. Evelyn wasn't able to tell us her doctor's name. I'll go ahead and call his office and leave a message. They are closed now, but the doctor wants us to notify him if any of his patients come to the hospital. His answering service will contact him if it is urgent."

Jeff thanked the nurse for her help and went back to Evelyn's room to update his wife. "We at least have an idea of what happened," he concluded.

"Mom," Jeff asked, kneeling on the floor next to her, "what were you doing at home before you fell?"

"It's none of your business what I do at home," she said harshly.

Jeff turned to Kate and whispered, "She is hiding something. I need to find out what is going on."

Jeff carefully held onto her hand. "Mom, I'm just trying to find out why you fell. You haven't fallen before and I want you to be safe at home."

Evelyn jerked her hand away from his grasp. "I don't need you checking on me," she replied hatefully. "Just leave—you've gotten me upset."

Jeff sighed. His mother's hatefulness toward him could often be ignored, but there were times when it stabbed him straight through the heart. "I'm sorry I upset you," he apologized.

Evelyn didn't respond but instead turned her head to face the wall. Jeff knew he had inadvertently upset his mother again, so he decided to leave her alone. He turned and slowly walked out of the room with his head slumped over.

"We can get through this together, Jeff," Kate said while gently grabbing onto his hand. "She's your mother and my mother-in-law. We will do everything we can to help her. Like I said, I have no problem taking care of her full-time."

"Looks like that's what we will have to do, even if she refuses," Jeff said with another sigh. "I've never wanted to do anything against her will. Mom was so good to me. After Dad had his affair, he just abandoned us and left Mom to take care of me by herself. I never saw him again, and I only have a faint memory of what he looked like. I'm not sure I could even recognize him now—he left us over twenty-five years ago. I was a kid and so confused, but Mom did everything in her power to give me a normal life. She made sure that I had food, clothes, and all the privileges she didn't have when she was a little girl. Dad never paid a dime in child support, but Mom worked two jobs just to support me." Jeff paused for a moment. Talking about his father often left him angry and confused. He used to blame himself for his father's leaving them, but Evelyn had assured him that he wasn't to blame. Jeff had heard through the grapevine that the woman his father ran off with had manipulated him out of everything he owned, and she left him a broken man. Jeff didn't know if the story was true or not. *Some things will always remain a mystery.*

A hint of optimism came over Jeff. "You know what, Kate? It's time for me to pay Mom back. I owe her so much for all she did. Now that I have a good job, I should have no problem affording the things she will need—physical therapy, a hospital bed—whatever it is. This will be a good experience for me."

They stopped by the nurse's station before leaving and found Nurse Donna.

"Is she going to stay overnight?" he asked.

"The ER doctor wants to admit her for observation. They will move her into a room shortly. If everything turns out fine, then she'll most likely go home sometime in the morning."

"Okay, thank you, Donna," Jeff said with another sigh. It was comforting to know she would get to stay in the hospital and be taken care of by professionals. In addition, he wouldn't have to worry about moving her to his house tonight. "Will you please call us after she is moved into her room?"

"Certainly. We have your number on file."

While walking back to the parking lot, Jeff said, "Before we go home, let's stop by Mom's house. I need to find out what she was up to."

"It's getting late. Can't it wait until tomorrow?" Kate asked.

"It won't take too long," Jeff replied as they got in the car and left.

CHAPTER FIVE

AFTER A FIFTEEN minute trip, they pulled into Evelyn's driveway. A light in the living room shone through the window. Jeff sorted through the various keys on his key ring as he neared the house. He found her key and unlocked the front door. The familiar, nauseous odor of trash took their breath away as Jeff pushed the door open. In the middle of the living room lay an old, three-legged stool that had been knocked over. A coffee table positioned near a sofa had a small trace of blood on its edge, and a trail of red dots stained the carpet. Next to it sat a rusty screwdriver. In the ceiling directly above, several small holes dotted the sheet rock.

"This must be where she fell," Jeff said to Kate, although the scenery spoke for itself. "I wonder what she was doing."

"Who knows?" Kate replied.

Jeff walked over to the stool and set it up straight and then picked up the screwdriver and placed it on the end table next to Evelyn's favorite recliner. He then went to the kitchen to make sure the stove wasn't left on.

"Wow!" Jeff said with a laugh after turning on the light. He had an unusual way of expressing his surprise. Rarely did something ever startle him, but there were those few moments in life when it did happen. "Come look at this, Kate."

Still staring at the holes in the ceiling, Kate casually walked into the kitchen. "What is it?"

"I just…." Jeff trailed off. On the kitchen table sat four place settings of Evelyn's fine china. Each plate was full of food, but it appeared that the meal—spaghetti and salad—had been left out for several hours as the spaghetti was cold and the lettuce had turned brown. Each chair was pushed up next to the table and the silverware had been delicately placed according to proper etiquette. It reminded Jeff of the ritual Sunday dinners he had with Evelyn when growing up.

"Who was she cooking for?" Jeff asked.

Kate approached the table and admired the formal setting. "I don't know, but it must have been someone important."

"This is new," Jeff said casually. "I've been checking on her at least once a week ever since she started to go downhill, and I've never seen her making meals—at least not like this." He walked over to the sink and turned on the hot water. He then put the drain stopper in and added some dish soap. "Will you turn the water off when the sink gets full? We need to clean this place up. I can't stand the smell of this garbage anymore, and tonight I'm going to do something about it. Mom won't like it, but I'm afraid she will get a disease from the bacteria she's farming."

"Okay, go ahead," Kate replied as she began gathering the plates, cups, and utensils from the table.

Jeff left the kitchen and went to his old bedroom. Covering his nose with his handkerchief, he took a deep breath and opened the door. Putrid fumes flew out from the room. Despite his protection, the smell entered his mouth and nose causing him to gag and cough violently. His eyes started to sting from the strong stench and finally Jeff had to go outside to the back porch to get some fresh air. The odor drifted into the kitchen causing Kate to gag and ultimately forcing her to escape outside as well.

"I haven't seen that room for several months," Jeff said as he panted for air. "How Mom can keep that smelly trash piled up in there is beyond me."

"I don't think I can go back in there," Kate said regretfully.

"That's fine. This has to be done tonight. I'm going to throw every one of those bags away," Jeff declared. "Her trash dumpster is in the driveway. Would you mind pulling it around here for me?"

"I'll do anything if it doesn't require going back inside," Kate replied.

Jeff put the handkerchief back over his nose and then pulled his shirt up to cover his nose and mouth. The pressure from his shirt forced the handkerchief to stay in place, allowing both his hands to be free. He took a deep breath and charged back into the house. He flipped on the bedroom light and there before him sat a mountain of white, fluffy grocery bags, each filled with garbage from days, weeks, and months past. Flies zoomed around their smelly paradise. Jeff reached down, grabbed a large armful of bags, turned around, and rushed out of the house.

Kate hurriedly pulled the dumpster over to the back door as Jeff exited. She flipped open the hinged lid and he dumped the bags inside. He wiped his hands on his pants and then removed his shirt from his nose. After taking several deep breaths of clean air, he put the handkerchief back over his nose, pulled his shirt up, and charged back inside for another load.

The process took a half hour to complete. Kate became nauseous from smelling the trash as Jeff brought the bags outside. She used a broom to stomp them deep into the dumpster to make more room, but there were just too many bags, so Jeff dumped the rest in a pile on the grass. He ripped his shirt off and spat on the grass as he tried to get the smell and taste out of his system. His pants and shirt were covered in nasty stains from all the basic food groups, and his hands had become sticky from the juices leaking out from the bags.

Although her husband was a gross, unpleasant sight, Kate couldn't help but laugh at his predicament.

"You're laughing, but remember you have to ride home with me," Jeff warned jokingly.

"You aren't going home without taking a shower first," Kate demanded.

"I guess I could," Jeff said. "But I've got nothing to change into."

"I'll find you something."

Jeff agreed and went inside to bathe. He hadn't used his mother's bathtub in years, but he was sure she wouldn't mind. *She won't be happy that I threw her garbage away though.*

The smell in the house was still present but not as strong as before. Kate found a can of air freshener under the kitchen sink and sprayed the entire bottle throughout the house. It temporarily eliminated some of the odor. Kate continued washing the dishes as she waited for Jeff to finish cleaning up.

After a ten minute shower, Jeff got out, wrapped a towel around himself, and saw that Kate hadn't brought him anything to change into. "Did you find anything for me to wear?" he yelled from the bathroom.

"Sorry, I forgot," Kate said. She dried her hands off and went into Evelyn's room looking for a bathrobe or some type of unisex article of clothing. After a long search, she came to the bathroom door.

"You have two options: this lovely yellow floral dress, or this pink bathrobe," Kate said, trying to keep a straight face.

"Is this the best you could do?" he asked, bewildered.

Kate burst out laughing as she hung the clothes on the door frame. "I could find you another dress if that's not your color."

"No," Jeff replied sarcastically. "I think I'll settle for this beautiful robe."

Kate snickered as she went back to the kitchen to finish cleaning. A few minutes later, Jeff entered, wearing the pink robe.

"You are cute," Kate said, still laughing.

"This stays between you and me," Jeff warned jokingly. He thought the situation was just as funny as she did, but even more so, it was embarrassing. "I just hope no one sees me when we leave."

"I'm ready to leave when you are. The dishes are finished and the kitchen is cleaned."

"Okay, let's go. But first, make sure no one is outside."

Kate laughed again. She went to the front window and peered through the curtain. "I don't see anyone.

"Alright, if the coast is clear then let's go home."

As they took the short trip home, with Kate in the passenger seat and Jeff driving in a woman's pink bathrobe, Kate asked, "Why do you think she keeps all that trash?"

"She said yesterday that she might need it. Her parents grew up during the Great Depression, and a lot of people from that generation had the habit of saving everything. Mom used to tell me how her parents saved coffee cans, jars, bags…you name it. She didn't like having the clutter in her house when growing up, and when she moved out on her own, she promised herself her house would always be clean. Now it seems that her memories of growing up in a cluttered environment have sprung forth again, while her recent memories fade away before they are ever formed. She's living in the past."

After they arrived home, Jeff and Kate were both exhausted and went straight to bed. Of course, Jeff hastily removed Evelyn's ill-fitting pink bathrobe and put on his comfortable pajamas. Samson, happy they had finally come home, hopped in the bed with them and lay down in his special spot in the middle of the mattress, right between his two servants.

CHAPTER SIX

TUESDAY MORNING came sooner than Jeff wanted. His deep sleep came to a sudden halt as the buzzing of his alarm clock sounded off. "Ugh," he grunted as he slammed his hand on the snooze button. He peered through one sleepy eye to check the time. *Six-o'clock already?* Last night's impromptu cleaning spree at his mother's house left him exhausted. He knew Kate would be tired as well, and he didn't want to awaken her. Besides, Samson would awaken her whenever he felt the need to do so. Jeff stumbled out of bed, turned off the alarm clock, and began his morning routine.

He went into the kitchen and Samson followed behind him, meowing incessantly.

"I know," Jeff said to his bossy cat. "You want a treat. Just give me a second!"

Samson replied with a high-pitched "meow" and raised his tail up, slightly curving it at the end. That long, black tail spoke all kinds of words for this cat, and over time Jeff had become fluent in the language of the feline. He gave Samson a handful of treats so the critter would stay occupied and not follow him around while he got ready for work. Jeff went to the refrigerator to get his pizza from the night before. He warmed it in the microwave and poured some orange juice. *The breakfast of champions.*

While in the middle of eating, Jeff received a call from Nurse Donna. "Good morning, Mr. Duncan. I just wanted to let you know that Ms. Duncan is stable. The X-ray showed a small fracture on her right arm. It is too small to require surgery, so an orthopedic doctor will put a sling on her arm later this morning when he arrives. The bone should heal itself. Also, Ms. Duncan's MRI came back; she did receive a minor brain injury to the frontal lobe. The MRI..."

"Brain injury?" Jeff interrupted. "How bad is it?"

"Well," Donna continued, "it's a small bruise. The doctor is concerned about it, but the MRI also showed something else that is even more concerning. Do you know what brain atrophy is?"

"No," Jeff answered, "but I don't like the sound of it."

"One of the symptoms of Alzheimer's disease and other types of dementia is the actual physical shrinkage of the brain. We cannot determine at this time how the injury on her frontal lobe or the atrophy will affect her, but being her closet relative, you will notice some changes."

Brain injury and shrinkage? Her personality changes had been difficult for both Jeff and Kate to adjust to, but they managed to adapt and let her hateful comments slide off of them. "This is upsetting to say the least," Jeff replied after a brief silence.

"I'm sorry to break the news, Mr. Duncan," Donna replied. "Dr. Norman read the MRI this morning. He compared it to the MRI he ran a year ago, and based on that comparison he said that Ms. Duncan's disease is progressing more rapidly than normal patients. He said he has never seen atrophy at such a fast rate."

"I don't know what to say," Jeff replied. "What can he do for her?"

"There are medicines she can take to slow down the deterioration and minimize anxiety and forgetfulness, but there is no cure."

Although he already knew there wasn't a cure to his mother's disease and that it would eventually take her life, hearing that there was no cure still brought everything to a dreadful reality. "I guess she will need the medication. I'm not sure she will take it, though."

"That could be a challenge for you," Donna said. "Your mother is okay at this time. The doctor hasn't made a determination yet on discharging her, but given her condition, he would most likely recommend sending her to a nursing home."

"No," Jeff replied sternly. "That won't be an option. I promised Mom that I would never let her go into a nursing home. That is her biggest fear."

"I understand," Donna replied sincerely. "If you can make arrangements for her to stay at home and be cared for, then the doctor will agree to discharge her home."

"My wife and I have already discussed doing that. Hopefully, it will work this way."

"Okay. Someone from here will call you when she is ready for discharge."

"Thank you for taking care of Mom," Jeff said as the phone call ended. He had lost track of time and saw that he had only a few minutes left until he had to leave. He quickly finished his pizza and juice, got dressed, and headed for the university.

The campus scene was different today. It was much busier as this was the first day of classes. Students walked along the sidewalk as they stared at their cell phones, most likely texting an unnecessary tidbit of information to their friends.

Jeff struggled to find an available parking space. *Shouldn't the campus have enough parking for their employees?* Finding a parking place had always been a frustrating task wherever he went, and the extra time he had to take today caused him to worry that he would be late for his first class. Traffic on the main street was bumper-to-bumper, and students were walking and riding their bikes right in front of his car. He had to slam on the brakes several times to avoid hitting the students. Jeff finally found a "visitor" parking place several blocks away from his office building. He got out of his car and hurried to his office as he dodged through the crowd of lost and confused students.

Jeff walked down the hallway toward his office. Before entering, he poked his head through Robert's door. "Good morning, Dr. Farris."

"Oh, good morning, Dr. Duncan. We missed you last night at the faculty party!"

Jeff had completely forgotten about the party. He had never been one to drink, but he definitely wanted to meet his new colleagues and hopefully make a good first impression. "I would have made it, but we had a bit of a crisis last night," Jeff replied.

"Is everything okay?" he asked.

"We were at the hospital—my mother fell at home, hit her head, and fractured her arm."

"How is she?"

"The doctor found that she has some serious health issues going on, and it will only get worse. We don't think it's safe for her to live alone anymore so my wife and I are going to move her into our home and take care of her there."

"I'm sorry to hear that," Robert replied. He turned back to his computer. "Of course, being an evolutionary biologist, I'm sure you understand what I mean when I say it's just the 'cycle of life'?"

Jeff waited to see if Robert would explain himself, but he didn't. "You mean the cycle of birth and death?" Jeff asked.

"Well, more so about the evolutionary cycle of life. You have a doctorate so you know what I'm talking about. The advancements in species come by natural selection. The weaker species die out while the stronger species thrive, advance, and become more complex. Sickness and injury are one of the determining factors for who is the weaker of the species."

Did he just say that to me? Not wanting to argue with his boss on the second day of his new job, Jeff briefly replied, "Yeah, we all have to die sometime I guess."

"When you said 'hospital' that reminded me of something I have never quite figured out in an evolutionary society: What is the point of having hospitals and nursing homes? In order for us stronger species to advance, why spend billions of dollars on healthcare to keep the weaker ones around? They have nothing to offer us; all they do is consume more money and resources. It's a mystery to me. I don't see why they don't mandate euthanasia. It sure would get the economy back in motion."

"I guess I never thought about that," Jeff replied, trying to figure out where this conversation was going. *Could my boss really be this heartless?* "Regardless, whether or not a person is weak, we still have an emotional attachment to them."

"Emotional attachment is evolutionary in itself. Our caveman ancestors grew close to one another because they had to rely on each other in order to survive. You see it throughout the animal kingdom," Robert replied, still typing on his computer. "I'm sure you have to get ready for your class. It was nice chatting with you." Jeff went into his office and sat down at his computer. The entire conversation had shaken his nerves. *How cold-hearted of him! My mother is very important to me. I don't care if she is weak.*

Jeff had five minutes to gather his lecture notes and textbook and walk to his first class: Introduction to Biology. He sat for an extra minute in his chair, trying to forget about the crude statements made by his supervisor. He distracted himself by reminiscing about all the years he had spent in school, awaiting the day when he would finally be on the other side of the desk. Today was the day, and no cruel or thoughtless comment would mess things up for him. He grabbed his briefcase and headed upstairs to the large lecture room.

The lecture hall was set up like an amphitheater. There were two doors at the top and bottom of the room. The room was divided into three sections, and each section held several rows of cushioned chairs and a long table in front of the chairs. Fifty students had already arrived to the class. Not much sound could be heard except for a few students quietly talking amongst themselves. The quiet scene reminded Jeff of the uneasy tension and silence at the beginning of each new semester when he was in college. Everyone was shy, and it took several weeks before the students started to open up and be friendly with one another.

"Good morning. My name is Dr. Jeff Duncan, but you can call me Jeff. I like to keep things informal," Jeff said with a friendly smile, hoping to ease the tension in the room. The students all stared blankly at him, and no one said a word. "Just to make sure, everyone in here has come for BIO 101: Introduction to Biology?"

A couple of students nodded their head. One student in the back of the class got up to leave. Jeff assumed he had come to the wrong class, but he didn't want to embarrass the young man on the first day, so he continued with his introduction.

"This is an introductory class as you may have already figured out," Jeff said. "We will be going over all of the basics of life. During the course of this semester, you will be learning about cells, genetics, and how life evolved."

A female student on the front row raised her hand. "Dr. Duncan, will you be teaching the theory of evolution?" A few students giggled.

"Yes, ma'am. Evolution will be taught in this class," Jeff said in a friendly but professional tone.

"I don't believe in evolution," the student replied. "I'm a creationist." The same students that giggled earlier laughed out loud. *At least the tension has eased.* Jeff looked up toward a group of young men in the back of the lecture hall.

"Guys, let's be respectful," Jeff said sternly. He then turned back toward the female student. "What's your name?"

"Jordyn Monroe," she replied.

"Jordyn, I respect your beliefs, and I would like to think these college-aged little boys will learn to respect you as well," Jeff said as he briefly glanced back up at the group of hecklers. "But in order for you to pass this class, you will have to demonstrate that you understand the concepts of evolution that I will be teaching. The assignments are geared to test what you will learn this semester, regardless of whether or not you believe it."

"Yes, sir. I can agree with that." Jordyn then wrote something in her notebook.

"That was a good question. Are there any other questions?"

A male student sitting amidst the hecklers shouted out, "Will we be talking about Noah's Ark?"

His friends continued laughing, and Jeff grew frustrated. *Ten minutes into the class and the clowns are already at work.* Jeff offered a quick response. "No, not in this class." The boy turned to his friends and laughed.

Jeff began going over the semester syllabus with the students, explaining the different topics they would cover and the assignments they would have to complete. "We will have four tests, and at the end of the semester we will have a comprehensive exam, so I expect you to take notes, read your chapters, and ask good questions. Also, feel free to come by my office if you need any help with an assignment or just want to chat."

After finishing the syllabus, Jeff began his short introductory lecture. "As already mentioned, we will be discussing the evolution of life…"

"You mean how a sky daddy made everything in one week, six thousand years ago?" blurted out another boy as the inevitable laughter reignited. Jordyn turned around and glared at the scoffers.

Jeff turned toward the boy, "Young man, please take note that you are in college now. This is not high school. I will not tolerate disrespect in this classroom. You and every other student on this campus are required to take this class no matter what degree you are pursuing, so keep your snide comments to yourself or transfer to another class." The young man's face turned red, and his friends quietly snickered at him.

"Now, as I was trying to say, today I want to give you a basic introduction to evolution. Generally speaking, all forms of life have evolved from earlier ancestors. Life on earth started in a simple form. Technically, I should discuss the origin of the earth and universe, but I won't spend much time on that topic in this class—it's something you can learn about if you take a geology or astronomy class. It is generally believed that the universe started with the Big Bang about fifteen to twenty billion years ago. The earth was formed about five billion years ago, so in this class, we will talk about what has happened starting from that time in history.

"The whole earth started out as a hot, molten mass at the beginning. Over time, the mass cooled, and the atmosphere formed. Rain in the atmosphere fell to the earth causing it to cool and form oceans. Over the course of millions of years there were chemical reactions taking place in these oceans. Imagine all of the different elements in the water we have today. The chemicals moved about, joined together, and broke apart— all types of random interactions occurred until one day the chemicals created amino acids, nucleotides, and simple carbohydrates. Over time, these chemicals polymerized—that is, they formed chain-like bonds. Then, as time went on, these bonds developed into large, cell-like clusters and eventually produced the first replicating molecule, similar to RNA. Then, this molecule, over more millions of years, produced the first single-celled organism. And there you have it, your first living ancestor. This is how life was first formed, from simple molecules to RNA to the first cell. There are different theories as to how the first living thing came into existence; I described only one of them. We will go over these in more detail in the coming weeks.

"Fast forward millions of years. This first single cell changed in structure and genetics thereby becoming more advanced. Over time, through natural selection and mutations, it replicated and produced another cell, and then another, until in a few generations we had our first multi-cellular organism. Things like sponges and small sea creatures were formed around this time period. Now, fast forward again. These complex critters turned into fish. These fish grew strong pectoral fins and stronger lungs, and then one day crawled out of the ocean and onto the beach. The fish had now developed the characteristics of an amphibian. Let's keep moving forward. This amphibian advanced into large mammals, then dinosaurs, then birds, and eventually, voila, you and me!

"What has caused life to thrive or die is an important concept you need to understand: survival of the fittest. Only the strongest of the animals survive. Weaker species die out while the strong ones live, breed, and advance. This applies to all life forms, and of course humans are the most evolved and therefore the most advanced of all animals. It kind of makes you proud, doesn't it?"

Jeff anticipated laughter from the students, but not many of them did as they were all busy writing down notes as fast as they could. *Either I said something informative or they are playing hang-man.* "That's a crash course on how we got here. We will go over this in more detail as the semester continues, but that is evolution in a nut shell. Any questions?"

The class continued writing down their notes. Jordyn raised her hand to catch Jeff's attention. "You mentioned the first simple molecules. How did they know to group together and form the RNA molecule?" she asked.

Jeff was surprised to find a freshman thinking at a much deeper level than he expected. "That's a good question, Jordyn. What it all boils down to is that chemicals bonded through random processes. There's no telling what kinds of combinations were created as the chemicals were forming and fashioning into different bond-pairs. Billions of reactions occurred in the ocean at the beginning. Who knows what other kinds of life forms were created and then died out? The RNA evidently was the strongest of the molecules because it survived and still exists today."

Jordyn wrote some notes on her paper and didn't respond with a follow up question. "Are there any other questions?" Jeff asked.

One of the hecklers spoke up. "How can an invisible God create something visible like RNA? Do you think he used a microscope?"

Frustrated, Jeff stared directly at the student and firmly replied, "Please understand that this is not a religion class. That is in another building, and if you want help signing up for one of those classes, then please consult with your student advisor."

The student cowered in his seat as his friends laughed at him. "Are there any serious questions?" Jeff asked. There was no response. *Are the students afraid of asking questions now?* "If not, then I will see you back in here on Thursday. Read chapter one in your textbook by then."

The students began gathering their things and exiting the room. Jeff sat at his desk for a moment as he watched the students leave. *I think I did well enough for my first class.* After packing her things into her book bag, Jordyn walked over to Jeff.

"Hi, Dr. Duncan," she said sheepishly. Jeff could tell she wanted to say more, but she waited on his response.

"It's nice to meet you, Jordyn," Jeff said as he stood up to shake her hand. Jeff towered over Jordyn, but he had his father's stature and had grown accustomed to being taller than most everyone he met. "I admire your courage to speak up in class. By the way, I'd like for the students to call me Jeff. 'Doctor' sounds like I'm stuck up."

Jordyn laughed. "Okay, Jeff." She paused and looked down at the floor. "I'm used to people scoffing at me for my religious beliefs. Thank you for standing up for me, and I hope you will continue to do so. I was homeschooled so today is my first experience of being around other students. It didn't go as planned."

"I'm sure this is a challenge for you," Jeff said with sincerity. "Listen, some of these students can be trolls. They just never grew up. And I will see to it that the students don't mock you. I'll remove them from class if necessary."

"Thank you," she replied. "I know I'm a minority here because of my beliefs, but that doesn't make me wrong."

"Listen, I go to church too, and I've been conflicted with what I've learned in church and what I learned in school. I see the evidence pointing to evolution, and it doesn't affect my faith at all. The evidence is very strong, but I would never disrespect you or anyone because of their beliefs. Of course, I will continue teaching evolution here—it's what I'm being paid to do."

"I appreciate your honesty," Jordyn said. "I know it's not safe to teach any theory in school except evolution. People get fired for teaching anything different, you know." She paused for a moment. "Maybe I shouldn't have said anything; from now until I graduate I will be the butt of all jokes."

"No, feel free to express yourself, Jordyn. If you have questions or comments, don't be afraid to ask them. Maybe the class will learn something from you. I'd love to have a classroom discussion on this origins debate sometime. It's helpful to discuss differing views and weigh the pros and cons of each side of the debate. It's the beauty of academic freedom."

"Okay, thanks for talking to me," Jordyn said with a friendly smile. "I'll see you on Thursday."

Jordyn turned around, walked up the stairs, and exited the room. She was such a well-mannered girl, and Jeff hated that the students made fun of her for her beliefs. He gathered his things and turned around to exit through the lower doors. As he stepped into the hallway, he was startled to see Robert standing right outside the doorway.

"Hello, Dr. Farris," Jeff said, wondering why his boss was standing suspiciously close to the door.

"Good morning, Dr. Duncan," Robert said rather sternly. "I'd like to speak with you in my office. Now!" He abruptly turned and walked away.

CHAPTER SEVEN

AFTER BREAKFAST, Kate busied herself cleaning the kitchen. The house was quiet except for the morning news playing. This was the first day she would be alone at home and not have Jeff to keep her company. Just last week, Jeff had heard the news that he got the job at Grogan University. Prior to that, she and Jeff spent most of their time together at home.

Kate used to work at her family home décor business. The store was a collaboration of her mother's interest in decorating and her father's interest in business. Her mother died from cancer when Kate was only a teenager, leaving her father with the burden of running the business and trying to raise Kate by himself. She helped her father all through her teenage and adult years. Her dream was to continue managing the family business one day when her father would ceremoniously give her the deed to the property. Those dreams were shattered before they came to fruition. One month ago, shortly after her twenty-eighth birthday, the failing economy forced the business to shut its doors.

Kate's income had helped support the family while Jeff was in school. The closing of the business left both Kate and her father in a state of depression and despair. They both felt like failures, but her father managed to find a job selling cars. Kate's financial hope came when Jeff got his job.

"There is nothing to do," Kate said to herself. She had always been occupied with her family's business, and now with that gone, she had nothing but time on her hands.

The telephone rang.

"Hello?" Kate asked, excited just to have someone to talk to, even if it was a telemarketer.

"Is Mr. Duncan available?"

"No, he isn't. I'm his wife—can I help you?"

"This is Nurse Robin from Grayson Regional Hospital. We are having some difficulty with Ms. Duncan."

"What do you mean?" Kate asked.

"She has been talking to someone in her room all morning, but no one is there," Robin replied. "We have tried to give her some medications to calm her down, but she refuses them. She actually struck one of our nurses."

"Oh, no!" Kate exclaimed. "I'll be right there."

"Thank you," Robin replied.

Kate grabbed her keys and left for the hospital.

* * *

"Why are you following me? Can't you see I want to be left alone?" Evelyn asked. "I've been trying to sleep for hours, but you won't stop talking!"

The man and woman continued their conversation, oblivious to Evelyn's complaints. She grabbed both sides of the pillow she was laying on and held it close to her ears, hoping to drown out the conversation, but to no avail.

"Stop it!" Evelyn yelled. "You have not stopped talking all morning!"

Nurse Robin came into the room. She lost count of how many trips she had made to Evelyn's room this morning. "Ms. Duncan, do you need any help?"

Evelyn could not hear Robin because of the pillow covering her ears. "What?" she asked.

Robin reached over and pulled the pillow away from her head. "I asked if you needed any help. I heard you yelling. You've been yelling a lot this morning, actually."

"No, I haven't," Evelyn replied sheepishly.

"Yes, Mrs. Duncan, you have," Robin said. "We keep coming to check on you, but you never tell us what's wrong."

"Because nothing *is* wrong!" Evelyn snapped.

"We are here to help you. Is there anything you need?"

"Just leave me alone," Evelyn said as she turned to face the wall.

Kate came into the room just as Robin was leaving. She put her purse in a nearby chair and stood next to the bed.

"Hi, Evelyn. How are you feeling?" she asked cheerfully.

"Who are you?" Evelyn asked, turning to look at Kate.

Prepared for her confusion, Kate responded without hesitation, "I'm Kate, Jeff's friend."

Evelyn stared at Kate for a few moments. "Who's Jeff?"

She paused. "Your son, Jeffrey," Kate replied, now getting more concerned. "You have a son named Jeffery. He's at work right now."

"Jeffrey? He's not old enough to be working. He's supposed to be in school," Evelyn replied worriedly. "Is he not in school?"

"He graduated already," Kate replied.

"Graduated! And I wasn't invited to the ceremony!" Evelyn yelled. Grief took over as she buried her face into her hands and wept. "Why didn't he invite me to his graduation?" she sobbed. Tears fell down her face, forming wet stains on the sheets.

Realizing that Evelyn had reached a new level of confusion, Kate did the only thing she knew to do: offer her mother-in-law comfort. Evelyn had attended Jeff's high school and college graduation but now lost all memory of those events, just as she had forgotten about his wedding.

64

Kate held Evelyn's head close to her side as she continued to cry. She rubbed her back and spoke reassuringly to her.

Robin came back to the room. "Is everything okay?" she asked, seeing Evelyn crying.

Kate nodded. "She's just upset today." Turning to Evelyn, she said, "I'll be right back, I need to go talk to the nurse."

Evelyn rolled back on her side as Kate met Robin in the hallway.

"What has she been doing?" Kate asked.

"All morning we have overheard her talking to someone in here. As soon as one of us nurses comes to check on her, she stops talking and denies having ever talked to anyone. The doctor will be in later to see her, and we will let him know about it."

"Who do you think she is talking to?"

"Who knows?"

"What can be done to help her?"

"There are some medications available to help calm her down."

"But she's been refusing them, hasn't she?" Kate asked.

"She has. That's been the problem all morning. We can't force patients to take medicine if they refuse."

"Something has to be done, though," Kate said, her voice becoming frantic as she envisioned taking care of Evelyn on her own in the upcoming days. "If she refuses, then she will just get worse and worse."

Having heard similar complaints from families before, and knowing there was no perfect solution, Robin replied, "Welcome to Alzheimer's disease."

CHAPTER EIGHT

AN UNEASY, nauseous feeling came over Jeff as he stood motionless in the hallway, trying to figure out why his supervisor wanted to meet with him. Not wanting to get in any more trouble, he hurried to Robert's office. Other faculty members passed by Jeff along the way, but they averted their eyes from him, causing an ominous feeling to fill the air. Arriving at Robert's office, he knocked on the door.

"Come in, Jeff. Close the door and have a seat, please," Robert said with an unusual gravity in his voice.

Jeff closed the door and approached the faux leather chair across from Robert's desk. He sat down, placed his briefcase on the floor, and nervously folded his hands together.

Robert didn't waste any time getting to the point. "Dr. Duncan, everyone is nervous on their first day on the job, and they are prone to stumble. In years past, I've been known to stand outside the doorways of the lecture halls and listen in on my staff to ensure they are teaching the truth. You are no exception to this, so this morning I stood outside your classroom. I cannot say you were nervous, but I can easily say you stumbled...a lot. It is clear to me you need additional training."

Jeff didn't like the sound of Robert's belittling tone. He had only covered the syllabus and given a brief introduction to evolution. *What did I do wrong?* Jeff didn't mind being evaluated because he always liked to have correction if it was needed. But getting this job was a great accomplishment, and keeping the job was now a necessity since Kate had lost her income from the family business. Not wanting to make a bad first impression, he asked, "Well, sir, I agree I'm new at this, but I'm open to suggestions. What did I do wrong? How did I stumble?"

"Dr. Duncan, I have no problem with your lecture this morning. You presented a good introduction to the fundamentals of biological evolution, and your ability to relate to the students impressed me. I trust your future lectures will be just as good. However, I am more concerned with how you handled that female student—the one who believes in that Bible nonsense."

"What do you mean, sir?" Jeff asked, all the while trying to think if he said something inappropriate to Jordyn.

"Here at this university, we believe in academic freedom, but we don't promote ignorance, and we don't want students mixing their religion in with science. They are two separate entities. I overheard you tell that student she could believe in her religious origins myth. This garbage she believes in is not good for the other students to hear about. She needs to keep her religion to herself. And that goes for you as well, Jeff. I don't know or care about your religious beliefs, and I'm surprised a man with your educational background is gullible enough to believe in fairy tales about some ancient old man in the sky who created everything. If I had known you were one of those, I would have weeded you out after the first interview. I guess I was wrong about you.

"You need to get your act together if you want to teach at this university. As of right now, with this religion of yours, I will never grant you tenure. Sure, it's many years from now before you will be eligible, but don't think for a minute I won't remember this. And don't get any ideas about suing the university for discrimination. I know all kinds of ways to get you fired. Lucky for you, I didn't sleep well last night and simply don't feel like doing the termination paperwork."

Jeff was furious with the demeaning comments, but he forced himself to keep a straight face. He thought he had handled everything quite well with Jordyn by allowing her to believe what she wanted to, while also informing her of what she would be tested on. But now, Robert was making threats of termination.

"Sir, I thought I handled the situation well," Jeff said, trying to stay professional. "Just because I have a religious background doesn't mean I believe everything I'm told. I'm an evolutionist, but I'm open to the discussion of other origin theories. In my graduate school, they enforced this type of academic freedom despite our religious beliefs. Students in my class were from all kinds of faiths: Hinduism, Judaism...."

Robert slammed his hands on his desk, causing Jeff to flinch from the sudden noise. "I don't care about the school you went to; and I really don't care about anyone's religious beliefs! Dr. Duncan, I forbid you from letting any student pass your class if they still believe in their imaginary friends by the end of the semester. If you don't make every student in there an atheist by the time they graduate, then you, sir, have failed as an educator! It shocks me enough that you earned a doctoral degree while holding onto these ancient fables."

Jeff was at a loss for words. He stared blankly at his boss until he managed to say, "Dr. Farris, one thing I do pride myself in is that I like to take correction from those in authority over me. So I'm asking you what I should have done differently."

Robert's face grew red. He leaned back in his chair and sighed as he looked out the window and watched the students passing by on their way to their next class. "Jeff, from now on, you tell that girl, and any other person with a ridiculous belief, that they will never be a scientist if they believe anything other than evolution. And this doesn't apply only to people wanting to be a scientist. If they want to pursue the medical field, anthropology, archaeology, paleontology, or any of the other science careers, they will never make it unless they change."

"I'll do better at…"

"And another thing, Jeff," Robert interrupted, "Do not discuss any other origin theory unless you are criticizing it. And never under any circumstance will you discuss the criticisms of evolution. We neither promote nor allow that type of discussion in this university."

"Yes, sir. It won't happen again," Jeff said, now forcing himself to remain calm. He glanced at his watch. "My next class starts in five minutes and I do need to leave."

Robert stood up and grabbed a satchel near his desk. "No, it doesn't start in five minutes. Not for you, at least." He put some papers in the satchel and slung it over his shoulder. "I'm not sure I can trust you with the other classes yet. I'm going to teach the rest of them in your place today. In the meantime, you go home and think about how you will make changes. Evaluate your faith and ask yourself how much you want to keep this job. For me, I haven't decided what I'm going to do about you."

"What do you mean? I'm not getting fired, am I?" Jeff grew increasingly worried.

Heading toward the door, Robert muttered, "I don't know," and then walked away.

Alone in Robert's office, Jeff let out a deep sigh and rubbed his hands over his face. *How could he reprimand me over something like that? I only did what I thought was right. I cannot lose this job!* He grabbed his briefcase and walked like a scolded puppy to his office nearby. He sat at his computer for several minutes as he processed the conversation and tried to calm down. Instead of spending the rest of the day teaching his other classes and meeting new students, he was chastised for a simple and innocent conversation and sent home. *This is not fair! He shouldn't have been eavesdropping anyway.*

A half hour passed, and Jeff's rage and blood pressure had finally returned to normal, although the nagging thought of pending disciplinary action never went away. He shut off his computer and left his office. He walked past Dr. Rhonda Matheson's office but didn't look inside to tell her, or anyone, good-bye.

"Jeff?" she asked quietly as he passed by her door.

Jeff rolled his eyes. He was in no mood to talk to anyone. He stopped and walked the few steps back to her office. She greeted him with a warm smile as her necklace with the silver cross glistened on her shirt.

"Can we talk for a second?" She asked.

"Sure," Jeff replied, trying to sound enthusiastic but clearly missing the mark.

Rhonda offered a sorrowful look and said, "I couldn't help overhear Dr. Farris having 'the talk' with you today."

Jeff wasn't sure how to respond. *Can I trust her or is she setting me up?* He closed the door and sat down across from her. "The talk?"

Rhonda continued, "I've worked here for eleven years now, and Dr. Farris has been the dean for well over twenty years. He is a very educated man and is dedicated to his profession. He loves his students and wants them to learn as much as possible during their four years here. However, Dr. Farris is very particular about his faculty. Most of the professors who have come and gone had graduate degrees and the same eagerness to teach as you do, but they couldn't tolerate his attitude. By that, I mean he has the occasional gruff demeanor that makes it hard for others to get along with him. I've seen many fresh, young faces come into this department only to leave by the end of the semester because of his personality. We have quite an embarrassing turnover rate, but it isn't like this at all in the other departments. Here in the science department, though, there are only three of us now who have tenure because the others left before they became eligible."

What have I gotten myself into? Shocked to hear about the high turnover rate, he asked, "What's made you stay here so long?"

"Let me be more open with you," Rhonda continued. "I and many other faculty members have had the same talk with Dr. Farris as you just had. It happened during my first month here. I'll admit that I almost quit. I went home in tears and considered not returning to work the next day, but then I remembered how hard I had worked in school to get to where I am, and I didn't want to let someone like him ruin me. Besides, the next college is over two hours away from here, and I didn't want to have to relocate or make a long commute every day."

"Did you also violate this hidden policy about allowing the discussion of alternatives to evolution?" Jeff asked sarcastically.

"As a matter of fact, I did," Rhonda said as she leaned back in her chair. "I'm sure you see this cross necklace I wear. You don't find many of these on college campuses, especially not here in the science department." Jeff looked at her cross again as she fiddled with it between her fingers. "My mom gave it to me on my sixteenth birthday. I have always been a very devout Christian and went to church every time the doors were open—at least I used to.

"You know, I remember that day so well when Dr. Farris chastised me. I told my class that evolution is just a theory, and a theory of course is just an explanation of the evidences. I was not criticizing evolution—I knew I was being paid to teach it—but apparently Dr. Farris thought I was teaching against the theory. He overheard my lecture, came into the class, and corrected me in front of all of those students. I was so embarrassed.

"Dr. Farris is a very smart man—no one can argue with that. I wanted to talk to him about intelligent design, but I was too intimidated, fearing he would give answers to everything I said and just shut me down or worse, talk me out of my faith. But Dr. Farris taught me something. Maybe he had high hopes for me or saw that my students liked me, but over time he showed me concepts in evolution that show its validity. It took a while for me to accept it, but I couldn't get past the evidence. Granted, when I was in school, my college professors never discussed intelligent design, so I guess you could say I was indoctrinated. Regardless, the evidence for evolution is all around us.

"I discussed this with my pastor at the time who knew I was a science professor. I asked him about creation from a biological perspective and he simply couldn't give me a satisfactory answer. It turned out that my pastor didn't believe in a literal creation, young earth, or any of the stuff I used to believe in. He said those stories in the Bible are more about life lessons instead of actual historical events. My pastor told me most of the stories in the Old Testament were metaphorical anyway and couldn't be relied upon since they were written thousands of years after the fact. Pastor Larry helped me understand that we need to accept the facts of science and interpret the Bible accordingly, and as far as our faith goes, all we need to do is be a good person and believe in Jesus Christ."

"Wait a minute," Jeff interrupted. "Did you say Pastor Larry?"

"Yes, do you know him?"

"Does he have a son named Bill Watson?"

"Yes, I think he is a pastor now," Rhonda replied. "I haven't been to church in a while, but I heard his son took over after Larry got sick."

"That's the church I attend!" Jeff exclaimed. "I guess he and Bill share the same beliefs because Bill gave a sermon this week about what you just said—about the Bible containing stories instead of real historical events."

Rhonda nodded her head in agreement. "Listen, Jeff. As I said, almost everyone has to go through 'the talk' with Dr. Farris. Just brush it off, go home, and get a good night's rest. Tomorrow he will calm down and talk to you like normal." She paused. "Did he threaten to fire you?"

"Yes, he did make the threat, but then he said he didn't know what he was going to do," Jeff replied.

"Keep your head up," Rhonda encouraged. "Just think about what I said. You and I both have our faith; and we also have our scientific knowledge. You don't have to deny one to keep the other. Just trust in Jesus, be a good person, and help others. That's the message of salvation." Jeff nodded. *That's what I've always been taught, at least.*

"Thank you. I needed some encouragement. It bothers me, though, that Dr. Farris has done this to so many others. I'm glad I'm not the only one, but still, how could he get away with such discrimination?" Jeff asked.

Rhonda sighed. "I told myself long ago that if I ever became the dean, I wouldn't care if a professor or student challenged evolution. I myself welcome academic freedom. It's a good way to grow, especially in the field of science. But back to your question: I know there are all kinds of laws about discrimination, but he thinks he is above the law while he is the dean." She paused for a minute and lowered her voice. "Have you ever heard the phrase 'money equals power'?" Jeff nodded. "You do know the name of this building, don't you?"

Farris Science Hall. "You mean, he owns this building!" Jeff exclaimed.

"Not exactly," Rhonda replied. "Dr. Farris' parents were wealthy, and they paid for this entire building we are sitting in. It goes without saying that Robert got promoted to dean because of his parents. You could say he has quite a bit of pull around here. He literally calls all the shots. Even the college president calls him 'sir.' This school is forever in debt to his parents for their donation of this building. No one in the administration would ever challenge the Farris family."

Jeff put the puzzle pieces together. "Politics, go figure," he replied with a gruff laugh.

"It doesn't affect just Grogan University. Some of my colleagues in the past tried to contact the higher-ups at both the state and federal level to make a complaint. Let's just say they used to be my colleagues."

"They got fired?"

"It's worse than that," she replied. "There were eight demoted professors who joined together to try to make a change and get something done about the discrimination and academic censorship. Not only were they fired, but their names were sent out to all of the colleges and universities in Tennessee. To this day, none of them are working as professors. I have heard that one of them became a truck driver because he could never find a teaching position, not even at the high school level."

Jeff's mouth fell open. "You mean they were banned from working in any school?" Rhonda nodded.

"It's easy to conclude that if I want to keep my job, I'd better do as I'm told or else. I dedicated my whole life to becoming a professor, and I can't afford to lose this job. This isn't fair, but until something better comes along, I'll have to obey the dictator."

"That's what we all had to do. To put it in evolutionary terms, you have to 'adapt to your environment,'" she replied with a grin. "Once you do, and Robert sees that you are progressing the way he wants, he will accept you. You will 'evolve' and he won't look down on you anymore. Do everything he asks and you will get tenure. That's the only way I get to wear this cross—I got tenure, and now he can't fire me over little things. Of course, I had to buy a longer chain so my cross would hide under my blouse. You can only see the tip of it now."

"It looks like you had to 'evolve' to adapt to your surroundings as well," Jeff said with a laugh. "Thanks for talking to me. I'll see you tomorrow, Rhonda."

Jeff smiled as he left her office. He began to feel better as he exited the building and walked to his car. It was reassuring to know he was not the only one who had been discriminated against, and he didn't have to put his faith on hiatus just so he could keep his job. Jeff had already concluded that a young earth and divine creation were unthinkable in the eyes of science, and he was okay with that. As far as his faith, he just wanted to live a good life so he would be saved from Hell. The little details in the Bible had never been too important anyway; much less make any sense to him.

CHAPTER NINE

JEFF ARRIVED home just as Kate pulled into the driveway.

"What are you doing home so early?" she asked.

"I was sent home by Dr. Farris. I got in trouble, and I don't know what's going to happen next," Jeff said sadly as he and Kate walked into their home.

"What happened?"

Jeff explained to Kate what he had been reprimanded for. "I did nothing wrong, but Dr. Farris believes otherwise. I'm so afraid he is going to fire me, and I'll never get a job teaching again."

"Don't worry about it, Jeff," Kate said, rubbing his back like she did with Evelyn earlier. "Maybe Dr. Farris was having a bad day and tomorrow he will apologize."

"That's not very likely according to what one of my colleagues said. What are we going to do about money if I get fired?"

"I don't know," she replied. "We still have a little bit left in the savings. We will work something out."

Kicking off his shoes, he asked, "Where did you go this morning?"

"The hospital called me because your mother was becoming difficult to handle. I went to check on her and try to help. The nurse said Evelyn's been talking to someone, but when asked who she is talking to, Evelyn just denies it."

"This is a new thing. We heard her talking the other day. At least others have heard it, too," Jeff said.

Kate nodded her head. "How about I fix you a nice lunch, and you go take a hot shower to relax. We will get through this. I'll find a job myself if necessary."

"A hot shower sounds nice. Would you make an omelet for me? Cheese and eggs always cheer me up."

"Sure," Kate replied with a warm smile. Jeff kissed her on the cheek and then went to the bedroom to prepare for his shower. She did cheer him up, but still, his joy and confidence were on the verge of being shattered as he awaited tomorrow's verdict of his employment.

Jeff turned the water up as hot as he could stand it and let his body soak in the relaxing heat. The steam filled the room, making Jeff think he was in a sauna. *As if I could ever afford one of those.* Several minutes passed by and then cold water began to pour out of the faucet as the hot water supply ran out. That was his cue that he had enough relaxation. As he stepped out of the shower, Kate yelled for him from the kitchen.

"Jeff! The hospital is on the phone and they want to talk to you."

"Okay, I'll be out in a minute. Tell them to hold on."

He wrapped a towel around his waist and quickly dried his face. He didn't see Kate standing in the doorway of the bathroom and holding the phone. A mischievous smile grew on her face as she said, "Nice body, hot stuff!"

"Opposites attract, you know," Jeff said in his usual dry manner. She jokingly punched him in the shoulder. One of the things he liked about Kate was her ability to take a joke and dish it right back at him, or at least hit him if she couldn't come up with a quick response.

Jeff took the phone and deactivated the hold button. "Hello, this is Jeff."

"Mr. Duncan, this is Nurse Joann from the hospital. I'm calling to let you know that Ms. Duncan will be discharged tomorrow morning. The doctor put her arm in a sling since the fracture was minor, but he still wants her to stay in the hospital for observation. Her potassium and blood sugar are a little low so we are trying to get it stabilized before she goes home."

"Okay. Do whatever is necessary to take care of her," Jeff replied. He was grateful to have one more day before his mother moved in with him. After having a rough morning, he didn't need any additional stress.

"There is something else I need to tell you," Joann added. "Dr. Norman is very concerned about her confusion and the rapid progression of her Alzheimer's disease. She has not been coherent since she arrived here yesterday."

"I understand. We already decided to let her move in with us," Jeff said with a hint of pride in his voice. "My wife stays home during the day while I work so she will be able to take care of her."

"That's wonderful," Joann replied. "Are you sure you can handle her?"

Feeling insulted, he replied, "Yes, I can take care of my mother. She's better off here than some nursing home."

"Okay, you can come get her tomorrow morning around nine o'clock. The doctor wants to see her in two weeks for a follow-up."

"I'll ask my wife to come get her tomorrow. Thank you for calling."

"Thank you, Mr. Duncan."

Jeff turned the phone off, laid it on the sink counter, and continued drying himself. Kate came back to the bathroom. "What did they want?"

"That was a nurse saying that Evelyn will be discharged in the morning. Will you have any problem picking her up at the hospital and bringing her back here?"

Kate replied, "No, I think I can manage it. She may think she is going back to her home so I'll have to convince her she needs to stay with us until she recuperates. That is, if she even knows who I am."

"This is true," Jeff said. "We better go to her house and get some of her things so she will feel at home."

"Okay. But let's eat first. I got your omelet ready: eggs, extra cheese, bacon, and mushrooms."

"Heaven on a plate," Jeff smirked. "Thanks for making it for me."

He finished dressing himself and went into the kitchen to eat. As he enjoyed his wife's cooking, he pondered the problems they would have with Evelyn moving in with them, especially since her mind had gotten worse. *It can't be that hard; she's my mother. What could possibly go wrong?* After lunch, Jeff cleaned up the kitchen while Kate put some suitcases and garbage bags in the car.

"This shouldn't take too long," Jeff said as they backed out of the driveway.

"I'm starting to have second thoughts about this," replied Kate. "I saw how bad she was this morning, and I don't know if I can deal with her confusion all day, every day."

"It will take some getting used to, but you have a lot more patience than I do, and I think you will do a great job."

After arriving at Evelyn's house, they were hit with the smell of garbage. Although the trash was gone, the odor had been absorbed into the carpet and onto the walls. Jeff carried the suitcases and garbage bags inside and placed them on the couch near the door.

"I should have brought some more air freshener," Kate said while gagging.

"I'll open all the windows. Maybe that will circulate the smell out of here."

Jeff proceeded to go to each window in the house. They had not been opened in years, so each one required some force before they would budge. Meanwhile, Kate took the suitcases and bags into Evelyn's bedroom. Evelyn kept most of her clothes in a dresser, but ever since her diagnosis, she

78

stopped organizing them and instead dumped them into whichever drawer was least full. Kate had offered to help her with laundry in the past, but Evelyn would refuse, and often she would wear the same clothes for several days in a row instead of washing them. Kate sorted through the assortment of unorganized clothes and put them into piles of shirts, pants, underwear, and socks.

After opening the windows, Jeff realized that there was no breeze or circulation coming from the hot August weather. He went to the shed in the back yard to get an old box fan he had stored when he moved off to college. He found the fan covered in dirt and grime. *I hope this works.*

Jeff returned to the living room and plugged it in. The blades made a grinding sound, but after a swift kick, they started to rotate at a slow speed, allowing enough circulation to disperse the stagnant air. Satisfied, he went to the bedroom to help Kate.

"What a mess," he said, seeing the piles of clothes.

"She would never let me help her organize her laundry, so now I have to sort through everything," Kate said tiredly.

Jeff knelt down to the floor and pulled out a drawer full of assorted clothes. He organized them into the piles Kate had started. "What's this?" he asked, reaching to the back of the drawer.

Kate stopped to look. Jeff pulled two old and tattered Feagan brand shoeboxes from the drawer and sat them on the floor. The Feagan brand had been out of business for decades and the boxes showed significant wear and tear from their old age. Pieces of duct tape held the torn cardboard corners together.

"I wonder what she has in here," Jeff said as he reached over and pulled the loose lid off the box closest to him. His eyes widened. There before him sat seven stacks of cash neatly stored in the old box. A one-hundred dollar bill sat on top of each stack. Jeff grabbed a bundle at random and fanned through it. All of the denominations in his hand were one-hundred dollar bills. He then grabbed another bundle and found that it, too, had the same denomination. A smile formed over his face as he admired the amount of money in his hands. He grabbed another stack...the same thing. His hands were getting full so Kate grabbed the four remaining stacks and verified that all of the bundles were full of one-hundred dollar bills as well.

"There must be at least two-hundred thousand in here!" exclaimed Jeff. "Where did she get all of this money? She has always complained about not having enough, but she has more here than I will ever earn."

He stacked the money neatly back into the box and removed the lid from the other box. "Wow!" he exclaimed. "There is just as much in here. Mom is wealthy!" Each stack in the second box also contained one-hundred dollar bills. In addition, Evelyn had stored her old check book registries, cancelled checks, and a credit card. Jeff reached into the box to look closer at the credit card. "It's not expired yet. No telling what she has bought with it. I hope she doesn't have a huge bill coming our way."

"That is a lot of money," Kate remarked.

"Who would have ever known she had this money stored up!" Jeff exclaimed. "Think of what we could do with it!"

Kate snatched the money out of his hands, stacked it back into the box, covered it with the lid, and put both boxes back into the drawer. "We aren't doing anything with it," she replied sternly. "This belongs to your mother, not us."

"It will be mine one day," Jeff remarked. "I'm in her will; everything will be given to me."

"When she dies," Kate clarified, "you will get everything. Until then, it all belongs to her and is only for her use."

"Why are you being like this, Kate? I might lose my job tomorrow, and we are going to need money to pay the bills."

"Be that as it may, I won't let you spend this on yourself."

"This is our chance to get out of debt and stop worrying about finances all the time. I'm sure Mom would never know if some of it was missing. She probably forgot about the money being here anyway."

"That's beside the point. Jeff, this is your mother's money, and we are not using it. She's bound to get a large hospital bill, and she will need to use this to pay for it."

"It won't be too expensive," Jeff reasoned. "She hasn't been in the hospital that long."

Kate didn't respond. She turned back to the clothes and packed them into the suitcases and garbage bags.

Still trying to convince her, Jeff added, "We don't have to spend the money, but if Mom is going to live with us, then it needs to be at our house for safe keeping. I wouldn't trust some of the neighbors over here. They might break in and steal it."

"We can take it to the house and store it there," Kate said reluctantly, "but we are not spending any of it on ourselves."

Close enough. Jeff stepped in-between Kate and the suitcase she was working on, opened the drawer again, and carefully removed both shoeboxes. "I'm going to take these out to the car," he said.

Frustrated with her husband, Kate carelessly stuffed the remaining clothes into the bags, tied the flaps in a knot, and dragged the bags to the car. She found Jeff leaning over the trunk sorting through the money. "Leave it alone, Jeff!" she snapped. "What has gotten into you? In a matter of minutes, you've become a money-hungry monster."

"Don't you see, Kate?" Jeff said slyly. "With this money, we can get out of debt, pay our bills, eat decent food, and get some of the things we've always wanted. You know how much you've wanted a new car, right?"

Kate sheepishly grinned. "Of course I want a new car. The one I have is on its last leg."

"Well, this is our chance!" he exclaimed. "There's something else, or should I say 'someone else' you've been wanting, too."

Kate laughed and hugged him. "I've wanted a baby for the longest time, but we were never able to afford one."

"So here is our chance," Jeff said. He wasn't at all ready for fatherhood, but he knew how badly Kate wanted to be a mother, and playing these cards with her would make her more agreeable to take the money to their house and use it for themselves. *It was willed to me, so it's basically mine already.*

Arriving home, Jeff quickly got out of the car, grabbed both of the garbage bags full of clothes, and tucked one of the shoeboxes under his left arm. Kate grabbed a suitcase, unlocked the front door, and held it open for Jeff. Before walking inside, he turned around to make sure no one was near his car because the other shoebox was still in the opened trunk. Dropping the garbage bags and putting the shoebox on the couch, he then hurried back to the car to grab the other shoebox and suitcase.

"I'll get some clothes hangers and put her clothes in the guest room closet," Kate said as he returned with the final load.

Jeff put the suitcase on the floor next to the one she had brought in. "I'm going to hide these shoeboxes under our bed. They will be safe there."

"Okay," Kate replied. She still wasn't comfortable having Evelyn's money at their house, even if it was for safekeeping. Her husband had become strangely greedy all of a sudden, and she didn't like it. Kate started sorting through the clothes but then realized they all had the smell of garbage and needed to be washed. She put the clothes back into their containers and one by one, carried the suitcases and garbage bags into the utility room where she would wash them. As she worked, Kate thought about how different it would be with someone else in the house. She wouldn't mind having the company, but taking care of an Alzheimer's patient would be stressful.

A half hour later, Jeff came running into the laundry room and eagerly squeezed Kate from behind. "What have you been doing?" she asked, although she knew he had to have been doing something with the money.

"You'll never guess how much money she had!"

"There's no telling," she replied, not showing much interest. "You guessed two-hundred thousand earlier, didn't you?"

Jeff laughed. "Not even close. Can you believe she has half a million in there! Kate, we won't have to worry about money for a long time! I can pay off our debts and buy any car you want!"

Kate smiled and said softly, "That is a lot of money. I wonder where it all came from."

"I don't know. I think she invested in the stock market back when she was working."

Kate wanted to remind Jeff that the money didn't belong to him, but she knew it would burst his bubble and he would get mad at her nagging; she instead decided to let him have his moment. "I think she will have enough clothes to wear for now. I grabbed a few dresses from her closet, and she has more in there if needed." Kate added a load of clothes to the washer, poured in the detergent, and set the dial. "I'm going to get the spare bedroom ready for her."

"There may be more cash over there, too," Jeff said, oblivious to his increasing lust for money. "Thanks for helping me get the house ready for her, Kate." She had noticed how much friendlier Jeff had been ever since he found the money. She tried to enjoy the pleasant change, but she knew it was only superficial. "Do you want me to help with the bedroom?" he asked eagerly.

"Nah, I can handle it," she replied. In reality, she just didn't want Jeff's company. She knew he would keep talking to her about what he would do with the newly found money. It did not belong to him; regardless, he would not listen to her. Kate took an extra-long time preparing Evelyn's room so as to avoid speaking to her husband. Jeff spent the remainder of the day counting and sorting the money several times and fantasizing about what he would do with it, all the while unaware of Kate's growing dislike of his decision.

CHAPTER TEN

WEDNESDAY MORNING arrived with Jeff waking up in a great mood, excited about going to school to teach for another day. Even if he got fired today, he would now have the financial stability to support him until he found a new job. Jeff got dressed, kissed Kate good-bye, and headed for the university.

He arrived at the school whistling a happy tune as he entered the faculty offices. Robert stood at the printer sorting through some papers he had just copied.

"Good morning, Dr. Farris," Jeff said in pleasant tone, hoping his boss would have forgotten about their conversation.

"Ah, good morning, Dr. Duncan," Robert said, peering at Jeff over his glasses. "Could we talk in my office?"

A chill shot down his spine. "Yes, sir," Jeff stammered while forcing himself to remain calm. Robert grabbed the rest of the papers and walked to his office, and Jeff followed behind.

"Have a seat," Robert said, gesturing to the chair in front of his desk.

Jeff sat down and put his briefcase on the floor.

"I'm sure you remember our conversation from yesterday," Robert said.

"You were right about what you said. I'm not going to allow the students to talk about other origin theories unless they are criticizing them. Evolution should only be taught and defended," Jeff replied robotically.

"That is what I wanted to hear, and that mindset will help you in the future," Robert said. "However, after thinking long and hard about our talk yesterday, I've made an executive decision. You're new, you're young, and you're immature. I know you are supposed to teach other classes today, but I'm removing you from all classes except the Tuesday and Thursday biology class. Your lab and other classes will be reassigned to my seasoned and more educated professors."

The overall shock caused Jeff to be speechless for a few moments. "I told you where I went wrong! I made the change!" he exclaimed.

"The decision has been made."

"But, won't that cut my pay? The university policy says I can't receive full pay and benefits if I only teach part-time."

"You're right, Jeff. It was a hard decision to make. I know you have a family and bills like the rest of us, but policy is policy. You will now be listed as part-time faculty. Your medical insurance and other benefits will be suspended until you are brought back to full-time." Robert changed his voice to sound friendlier and offer a glimpse of optimism. "Like I said, this is only temporary. Once you find yourself and stop believing in those silly Bible stories, I'll let you come back full time."

"Are you saying I can only teach introduction to biology now?"

"Yes, Dr. Duncan. I'd rather you not even teach that, but since you already started with that class, I'll let you keep it. Maybe you'll learn a thing or two yourself." He gave a fake smile and turned to his computer. "By the way, you can go home now. You will not be needed today."

Jeff grabbed his briefcase and stood up to leave. The growing rage inside caused his body to tremble. He didn't turn to tell Robert good-bye or even thank him for the correction.

As he reached for the door handle, Robert said, "Remember, Jeff, I'll be watching. Don't let your little creationist friend have any hope. Use the evolutionary truths to destroy her beliefs and turn her into a real scientist. Don't allow her to pass the class until she gets serious."

Jeff didn't respond to those last remarks. He exited Robert's office and hurried into his own office, closing the door behind him. He dropped his briefcase into a chair and stomped his feet on the carpeted floor as he walked toward his desk. Anger had overtaken him. He collapsed in his chair to process his thoughts.

I didn't do anything wrong! I told Jordyn that she can believe what she wants to believe, but I never said evolution was incorrect. I believe in evolution. The evidence supports it. Robert is accusing me of being some type of religious fundamentalist! I used to believe some of the things in the Bible about the origins of the earth, but that was all done away with when I went to college. Besides, even Pastor Bill doesn't believe in a literal creation, much less teach that the Bible is true. He spends more time at church entertaining us with music than teaching about God.

What am I going to do? I can't go for a semester as a part-timer! I need the money and insurance! I have bills and a mortgage and a car payment, and now there is this whole ordeal with taking care of Mom. Why did this have to happen now?

Embarrassed because of his demotion, Jeff left the office. He walked slowly, boiling with anger while replaying the conversation over and over again. He didn't understand how he had violated any written policy. It wasn't as though he passed a student that was failing or committed some other academic violation. Jeff had spent time critiquing his lecture from yesterday to make improvements, and he had a plan for how he would respond to any student who wanted to bring religion into the discussion. That was of no use to him now that he had only one class to teach. *Where is the academic freedom?*

He got back in his car and slammed his hands on the steering wheel. It hurt to do that, but he had to let the steam out somehow. Jeff tried to collect his thoughts, but a dark cloud of rage fogged his mind. In utter desperation, he began to pray.

"God," he whispered, "I know we don't talk much, but I'm having trouble believing everything I've been told about you. If you are real, then why am I suffering like this? I prayed to you for a job, and I got the job, but now you took almost all of it away from me! And why does Mom have to suffer like this? She's always been a good woman. I thought you were a loving God. She never did anything to deserve this! Lord, God, Jesus, whoever you are, I am simply struggling now to find any evidence that you are real. What evidence is there for your existence? Everything I see has been explained through science, and there is no need for supernatural explanations anymore. It worked on me as a child, but now I'm an adult. What is the point of your existence anyway? Show me something already!"

Jeff raised his head and looked up at the sky through his windshield. The tops of the Appalachian Mountains had disappeared into the increasingly cloudy sky. He laughed at himself. *I can't even see this God. Where is He anyway?* No obvious answer came to him. Discouraged, he started his car and headed for home, all the while pondering his prayer. *Does God even listen?*

Jeff had grown up in church and always believed everything he was taught without question. He was active in the youth group and many of his weekends during his teenage years were spent doing "servant evangelism" where they did community service as a means of spreading the gospel. His youth pastor, Allen, who came from an older generation but still felt youthful enough to handle teenagers, always talked about Jesus. Jeff wanted to learn more, but no one could ever answer his questions. He would ask Allen about the origin of life, the purpose of life, who created God, where heaven is located…but his unequipped youth pastor would oftentimes be stumped and give an ambiguous answer, which left Jeff with even more questions. When he graduated from high school and began college, Jeff was ready for a break from all things church-related. He was eager to be on his own and discover for himself the answers to life's questions instead of being told to "trust in Jesus and don't ruffle any theological feathers."

Jeff pulled into his driveway just as Kate was leaving. She stopped the car and got out to see why he was home early again.

"Please tell me you didn't get fired," she said anxiously.

"No, I still have my job," Jeff replied. "But now, I only have one class. The jerk said he couldn't trust me with any other classes so he reassigned them. I really don't want to talk about it right now."

"That's terrible. At least you are still employed." Kate was still upset over Jeff wanting to use Evelyn's money, but now she was angry that her husband had been let down again, and she felt sorry for him. "Maybe that boss of yours ought to retire. He's taking all of this way out of proportion." Jeff liked that Kate was agreeing with him. "I'm going to the hospital to get Evelyn. Do you want to come?"

"No, I'm going to go inside and relax for a little bit—I still need to cool off from these two bad days I've had. I thought it was great to get this job, you know? Straight out of college and already employed—that doesn't happen often, but so far this has been nothing but trouble," Jeff said mournfully. "I hope Mom doesn't give you a hard time. Call me if you need help."

"I will," Kate said as she drove away.

Jeff went inside and Samson got off the couch and sauntered over to him. "Yes, I'm home early," Jeff tried to explain to his feline companion. He rubbed his head on Jeff's clean pants leg, leaving behind a few strands of black fur. Jeff went to the bedroom to change, and as always, Samson followed closely behind.

Jeff lifted the bed comforter up and peered underneath the bedframe. There sat the two shoe boxes full of money. He pulled them both out and looked inside to make sure the money was still there, and of course it was. *It's not going to walk away, Jeff.* The sight provided a sense of comfort to know he had financial security. He picked up one of the bundles and fanned the edges in hopes of bringing himself some joy and reassurance. Jeff grinned, thinking how safe and secure he would be with the new found money. It made his demotion not seem like a problem after all. He already knew how he would make changes in his teaching style so that next semester he could work full-time again. Jeff put the money back in the box, slid them both under the bed, pulled the comforter down, and then went back to the living room to wait for Kate and Evelyn to come home.

They arrived about an hour later. Kate pushed the door open and held onto Evelyn's non-injured left arm to ensure she wouldn't fall. Seeing Evelyn frail and disoriented, wearing a sling on her right arm and a bandage on her forehead, Jeff got up to help her inside. "Hi, Mom. How are you feeling?" he asked.

"This isn't my home," Evelyn said as Kate helped her walk over the threshold. "I told her this wasn't my home but she insisted I come inside. I want to go home! Take me home!"

"Remember what we talked about in the car, Evelyn?" Kate said with a somewhat childish voice. "We want you to live with us for a little while until you feel better."

"I feel fine. There's nothing wrong with me. Take me home!" Evelyn quickly responded.

Kate didn't anticipate Evelyn agreeing with her, but she at least wanted to make the effort. She and Jeff carefully walked with Evelyn over to the couch. Kate sat down and slightly pulled on Evelyn's arm so she would sit next to her, but instead Evelyn positioned herself at the opposite end of the couch. "We just want to spend more time with you. We have all of your things here that you need. Don't you want to stay with us?"

"No, I want to go home. I have important things there!" Evelyn said. Her body shook from the anxiety, and a worried expression filled her eyes. "Take me back! I don't even know who you people are!"

Jeff sat down on the couch next to his mother. "Mom, Dr. Norman wants you to stay with us for just a little while to make sure you don't fall again. You have to go back to see him in two weeks; maybe then he will let you go back home." *That's not going to happen.*

Evelyn gave Jeff a curious look. "Why are you calling me 'Mom'? I don't know you, and I don't know why she brought me to this place. Take me home, or I'll call the police and have you both arrested."

Jeff paused. "Mom, don't you know who I am?"

"No!" she barked. "Quit calling me 'Mom.' I have one son and he is just a little boy. He's at home now by himself and I need to go check on him."

"But, I am your son," Jeff pleaded.

"You're a grown man. My Jeffery is just a child."

Tears formed in the corners of his eyes, so he stood up to leave the room. Kate followed behind him.

"Jeff, she doesn't recognize us anymore. The combination of the head trauma and Alzheimer's has made her lose all memory of familiar faces."

Jeff wiped away the tears. "No, I won't accept that."

He turned around and went back to the couch. He slid the coffee table out and knelt down in front of his mother. "Mom, I am Jeffery, your son. You raised me all my life and now I'm a grown man."

Evelyn gave Jeff a blank look. Her mouth opened a little bit and quivered as she tried to form the right words. "My son isn't grown up. He's just a little boy, and he's at home waiting for me!" She then reached for the cordless phone lying on the coffee table in front of her. "I'm calling

Jeffrey right now. He needs to know where I'm at. Maybe his daddy is at home too, and he will come and rescue me." *Good luck with that, Mom. Dad never cared about you or me.* Evelyn picked up the phone and began pointing her fingers at different numbers, clearly confused on which ones to dial. After a few moments, Evelyn dialed Jeff's home phone number. *Why is she calling here?* Jeff glanced at Kate, hoping she would have a new idea on how to persuade Evelyn to stay at their home.

"It's busy," Evelyn said after a few seconds of holding the phone up to her ear and listening to the aggravating busy tone. "I'll try again in a minute."

Jeff sighed and rubbed his hands over his face. "Mom, I am Jeffrey. I'm 35 years old now. The reason the phone line was busy is because you dialed the very phone you are using." He grew irritated but tried not to show anger toward her. She couldn't help how her mind had deteriorated.

Jeff then thought of a clever trick. "Mom, ask me any question about Jeffery, and I can answer it. This will prove I am your son."

Evelyn laughed. She put the phone down on her lap. "Okay, I'll ask you one thing that only he could know. I'll prove to you that you aren't my son, and then I'm calling the police."

"Ask away," Jeff said as he repositioned himself on the floor.

"What was Jeffrey's favorite pet?" Evelyn asked smugly.

Jeff knew the answer immediately. It was Roscoe, his cat Evelyn got him when he was six years old. Roscoe lived with the family until Jeff turned eighteen. Although he lived a rather long life, Roscoe was playful and lovable up until the day he died.

"It was an orange tabby cat named Roscoe. He lived with us for twelve years and died of kidney failure," Jeff confidently replied.

Evelyn paused. Her mouth hung open and her eyes widened. She replied, "Well, that was just a lucky guess. I don't care if you know about some silly cat. You are not my son. I'm going home."

Evelyn began to stand up. Jeff had had enough. He growled through his teeth like an angry dog and got up from the floor. He stomped back to his bedroom and slammed the door, causing the walls to shake and the wedding pictures in the hallway to slide back and forth. He punched his fist into the bed. This had been his coping mechanism for many years—hitting something soft to relieve aggression. With all the problems he had with his job, the last thing he needed was a contrary mother.

"That's just like Jeffrey does," Evelyn said after watching her son storm off. "He gets so mad at me when I tell him something he doesn't want to hear. He marches off and slams his bedroom door, but then he comes back out in five minutes to apologize. And just like that, we get along as though nothing happened."

Kate had difficulty grasping Evelyn's immense level of delusion. The Alzheimer's disease had blinded her from seeing her own son. "Evelyn, that is your son," Kate said in a calm but firm voice. "He knew the name of his cat, how long it lived, and how it died. He even slammed the door just like Jeffery. Can't you see?"

"He's not my son. My son is just a little boy. You and that man are trying to fool me, but you aren't going to do it. I might be old but I still have my mind! The doctor said I'm in the best shape ever!"

Behind the bedroom door, Jeff could hear his mother's proclamation. *She's not in good shape at all. This is the worse she has ever been.* Knowing that he was fighting a losing battle, Jeff came out of the bedroom a few minutes later. "Alright, if you want to go home, then just leave. Your doctor will not like it, but I give up on convincing you to stay," Jeff said. He was flabbergasted, and any other time he would

93

be yelling, but since this was his mother, he tried to soften his voice. He turned toward his wife. "Let's take her home."

"It's not safe for her there. She's not able to take care of herself with her mind like this," Kate said in a hushed whisper.

"We can't hold her against her will. She'll call the police on us next." Jeff wondered if Evelyn could even remember the correct number for the police department.

"Take me home, or I'll call the police!" Evelyn declared.

"Let's go," Jeff said. They headed for the door, and Evelyn slowly followed behind.

CHAPTER ELEVEN

"THIS ISN'T my home. I don't know who you people are. My son Jeffrey is at home waiting on me." Evelyn continued with her common phrases as she walked behind Jeff and Kate to the car. Jeff ignored her and bit his tongue as he helped her into the back seat. *I'm so tired of her repeating herself. Why does she do this?*

She continued to mutter as they drove to her home. Jeff felt the veins in his forehead throbbing. The tension could be cut with a knife. He didn't want to say anything to his mother because she would just argue more with him. Despite the overwhelming frustration, both Jeff and Kate had mutual concerns over Evelyn's safety when she would soon be on her own. "I'll call the doctor to see what he suggests," Jeff whispered to Kate as they pulled into Evelyn's driveway. He opened the back door and helped his mother out of the seat.

"You sure are nice for a stranger," Evelyn said as she turned to face her house. "This is more like it. Thank you for bringing me home. Those crazy people were going to keep me at their house all night. That one man tried to fool me into thinking he was my son! Can you believe the nerve of some people?"

A perturbed expression fell on Jeff's face. Kate looked back at him, reciprocating a similar countenance. They knew what the other was thinking: Evelyn had completely forgotten that "those crazy people" were the very ones who had just brought her home and were now standing next to her.

As they walked to Evelyn's house, Jeff reached into his pocket and pulled out his set of keys containing one for Evelyn's front door. He stuck the key in the lock, turned it, and opened the door for his mother. Evelyn suddenly turned to him and asked, "How did you get a key to my house?"

Without missing a beat, Jeff replied, "I know your son really well. He let me borrow a key." *I hope she buys that one.* Kate turned away so Evelyn wouldn't see her suppressing a laugh. Before Evelyn could answer him, Jeff turned on the light so she could see the inside of her home and hopefully be distracted from the thought that her "child" had been spending time with an unknown, older man.

"Home sweet home," Evelyn said as she walked in.

"Evelyn, can I fix you something to eat?" Kate offered.

"I don't know who you are or how you know my name, but I'm home now and don't want any company. I will ask you kindly to leave," Evelyn replied.

Kate turned to Jeff and said, "One of us needs to stay here with her for a little while. She can't be left alone."

"We are strangers to her," he replied. "She won't listen to us. She's lived here alone for all these years; what's one more day going to hurt? Let's just contact the doctor and see what he wants us to do."

Kate sighed. "She's your mother. I don't like the idea, but there really aren't any good options. She will just argue with us or kick us out of the home."

Jeff and Kate both told Evelyn goodbye. "Thank you for bringing me home and getting me away from those people," she told them as they left. While driving back home, Kate called Dr. Norman's office for advice, but no one answered so she had to leave a message with his nurse.

As soon as Jeff and Kate got home, the phone rang.

"Hello?" Jeff answered.

"Jeffrey, this is your mother. Someone tried to kidnap me today. I don't know who they were, but they took me to a strange house. I threatened to call the police on them so they brought me back home."

The increasing tension in his forehead finally caused a violent headache to form. While Evelyn talked, Jeff scrolled through the missed calls on his phone and saw that she had already called him five times since they left her house. "Mom, I was just at your house. I am the one who brought you home."

"When did you come by?"

"Just fifteen minutes ago!"

"I don't remember seeing you. I would have remembered if you came to my house, Jeffrey. I may be old but I'm not crazy," Evelyn said.

Am I a small child to her or an adult? Now I'm confused. Changing the subject, Jeff replied, "Do you need something, Mom?"

"I've been robbed! Someone stole my clothes and some very important boxes. I have nothing to wear. My garbage is missing, too! You have to come over here!"

Very important boxes. Jeff shuddered. His immediate thought went to the two shoe boxes tucked away under his bed. *How could she even tell what was missing?* "Okay, I'll be right over." Jeff thought maybe Evelyn would recognize him since she was expecting him to come over. If she did indeed recognize him, then hopefully he could convince her to stay at his house.

"Okay, Jeffrey. Hurry over; I don't know if the burglars are still here. They may be hiding.

He updated Kate about the phone call, and she agreed to come with him. They got into the car and drove back to Evelyn's house. Jeff got his key out and began to unlock his mother's door, but then he stopped himself. *She might think I'm a burglar.* He decided to knock instead.

Evelyn's familiar warm smile and twinkling blue eyes greeted him. "Why are you knocking, son. You know you can come on in. But be careful because the burglars may still be in here."

Jeff gave another confused look at Kate, and she did the same to him. "Weren't we two complete strangers to her just a half hour ago?" he rhetorically asked his wife.

"She has me all confused now," Kate laughed.

Jeff entered the house and followed Evelyn to her bedroom. "See here?" Evelyn said as she pulled open her dresser drawers. "Someone has come and stolen my clothes, my socks, and my underwear. Why would anyone want my underwear? And all of my trash is missing. I needed to sort it before I threw it away." Standing beside Jeff, Kate began to speak up, but Evelyn interrupted. "And in this middle drawer I had two important boxes. I have to have those boxes, Jeffrey. Do you see them anywhere?" Evelyn looked at Jeff through worried eyes, hoping he could find the boxes for her.

A nauseous feeling entered Jeff's stomach. He decided to tell her the truth although he wasn't sure if she could handle it. "Mom, when you were in the hospital, the doctor requested that you live with us until you got better. We came over here last night and got your clothes so you could stay at our house."

"When was I in the hospital?" Evelyn asked with a look of pure innocence.

"Since Monday night. Today is Wednesday, and you were discharged this morning," Jeff replied with a sigh. He wasn't sure how much longer he could deal with her short term memory loss.

"I wasn't in the hospital. Where are my boxes?" she asked.

Jeff bit his tongue again. *She will hate me forever if she finds out I took them to my house.* "What was in them?" he asked.

"They have my life savings. I've saved money in it ever since your daddy left us. I never wanted to put it in the bank because I was afraid that cheating crook would steal it from me. Oh, I have to have that money to live on!" Evelyn became tearful.

"Mom, I don't see any of the money here. How about we do as the doctor ordered and you come stay with us for a while?" Jeff suggested, hoping he could change the subject and get her back to his house where she would be taken care of. "It's not safe for you to be here if the burglars are still inside." *That was a long shot.*

"Well, I want to keep looking, but I guess I can stay with you for a few days," Evelyn replied. She opened the dresser drawers again to see if she might have overlooked the boxes, but each dresser was completely empty. A guilty feeling came over Jeff since he omitted some truth, but he didn't want to upset her anymore. They walked out and waited in the living room as Evelyn continued searching for her money.

"This is the part where I say 'I told you so,'" Kate remarked. "Why didn't you tell her about the money? She's your mother!"

"If she finds out that I took her money, she'll never forgive me. Besides, the money is safer with me." *Did I lock the door when I left home?*

Kate let out her token sigh of disapproval, but she refused to start an argument with him. "Just tell her you took it to our house for safe keeping. She's going to keep looking until she knows where it is."

"This is not going to be good," Jeff said as he cautiously walked back into the bedroom to make the confession. Standing at a safe distance from Evelyn, he calmly said, "Mom, your money is at our house. We took it over there so you would have it with you when you came to live with us."

Evelyn quickly turned toward Jeff as her worried face transformed to rage. "You stole it!" Evelyn yelled. "That is all the money I have to live on. I keep it hidden here so people like you won't take it!" Jeff had never seen his mother so angry. Her face turned brick red, and she shook with anger.

"I'm calling the police. I can't believe my own son has stolen from me." She walked out of the room and toward the telephone in the kitchen.

"Mom, I'm sorry!" he pleaded as he followed her out of the room. "I didn't want it to get stolen from here while you were in the hospital."

"I have never been in the hospital! Why do you keep saying that?"

Pointing at her arm, Jeff asked, "Then how do you explain that sling on your right arm? You broke that arm when you fell here the other night. Don't you remember?"

Evelyn then turned her head and stared at her right arm. "Oh, you're just trying to fool me. Someone must have put this on me when I wasn't looking."

Good grief! "Then why is that on your wrist?" Jeff asked, pointing at the laminated hospital bracelet she still had on.

Evelyn slowly lifted her wrist up to eye level. She squinted to read the small print and then shook her head. "I don't know how you got that on me, but you better take it off! I'm not playing anymore of these silly games with you, young man. I'm calling the police right now!" Evelyn picked up the phone, looked at a list of numbers she had taped to the wall, and called the Grayson City police station. Jeff just shook his head.

"Let's leave," he said quietly to Kate. "She's just too much for me right now. I thought we could work this out, but it's not going to happen, and now she's calling the police on me. They left the house and hurried home. *What am I going to do with her?*

CHAPTER TWELVE

OFFICERS TOM BAKER and Alex Carlton rang the doorbell. Evelyn slowly opened the door. "Can I help you?"

"Ma'am, we are with the Grayson City Police Department," Tom said. "I understand you wanted to report a theft?"

Evelyn stared at the two men in uniform and took a moment to answer. "Did someone call you?"

"According to our dispatcher, you called us, ma'am. How can we help you?"

"I didn't call the police," Evelyn said. "My son lives here, but he's too young to use the phone. You must have the wrong house."

Tom leaned back so he could get a better look at the address above Evelyn's door. He stepped away to contact the dispatcher who verified that they had come to the correct home. "Ms. Duncan, the dispatcher said we were at the correct address. May we speak with your son?" Because of her confusion, Tom sensed there may be another problem at hand.

"He's just a little boy; he won't have much to say. He won't mind talking to you though." Evelyn stepped aside and motioned for the two officers to come in. "Let me go find him." Evelyn walked to the kitchen and stayed there for a moment, and then turned and went to look in the two

101

bedrooms. She then went back to the kitchen. After several minutes, Alex approached Evelyn.

"Ma'am, do you not know where your son is?"

"He was just here, and he had a friend with him, but I can't find either of them," she said as a worried expression came back to her face.

Tom asked, "How old is your son?"

"He's about eight or nine now; I don't keep track anymore—he's growing up so fast!"

Tom had assisted many senior citizens during his career, and his past experiences had helped him become aware of the symptoms of dementia. He asked Alex to step outside with him. "I've seen this before," Tom said to his partner. "We need to find a family member to take care of this lady or get her into a nursing home. I'm calling dispatch to send out a social worker."

"Sounds like a good plan," Alex replied. "Let them deal with her instead." Alex had been on the force for about five years, but he still hadn't fully grasped the principle that police work involved more than arresting criminals. The duties were to serve and protect, and that didn't always require the use of handcuffs and stun guns.

Tom called his dispatcher again and requested to have a social worker sent to the home. A half hour later, Clarissa Young, an employee with the Tennessee Department for Elder Abuse and Protection, pulled into the driveway, and Tom updated her on the situation.

"We need to find a family member," Clarissa said. "Any idea who her relatives are?"

"She said she has a child in the home but doesn't know where he is. If this lady is still giving birth to children at her age, then we need to give her an award." Tom could always use his sense of humor to lighten up tense situations.

"I'll go talk to her for a minute and see what I can find out," Clarissa said as she entered Evelyn's home. There, she found her sitting on the couch, staring blankly toward the kitchen. "Good afternoon, Ms. Duncan," Clarissa said as she introduced herself. "I've come by to check on you. How are you feeling today?"

"Oh, I'm doing well," Evelyn replied casually.

Clarissa asked, "Do you live here by yourself?"

"My son lives here with me."

"Do you know where he is?"

"I saw him here not that long ago with his friend. I don't know where they went."

"What's his name?"

"Jeffrey Duncan."

"Does he work anywhere?" Clarissa asked, hoping to finally get some contact information.

"Jeffrey doesn't work; he's just a little boy," Evelyn laughed, but then her worried expression came back. "I can't find him and he left without telling me where he was going. Will you find him and tell him to come home? I'm worried sick about him."

"Yes, I will try to find him." Clarissa went back to the police and told them the son's name. Alex called the dispatcher to gather more information on Jeff. Through a quick computer search, the dispatcher produced an address and phone number. Alex then called Jeff's residence.

"Hello," Jeff answered.

"Hello, this is Officer Carlton with the Grayson City Police. Am I speaking with Mr. Jeffrey Duncan?"

Jeff immediately knew what had happened. His mother, the only person who still referred to him as "Jeffery," had successfully called the police. "Yes, sir. How can I help you?"

"Are you Evelyn Duncan's son?"

"Yes, sir."

"My partner and I were called to her home. She had reported a theft, but when we came to the house, she denied ever calling us. Your mother appears to be very confused."

"Is she okay? Did something happen?" Jeff tried to sound surprised.

"Yes, she is okay for now, but it appears she has dementia or something. We have social services here helping us. Can you come to your mother's house?"

Not social services! "Uh, yes, sir, I'll be right over." Jeff hung the phone up. Kate had been standing in the room listening to the conversation. "Mom called the police and reported a theft, but the officer said that Mom forgot she called, so maybe she didn't report us after all. I'm not really sure what's going on but they want me to go over there. Social Services are involved also. That's the last thing I need. Will you come help me convince Evelyn to stay here with us? If she doesn't, then that social worker will put her in a nursing home, and you know what that means."

Kate gave a confused look. "What?"

"The money will be gone! Nursing homes are expensive. She will have to sell her house and spend all of her savings to pay for the nursing home," Jeff replied nervously. "That house belongs to me, and that money is mine, too. We can't lose it. I need this until I go full time at the university! We can't afford to lose her to the nursing home!

Jeff and Kate hurried over to Evelyn's house again. The two police cars parked near the curb still had their lights flashing. The mere sight of the flashing blue lights added to Jeff's anxiety. The two officers and the social worker were on the porch talking, and Evelyn stood in the doorway nearby with the confused expression Jeff had seen many times lately.

"There's that man again!" Evelyn said harshly, pointing toward Jeff when he got out of his car. "I told you not to bother me anymore, you imposter! And stay away from my son!"

Jeff got out of the car and put on a fake smile. "Mom, it's me. Remember?"

Tom approached Jeff and introduced himself. "Sir, your mother is very confused. She doesn't seem to be in immediate risk of harm, but I don't think it's safe for her to be here alone. The state social worker also agrees."

Jeff updated the officers and social worker about all that had transpired from the hospital stay to the ongoing battle of trying to get Evelyn to live with them. "What complaint did she make to you?"

Tom replied, "She told dispatch that someone stole her money and clothes, but after we arrived, she denied calling us. I've dealt with many people who have dementia, and they often misplace things and blame others for stealing it."

A wave of relief came over Jeff as he realized they didn't accuse him of stealing anything. "Her doctor didn't want her to stay by herself," Jeff said. "My wife and I came over here yesterday afternoon, filled up two suitcases and some garbage bags full of clothes, and took them over to our house so she could live with us, but like I said, she thought we were strangers. We brought her to our house this morning, but she refused to stay. She will recognize me one minute, and then call me a stranger the next. Sometimes she thinks I'm a child while at other times remembers I'm an adult. Do you have any suggestions?"

Clarissa joined the discussion. "She doesn't need to be here alone. Do you think we can somehow convince her to stay at your house tonight? Maybe tell her 'this nice young couple' wants to help her out?"

"I'll try anything," Jeff said. "We are prepared for her to live with us, but getting her to stay has been the hardest part." Clarissa went back to the porch to talk to Evelyn. He watched his mother's expression turn from worry to sadness, and then she nodded her head in agreement. A few moments later, both Clarissa and Evelyn walked over to Jeff, where he was waiting by his car in the driveway.

"She has agreed to stay with you for a few days," Clarissa said. Evelyn walked to the side of Jeff's car, and Kate helped her get into the back seat.

"We will take her home and do what we can to help her," Jeff said to Tom and Clarissa. "I'll call her doctor again to see if there is any medicine available to help calm her down."

"Okay," Tom said. "Hopefully this will work out for everyone."

As they began the drive back to Jeff's house, Evelyn said, "I still don't know you, but that girl threatened to put me in a nursing home if I didn't obey her," Evelyn said. "I'm never going to a nursing home. I'll go to your house until they all leave, then I'm coming straight back home. I wish everyone would just leave me alone!"

The social worker threatened her? "Mom, I am your son!" Jeff said, looking directly at Evelyn in the back seat. "Why don't you recognize me?" He turned his attention back to the road. "You raised me and now you don't even remember me." A mixture of anger and rejection filled his emotions.

"Jeff, she can't help it," Kate said quietly so Evelyn wouldn't hear her.

Evelyn replied, "My son is a child. You are not a child, and you better stay away from him or else!" For the rest of the ride home, Evelyn muttered incoherent things to herself.

Dreading her confusion and disorientation when they got home, Jeff came up with an idea. He whispered to Kate, "Do you have any of those sleeping pills leftover from the last time you got sick?"

"Yes, why?"

Jeff nodded his head to the back seat. "We have to do something for her until the doctor can help us. If we can just get her to rest for the night, that will give us time to settle down, make a plan, and get some rest ourselves."

Kate frowned. "That is just cruel. What has gotten into you?"

"Do you have a better suggestion?"

Kate didn't reply, but instead turned and stared out the window. After a few moments, she reluctantly mumbled, "They're in the back of my medicine cabinet."

"Get them out when we get home. Figure out some way to make her take a few," Jeff said hastily, unaware how desperate he had become. At first he was excited to be able to take care of his mother and pay her back for all of the support she had single-handedly provided him as a child; now the excitement had disappeared as the difficult and harsh reality came into full view. This was supposed to be a time to rekindle, but instead it had become a time of struggle and hardship.

When they arrived home, Kate got out of the car first and went inside to the master bathroom to look for her sleeping pills. Meanwhile, Jeff helped Evelyn walk into the house. "Like I said, I'm only here with you people until the police leave my home. Don't plan on me staying too long," Evelyn said hatefully as Jeff held onto her uninjured arm and helped her walk inside. Although she had not injured her legs, she walked with a limp ever since she had come home from the hospital.

Inside the bathroom, Kate found the bottle of prescribed sleeping pills. She had ten small capsules leftover from her recent illness. Assuming Evelyn wouldn't take pills from her, she decided to break open two capsules and pour them into a glass of water. After stirring the concoction, tiny blue particles floated around inside the glass. The medicine would definitely put Evelyn to sleep and give her and Jeff some time to relax and make a new plan.

She carefully held the glass in her hand and stepped out of the bathroom, but then came to a sudden halt. "This is a human being," Kate whispered to herself. "I'm not going to drug her just to get her off our backs for a while." Disgusted with herself, Kate dumped the water in the sink and flushed the remaining capsules down the toilet.

Jeff had talked Evelyn into sitting down on the couch as he sat next to her. "Do you want to watch some television?"

"No. I want to be left alone. I don't trust you people," Evelyn said with the ever-present hatred in her voice.

Kate came into the living room and walked passed Jeff. "The sleeping pills?" he whispered as he stood up to follow her into the kitchen.

"I…don't have anymore," Kate replied. She felt comfortable with her reply because in all truth, she didn't have any pills now that she had disposed of them, but Jeff didn't have to know that.

"How are we going to get her to calm down now?" he asked angrily.

Kate ignored his attitude and went back into the living room. "Ms. Evelyn, we have a guest bedroom for you. Would you like to go in there for a while?"

"I usually take an afternoon nap," Evelyn replied. "Where is the room?"

She walked over to the couch to help her mother-in-law stand up. Slowly and carefully, she walked Evelyn down the hallway. Kate had left the master bedroom door opened when she left the bathroom a few moments ago, and she then noticed the comforter on the bed had gotten stuck under the mattress. Her hasty bed making skills resulted in Evelyn having full view of the space beneath the bed where her life savings sat inside two shoe boxes.

"Those look familiar," Evelyn said as she stopped in the hallway and peered at the contents under the bed. "I have some boxes just like that at my house somewhere. Either someone stole them or they went missing, but I can't seem to find them. Would you mind if I go look at them more closely?"

Overhearing his mother, Jeff hurried to the hallway where Evelyn and Kate stood. He briskly passed by the duo and went into the bedroom, shutting the door behind him. *She doesn't need to know they are here.* Jeff quickly pulled the comforter out from the mattress so it would drape down to the floor and hide the boxes. When he came out of the room, Kate had already taken Evelyn into the guest room.

"Ma'am, you have been very nice to me, but I'd like to be alone for a while," Evelyn said to Kate.

"Okay, we'll be in the living room if you need us," Kate assured her as she gently patted Evelyn on the shoulder.

"I need my missing money," Evelyn said. "If you come across it, let me know."

Kate didn't respond, knowing that if the conversation continued she would be forced to lie in order to please Jeff, or tell the truth, which would incriminate her husband. Jeff stood nearby as Kate entered the hall and closed the door. Her eyes penetrated his soul.

"You are a thief," she scolded. "Your mother is worried sick about that money. I want it out of here!"

"I've given good reason to keep that money here, and it isn't leaving," Jeff replied in a hushed, angry voice. Not wanting to argue anymore, he went into the living room and vegetated in front of the television. He wondered if he should somehow lock Evelyn in the room so she wouldn't wander around the house, or even worse, go into the master bedroom and snoop around. *I'll deal with that later.* Kate stayed in the bedroom, and they didn't speak for the rest of the day.

CHAPTER THIRTEEN

JEFF FELL asleep on the couch only to awaken early Thursday morning to a metallic clicking sound. He turned on the lamp nearby. At the front door stood his mother fiddling with the locks. She struggled with the basic task of unlocking the door, which had a lock on the door handle and a deadbolt above it. Evelyn unlocked the deadbolt first and then pulled on the door. She then turned the deadbolt back to "lock," thinking that turning it in another direction would release the latch. She pulled on the door again but it didn't open. Evelyn turned the deadbolt a third time and pulled the handle, but the door remained locked. Jeff watched helplessly as Evelyn went back and forth unlocking and relocking the deadbolt, tugging on the handle each time. *If she figures out she just has to unlock the handle, she will escape, and we will have a big mess.* She grew frustrated and muttered to herself.

"Where are you going, Mom?"

The voice startled her and she turned around to face Jeff. "I'm trying to get home!" she exclaimed. "I've somehow ended up in this house and I don't know where I am. I haven't seen my son all morning, and he needs me to make his breakfast." She turned back to the door and continued pulling on the handle.

Jeff sighed. *Not this again.* He wasn't ready for another battle of wits. He tried again to be straightforward.

"Mom, I'm your son. You are living at my house now. The doctor wants you to stay here with us."

Evelyn turned around to look at Jeff. "Sir, I've never seen you before. I don't know how I got into your house, but will you please help me get out of here?"

She turned back to the door. It saddened Jeff to see his mother have such mental decline. This same woman who had the ability to heal his skinned knees with a magical kiss and wipe away his tears with a warm hug when he was a child had now become so mentally impaired that she could not perform even the simplest of tasks. Jeff went to the bedroom to awaken Kate.

"Mom is awake and trying to leave, and I have to get ready for work. Would you mind watching her until I get back?" Kate was sound asleep. He knew she was exhausted and probably still angry at him. He wanted to let her rest, but he really needed her help.

Kate rolled over on her side, opened her eyes, and looked up at Jeff. "Okay." Her one-word response signified that she still wasn't happy with him. She fluttered her eyes as she tried to force herself awake. Samson hopped onto the bed to prod her along. Jeff got his clothes out of the closet and started to get dressed. In the living room he could still hear Evelyn tugging on the door and muttering to herself.

Kate put her bathrobe on and went to the living room. "Ms. Evelyn, can I help you?" she asked in a friendly voice.

Evelyn let go of the door knob and turned to face Kate. "Ma'am, I'm trying to get home, but I can't seem to open the door. Will you help me?"

Kate feared opening the door for Evelyn because she would go outside and never return. Kate thought of a distraction. "Yes, I'll help you open the door, but will you sit down and eat breakfast with me first? I'm hungry."

"I'm in a hurry to get home. I need to check on my son," she politely replied, although the anxiety in her voice made her sound angry. "Thank you for the offer, but I really need to go."

Kate thought for a minute. "Excuse me; I need to go get something." Kate hurried to the bedroom and got Jeff's cell phone. She then whispered, "She wants to check on her 'son.' Here, I'm going to tell your mother that I'm calling her house to check on you. I'll call your cell phone instead, and when you answer, tell her you are okay. Just play along."

"Sounds like a plan. I'll do whatever works," Jeff said as he muffled a laugh and put the cell phone on the nearby night-stand.

Kate went into the kitchen, passing by Evelyn who had already turned back to the door. Kate put some bread in the toaster and cracked open a few eggs. She then turned the coffee maker on. "Ms. Evelyn, I'm not sure what's wrong with the door—I'll have to call a repairman to come fix it. In the meantime, how about you come eat breakfast with me? I'll have some coffee ready shortly."

Frustrated and exhausted, Evelyn replied, "I've been trying to get out of here for some time now. I give up. That door must be broken." The aroma of freshly brewed coffee provided a brief distraction. "Now that you mention it, I wouldn't mind having some coffee."

"If you would like, since we are locked in here, I can call your house to check on your son," Kate suggested, hoping Evelyn would agree.

"Oh, that would be wonderful," Evelyn said gratefully. "He needs to get ready for school. I hope he is okay."

Kate grabbed the cordless phone. "What's your phone number?"

Evelyn paused as a surprised and confused expression formed on her face. "Well, I completely forgot it!" Evelyn laughed. "I've been so confused and nervous all morning—I just can't recall it right now."

"That's okay, Evelyn. I'll look it up in the phone book." Kate grabbed the Grayson City phone book and flipped back and forth through the pages as though she were searching for Evelyn's name. "Here it is." She then dialed Jeff's cell phone.

Jeff had overheard the conversation and suddenly remembered that his phone had not been set to silent yet. He reached over to his night stand, grabbed the phone, and quickly triggered the "mute" switch. At that very moment, his phone vibrated. He tip-toed over to the bedroom door and closed it so Evelyn wouldn't hear him talking.

"Hello?"

Kate began her charade. "Hello, this is Kate Duncan. I'm calling on behalf of Evelyn Duncan. May I speak to Jeffrey?"

"This is Jeffrey speaking. How can I help you?" Jeff had to muffle another laugh. He was surprised at how well Kate got into character.

"Your mother would like to speak with you." Kate handed Evelyn the phone.

"Jeffrey, this is your mother," Evelyn said with pressured speech. "I'm locked in this house with this nice young couple. I don't know where I'm at, but I'm trying to get home. You need to get dressed and get to school, okay?"

Jeff raised the pitch of his voice in hopes of sounding more like a pre-pubescent child. "I am, Mommy. I'm getting ready for school right now." Jeff grinned at the irony that he literally was getting ready for school. "And don't worry, I'll eat breakfast too."

"That's a good boy," Evelyn said. "I'm so sorry I'm not there to help you."

"It's alright, Mom. You raised me well and I can take care of myself."

"Oh, how sweet of you," Evelyn smiled as she wiped away a small tear. "I'll see you this afternoon when you get home. I love you!"

"I love you too, Mommy. See you this afternoon." Jeff smiled as he hung up. He decided he could get used to playing these types of games with his mother if that's what it took to keep her pacified at their house. *And to keep her money.*

Evelyn handed the phone back to Kate. "That's a good boy I raised. He'll make a fine husband one day."

Kate grinned. "I bet he will."

Evelyn sipped her coffee just as Jeff finished getting dressed. He walked over to Kate at the dining room table and kissed her good-bye. Kate purposely avoided eye contact with him so he would know she was still angry. He ignored her silent treatment and cautiously gave his mother a side-hug where she sat at the table. "See you in a few hours, Mom."

Evelyn gave Jeff a funny look. "I'm not your mother. I think I would know my own son. I just talked to him on the telephone, and you sound nothing like him."

Although he knew she didn't recognize him, her words stabbed him like poison arrows. Jeff faked a smile and went to the door. He grabbed the handle and suddenly remembered that Evelyn thought it was broken. He nonchalantly turned around and went to the back door to leave, hoping his mother wouldn't realize there was another way to exit the house.

After he left, Evelyn asked Kate, "Who was that man?"

Kate responded, "That's my husband."

"Oh, so you're already married? Well, I guess I'll have to find Jeffery someone else to marry when he gets older."

Kate turned her back to Evelyn so she wouldn't be seen suppressing a laugh. Through her and Jeff's teamwork, they were able to calm Evelyn's anxiety, at least for now.

CHAPTER FOURTEEN

JEFF ARRIVED a half hour early to his office. Robert Farris had his door closed, but Jeff could see the light was on in his office as it shined through the decorative, blurry window. He still harbored bitterness toward Robert and had no intention of talking to him. Jeff quietly entered his office and closed the door. He sat down at his desk and began checking his emails on the computer. There were no new messages, but it at least gave him something to do until his class started. He had created a folder on his computer entitled "lectures." He opened it to review what he would discuss during class today but then realized he hadn't created a lecture yet. It was on his list of things to do yesterday, but with his unexpected demotion and the stress at home, he had simply forgotten. Jeff panicked. *This is not how I want to start my day! I have to prove myself if I want to keep this job.*

The creaking of Robert's door sounded. *Don't come in here!* Jeff could see Robert's short frame through the blurred window of his door. Robert walked by Jeff's door and stopped. *Great, he's coming to chastise me again.* He paused by the door for a moment and then continued down the hall. *Good, he's gone. I really don't want to see his face right now.*

Jeff regained his composure and went back to the real problem at hand: today's lecture. He scrambled to come up with a topic on such short notice. All he had really discussed with his class so far was the basics of the evolutionary theory, and then he had the fateful encounter with the creationist.

That gave Jeff an idea. He decided to redeem his credibility by undermining creationism. Robert said we could only talk about other origin theories if we critique them. *If Robert wants to eavesdrop, he'll be sure to respect me when he hears me destroy the creationist arguments.*

He had twenty-five minutes left before his class started, and this would allow him enough time to throw together a lecture. Jeff thought back to everything he had been taught about creationism. During graduate school he took an elective course called "Alternative Views on Origins" in which different speakers came to the class to talk about intelligent design, creationism and other religion or philosophy-based views on life's origin. After each presentation, the class and professor would drill the guest speaker with tough questions until he or she would get stumped. It became a game among his classmates.

He searched for "creationism" on the Internet and found a multitude of websites. Most of them were from religious organizations, but others were from secular sites. *These religious websites will be biased.* He clicked on a secular webpage entitled: "An Overview of Creationism." *This should be a good refresher.* Jeff scanned a few articles and jotted down some notes on the basic concepts of creationism.

While working, his mind wandered back to when he was a child attending Sunday School at Everlasting Glory. The church's small congregation resulted in the Sunday School classes often being grouped together with multiple age levels. There were only three or four adults who had volunteered to teach the different age groups. Although they had good intentions, they were grossly lacking in their ability to defend what they taught.

Back then, all of his Sunday School teachers taught that God created everything in six literal days. His teachers also taught him about Noah's Ark and the worldwide flood along with the other common Bible stories. As a child, Jeff believed it all at face value, but as he grew older, he began to ask questions. He would ask his teachers how God could have created everything while the theory of evolution he had learned about in public school showed how everything came into existence naturally. He would also ask how Noah fit all of the animals on the ark, how Noah could build such a large boat, and so on. They were honest questions, but the teachers were not able to respond. Instead, they brushed him off and replied with "just trust in Jesus."

One of his teachers had gotten so frustrated with Jeff's questioning that she told Evelyn that he was causing a disturbance in the classroom. When Jeff and Evelyn got home after church that day, Evelyn scolded him for causing problems, yet she never asked him what he had specifically done. *I just wanted an answer. Why did she punish me?* He could never get the solid answers he was looking for, and the time finally came when Jeff concluded there were no real answers, so the stories he had learned during his youth were probably not even true. Even now, with Pastor Bill himself saying that the stories in Genesis are just moral lessons, Jeff felt sure he had come to a rational conclusion. *Just believe in Jesus and you will be saved.*

The bad memories of his church experience left him feeling bitter. *All those wasted years of teaching me something they couldn't even prove.* Jeff's daydream helped him prepare his mind and attitude for the upcoming class. He finished writing his notes, grabbed his briefcase, and stepped out of his office. Robert's door was still open. Jeff glanced down the hallway but saw no sign of his eavesdropping boss. He quietly left the faculty offices and went to the lecture hall.

He arrived on time for class. Everyone sat in the same place—the group of male hecklers stationed in the back, Jordyn the creationist sitting alone on the front row, and everyone else scattered about.

"Good morning, class. I'm glad to see everyone is awake and not wearing their pajamas." No one laughed.

117

Tough crowd today. "You'll recall during our first class we talked about the evolution of life, and there had been some discussion of what's called 'creationism.'" A few of the hecklers giggled. "Now remember we shouldn't poke fun at others for having differing viewpoints, even when the cards are completely stacked against them."

Jordyn looked up from her notes. Jeff made eye contact with her, cleared his throat, and focused his attention on other students. He didn't hold a grudge against Jordyn for bringing up her religious beliefs, but then again, had she just kept them to herself, Jeff would never have had the conversation with her, he would have never been reprimanded by Robert, and he would never have been demoted. This deductive reasoning gave him some sense of bitterness toward Jordyn. Still, she was a nice girl and deep down Jeff still believed she had the right to express herself. Regardless, today he had the important task of proving himself to his boss.

Jeff began his lecture. "The truth is that those who believe in creation are either unaware or willfully ignorant of the evidence for evolution. They ignore the scientific truths and instead hold onto their faith, which they base on the words from a Sunday morning preacher whose source is an old, unreliable book. Let me start by going over the basics of creationism. Creationists, as they are called, believe the God of the Bible created everything we see today. There are two camps of creationists: those who believe the earth is old, and those who believe it is young. They are sometimes labeled as 'Old-Earthers' and 'Young-Earthers.' Now those that believe the earth to be old—and when I say 'old' I mean billions of years, like the geologists say—they at least have better arguments for their beliefs which line up with the uniformitarian principles of geology. The young earth view, however, is very easy to dismantle. These people believe God created everything in six, twenty-four hour days."

A student in the back of the class spoke up, "I thought you said we weren't going to talk about religion in here."

The question caught him off guard. "I did say religious discussions were to be held in the religion classes, but the more I thought about it, I feel this is an important topic since we will be discussing origins in this class. I want to get all of this out of the way and not let it distract us from real science. During this semester I will demonstrate to you that evolution explains everything with scientific evidence, but today I will show you that the creationist viewpoint is based strictly upon a person's religious faith, or outright ignorance, in spite of the evidence.

"Now," Jeff continued, "these 'Young-Earthers' base their young age of the earth on the genealogies recorded in the book of Genesis. They claim if you count the years that people lived, you come up with an age for the earth ranging between six-thousand and ten-thousand years. Of course, you first have to assume the Bible is true and correctly translated. I'll confess I grew up in church and was taught all of these things, but none of my teachers were able to prove any of it to be true. They expected me to believe it 'for the Bible tells me so.'" Jeff sang to the tune of *Jesus Loves Me*, and the class started laughing. "But seriously, as a scientist, I cannot accept things because a person or old book told me to. I need evidence, and no one, regardless of their background, should ever be told what to believe.

"To believe in creation, you have to believe in a God. But what evidence is there for God anyway? And if you were to find that evidence, how would you know which God was the correct one? Doesn't Hinduism have millions of gods? Maybe one of them is the real god, and he or she created everything instead of the Judeo-Christian God. Or what if it is the Christian God? How would you know which of the thousands of denominations is the correct one to follow? I might add that many ancient cultures and religions have similar myths on origins. It goes to show that folklores get passed down and shared from culture to culture, but there is no scientific evidence to support them. That's why they are called myths.

119

"Class, I'm not here to debate God. I have my own beliefs, but this is a science class, and we only study the natural things—the things that can be tested and proven with experiments. Let me go over some of the evidences we have of evolution that clearly disprove creationism. The Bible states that the sun, moon, and stars were created after the earth. But the Big Bang Theory shows strong evidence that the sun, moon, and stars were created before the earth. Here is another one: The Bible says birds were created before the reptiles, but our fossil record shows that reptiles came first, and the birds evolved from them. In fact, that is what happened to the dinosaurs: through natural selection and mutations, they evolved into birds. Those little flying critters in your back yard are actually the ancestors of giant dinosaurs that roamed the earth sixty-five million years ago!

"The fossil record we have is clear evidence that life has evolved from simple organisms to more advanced life forms. You can't argue with the bones!" Some of the students laughed. "This brings me to my next point. Has everyone heard the story of Noah's Flood?" Many nodded in agreement. "Well, for those who haven't, it is also recorded in Genesis. Simply put, the story is about a man named Noah. God told Noah He was going to destroy the entire world, and He wanted Noah to build a big boat to put the animals on so they would be saved from a global flood. There are so many problems with that story, but just like the creation myth, Christians believe in it despite the absurdity. For example, where did Noah get the wood for the ark? Didn't he build it in the Middle East? There aren't too many trees over there, you know; it's mostly desert. And how could he fit all the animals on the ark? There are millions of species in existence, and no boat could ever be big enough to hold them all and still survive a flood. The story of Noah's ark just doesn't hold water.

"Did you know there are over three-hundred other flood legends from cultures all across the globe? Who is to say the legend recorded in the Bible is the right one? Isn't that kind of arrogant? What if one of the other flood legends were the real one and the Bible copied from it? Some historians say the Bible copied things from other religions. Back then, it was a common practice to borrow ideas and customs from neighboring cultures. It was a battle of the gods, I guess you could say. Besides, there is no evidence of a worldwide flood anyway. In the Bible, it was just a story about God not liking how people were acting, so He destroyed them.

"Class, when you base your beliefs on some book supposedly written thousands of years ago, you have to sacrifice logic and reason for it to make sense; otherwise the entire basis for your faith is called into question. Why not choose science? It will never contradict itself!"

One of the boys from the group of hecklers raised his hand. "Uh, Dr. Duncan?"

"Yes, you have a question?" Jeff responded, looking up at the student.

"Yeah, well, uh, I have a friend who believes in that stuff. I've tried to talk to him about it, saying that science has proven the Bible to be false and that all life came from a common ancestor, but he won't believe me. He said the fossils are evidence of the global flood you talked about, but I told him the animals died and were gradually buried by dirt and rocks over millions of years."

"You are right," Jeff replied. "See, the fossils of dinosaurs, for example, have been dated to be about sixty-five million years old, as I said earlier, and all of the rock layers above and below them have also been dated to be millions of years old. If your friend thinks the animals were buried by flood waters, ask him how he can answer to the radiometric dating methods that prove the fossils are old."

The student grinned, "Okay, I'll try that and maybe he will finally shut up. Thanks!"

Jeff continued with his lecture. "Let me be open with you, class. As I said, I was taught all of those stories when my mother dragged me to church as a kid. The teachers could never answer the questions I had, so I just chalked it up as a fable or some vague moral lesson and forgot about it." He saw a lot of students gazing at him as though he had said something they had all been wanting to hear for a long time.

He began to close. "I don't get why some people hold onto these old stories. I think we should all have the right to our own opinions, but when you compare opinions with facts, the argument is settled before it even begins. I conclude that we should let the creationists have their legends and stories. But as for me and my house, we will listen to the facts!" A roar of laughter filled the room. Jeff was surprised anyone would catch his Biblical play on words.

Jeff laughed along with the students. In the corner of his eye, he saw Jordyn grab her book bag and hastily put her things into it. When she finished, she stood up and pointed her finger at Jeff.

"Dr. Duncan, you told me you would be respectful of my beliefs. You said you would defend me when people mocked me, but you lied! Now, even you are laughing at me!" Silence fell across the room.

"Please, Jordyn," Jeff said, still with a smile on his face. "We are just having a little bit of fun."

"You're having fun at my expense! Where did you get your source of information for today's lecture? Everything you said was filled with lies and half-truths! I can provide a counter-argument to every point you made. You have not talked about the secular faulty assumptions, the worldview-based interpretations of the evidence, geologic evidences for the flood, the proof of the Bible's reliability...it is clear you have not thoroughly studied both sides of the issue. You have completely misrepresented creationism and made me look like a fool!" Jordyn grabbed her bag and hurried up the stairs toward the back of the classroom. She pushed open the door and let it close with a loud bang. After she left, several students snickered silently and whispered among themselves.

One of the hecklers broke the tension. "Professor, do you think she left to go pray to her sky daddy?" Several of his friends broke out in laughter.

"Alright, everyone calm down," Jeff said. He didn't like that Jordyn left the classroom upset, but he knew he had to choose between pleasing each and every student or pleasing the person who signed his paycheck—Robert. Although Jordyn was mad at him, he hoped she would at least consider the things he lectured about today and maybe she would reconsider.

"I think we had a good discussion today and look forward to many more next week. We will meet again on Tuesday. Please be on time. I noticed some of you coming in late today. To God, a day is like a thousand years and a thousand years are like a day, but here in the real world, a day is only twenty-four hours long, so set your alarm clocks accordingly and be here on time." The students laughed again. Jeff smiled as he gathered his notes and headed for the door.

As Jeff exited the lecture hall, he was greeted by Robert, who slowly clapped his hands and offered an affirming smile. He had been listening in again, but this time he had a more pleasant demeanor. "Nice improvement, Dr. Duncan. It looks like there is hope for you after all."

CHAPTER FIFTEEN

"PLEASE, GET this door opened! I want to go home now!" Evelyn pleaded as tears rolled down her cheeks.

Kate had lost her patience. For over an hour Evelyn had been asking to go home. Knowing it was not a feasible or safe decision for her to leave, Kate used every distraction she could from offering more food and coffee to taking a relaxing bath. Nothing would satisfy her, and Kate had run out of ideas. Evelyn demanded to go home.

"You cannot leave until we get the door fixed," Kate said sternly. "I've told you this many times already. It won't open."

"Fix it!" Evelyn ordered.

"I can't until Jeff comes home," Kate said, although she knew a simple turn of the door handle lock would give them both what they wanted. "Why don't you go lay down for a few minutes and I'll call the repairman?"

Evelyn scowled at Kate as she turned away and walked down the hall toward the bedrooms. Kate was grateful to distract her and finally have peace and quiet. She busied herself in the kitchen cleaning up a few crumbs leftover from breakfast. Unbeknownst to her, Jeff had left the master bedroom door opened, and Kate had been too preoccupied with Evelyn to go through the morning routine of making the bed.

* * *

"Thank you, sir," Jeff replied to Dr. Farris' compliment as they walked to the faculty offices.

"I see that your creationist got mad because you tore apart her fairy tales. The truth is, if she can't handle the facts, then she can't handle the real world," Robert concluded. He gave a friendly wink to Jeff and then went to the staff lounge.

Jeff went back to his office. He paused for a moment and grinned. He was glad he made an improvement and met his goal. Maybe he and Robert would be able to get along after all, and hopefully he would get to teach more classes and go back to full-time status sooner than expected. He checked his cell phone and saw where he had missed a call from Kate, so he called her back.

"When are you coming home?" Kate asked frantically. "The police are here again!"

"What!"

"Your mother called the police on us!"

"Why did you let her use the phone?" Jeff asked, not realizing he added insult to injury.

"Don't blame me!" Kate yelled. "You have no idea what I've been going through all morning with your mother! She has been asking me to take her home ever since you left. I've tried every distraction I can think of. I kept telling her I had to wait until you came home. And then she said you were at home alone and she needed to go check on you, but I told her you were in school. She is just so confused. We've been going back and forth with the same conversations. It's as though she forgets everything we talk about; but I'm starting to think she picks and chooses what she wants to remember. She is quite the manipulator.

"Jeff, I'm about to pull my hair out! I just can't take care of her. I know I said I would do it, but now I know that I can't. I asked her to go lay down, and when she walked down the hall she went into our bedroom and found her money."

"She did!" Jeff yelled. "Why didn't you make the bed?"

"It's not *my* fault!" Kate snapped back. "You left the bedroom door opened this morning, and I haven't had a moment's rest since you left. She somehow remembered seeing her shoeboxes under our bed yesterday. She pulled them both out, brought them to the kitchen, and then accused me of stealing her money. After that, she went into a rage. She's knocked pictures off the wall, thrown a pillow at me, and tried to kick the cat. When I went to pick the stuff up, she went to the phone and dialed the operator. The police are talking to her in the living room, and they want to speak with you."

Jeff shuddered. "I'm on my way." He closed his eyes imagining what he would encounter at home. He began thinking of a better alibi to tell the police instead of, "I kept the money here to keep it safe." Jeff hurried to his car and began the commute home. Although he had more confidence about his job stability, the reality of having to again deal with his contrary mother triggered a sense of hopelessness.

As Jeff made the slow exit through the congested college traffic, a nearby tree in the university commons area caught his attention. Three students sat under the tree, each with a Bible opened. *A Bible study on campus?* Seeing the roots poking out from the ground, Jeff was suddenly reminded of the tree in his dream from a few days ago. The thoughts of the mighty tree breaking at the roots and crashing down to the earth had nagged his mind several times since that Sunday afternoon nap. Even worse, a sense of loathing came as the images of the ground sinking into a fiery abyss frightened him. Still, although he could find no meaning from the dream, he had tried to figure out why the memory kept haunting him. *It was just a dream, and science has shown that dreams have no meaning.*

As the traffic began to speed up, he distracted himself from the pending anxiety awaiting him at home by reviewing his lecture in his mind, which ultimately led to him reflecting on his religious upbringing. *Could it be that everything I had been taught in church was just moral stories borrowed from other religions? If the beginning of the Bible isn't true, then what about the rest of the stories? What about the wars, the kings, the prophecies...what about Jesus?* Jeff had always believed Jesus was a real historical figure. He never had any doubt—until now.

Jeff arrived home to find Officer Tom Baker at his house again. After stepping out of his car, Tom greeted him.

"We meet again," Tom laughed, although he had a serious expression.

"What's the problem this time, officer?"

"Well, Ms. Duncan is still quite confused, but she called us this morning and said she had found her money in your house. This is the second time in a row she has reported theft. She called us yesterday about it but then had no memory of making the report, and we couldn't conduct an investigation. Do you know anything about the money she found here?"

Jeff thought how he could respond and appear innocent. "Oh, you mean the money in those boxes?"

Tom replied, "Yes, she showed us two really old shoe boxes. There must have been hundreds of thousands of dollars in there. She said it was her life savings."

Jeff faked a laugh. "Yes, that is her money. You see, officer," Jeff stammered, "she was in the hospital recently, and while she was gone, my wife and I went to her house to get some clothes and things so she could stay at home with us. The doctor wanted her either in a nursing home or to live with us. While we were at her house, we found the money and figured it would be safer with us. I didn't want anyone to steal it from her. Someone could have broken into her home and taken it."

"Do you know how much is in there?" Tom asked.

"No, I haven't counted it," Jeff lied. His voice quivered as another chill crawled down his spine. "It's none of my business. I just wanted to keep her money safe here.

Her house is old and the door locks don't always latch. You can't trust some of her neighbors, you know."

"Well, let me be frank with you, Mr. Duncan. I have to cover all my bases so I must ask: Have you taken or have you planned on taking any of that money for yourself?"

"No, sir!" Jeff quickly responded. *Did I respond too fast?* "That is her life savings and all she has to live on except for her monthly pension."

"I had to ask. Financial exploitation of the elderly is a common crime because it's so easy to do, especially when the victims are as confused as your mother is. Well, what do you plan on doing with her? She said she doesn't want to stay here any longer. I'm not too sure she would be safe alone given her current state of mind."

Jeff replied, "I have to take her back to the doctor. Maybe he can give her something to calm her down."

"Okay, let's go back in and we'll try to talk her into going to the doctor today. She's pretty wild right now!" They went back into the home. Evelyn stood in the living room with both shoe boxes at her feet along with her clothes carelessly stuffed into the garbage bags.

"That's the man, officer!" Evelyn yelled, pointing at Jeff. "He's the one who tried to take my money. Arrest him!"

Her accusatory finger was intimidating, but Jeff felt like he had a good alibi. Tom turned to Evelyn and replied, "Ma'am, he said he was keeping the money here for safety so no one would steal it. He said he has not taken any of it and never planned on doing so. I can't arrest an innocent man."

"There's nothing innocent about him!" Evelyn quickly replied with a fierce anger. "He's kidnapped me, taken my clothes, taken my money…what else will he have to do before you see that he is a criminal?"

"Ma'am," the officer replied. "Do you not recognize that this is your son? He claims to be your son."

"I have told you! My only child is a small boy, and he's been at home alone all this time. You have to take me home. He needs me!"

"Would you be willing to go to the doctor today," Tom asked.

"The doctor?" Evelyn asked. "I'm not sick."

Turning back to Jeff, "I can't make her go unless she is a danger to herself or others. Although she is angry, I don't see her as being homicidal."

Kate spoke up, "Would you like me to take you home to check on your son?" Now, even "patient Kate" was eager to have peace and quiet in the home.

Evelyn turned to Kate, "Yes, please take me home. Help me carry my things."

Jeff looked at Kate worriedly, but he had to regain his composure so the officer wouldn't get suspicious. He didn't want to lose the free access to Evelyn's money, but there was no way he could talk her into keeping it at the house with him. *I have to get another plan.* Kate helped Evelyn pick up the boxes and bags and then walked with her to the car.

Kate whispered to Jeff, "If we can get her mind off having you arrested, it will at least be some progress." Jeff sighed but nodded his head.

As Kate and Evelyn got into the car, Tom informed Jeff, "You need to do something to help your mother. It's not safe for her to live alone. Her mind is severely impaired—she has one of the worst cases of dementia I've ever seen. If you'd like, I'll contact the social worker to have her help you."

"She won't go see the doctor, but I'll call to see what he suggests," Jeff quickly responded. He did not want to get social services involved again. *They will just throw her into a nursing home, and I'll have to say "good-bye" to my inheritance.* Jeff didn't want anyone else interfering. The money, and everything for that matter, would be his when Evelyn died. *What harm would there be in using my inheritance now? At least Evelyn would be able to see the joy I had with my bills being paid off. But she doesn't know who I am anymore.*

Tom's radio sounded, and he was dispatched to assist with traffic control at a house fire. Jeff watched as Kate and his mother drove off in one direction toward Evelyn's house, and the officer went in the opposite direction with his lights flashing and siren wailing. Jeff tried to process all that had transpired. Something had to be done to help calm his mother down. She would not be safe at home by herself, but she refused to live with Jeff. The nursing home option was out of the question. *I will not lose my inheritance.*

CHAPTER SIXTEEN

DEEP DOWN, Jeff really missed his mother. She had always been such a good provider and nurturer. She raised him well and even worked two jobs so she could support him and his education, and that was more than his father ever provided. After his father, Glen Duncan, abandoned the family, Jeff never saw him again, and Evelyn never received child support. Not once did Glen visit Jeff on his birthday or at holidays, much less pick up the phone and call him. Despite his father's gross lack of provision and their dwindling emotional bond, Jeff still wanted to know him and spend time with him. He had yearned to have those moments other boys had with their fathers, like learning how to fish, catch a baseball, and shave their first peach-fuzz mustache. Jeff often had asked his mother when his father would return, but Evelyn, with a tear in her eye, could never provide a definite answer. Jeff had needed a male role model as he grew up, and he struggled with self-identity for many years. Evelyn had wanted her husband to return home for the sake of their son, but he refused. Glen had tried to divorce Evelyn, but she didn't believe in divorce and she refused to sign the legal papers he repeatedly mailed to her. After all these years, they were still legally married on paper, but not at all engaged.

With Kate and Evelyn gone, Jeff went back inside to clean up the aftermath of his mother's rampage. Kate had gotten most of the things picked up, but there were still a few items tossed about on the floor. He picked up some pictures and stacked them along the wall where they normally hung. A pillow lay on the floor in the kitchen. Jeff walked over and grabbed it, then went back to the living room and tossed it on the couch. There were some other things that needed to be picked up, but Jeff instead lay down on the couch and closed his eyes with hopes of clearing his mind.

As he tried to process the excitement and recent changes in life, his mind wandered back to his morning lecture. *What if God really is just a made up entity? If He is real, then why does He allow suffering? What did my mom do to deserve this Alzheimer's disease? Maybe people in ancient times invented a god to explain things they couldn't understand. We know now what those people back then didn't know. Science has shown us how life was formed, and there was never any need for divine intervention. It was all just made up.*

Jeff sat up on the couch and rubbed his hands through his hair. His Bible, the one his mother had given him as a high school graduation gift, sat on the nearby coffee table where he left it last Sunday. The brown leather covering was in mint condition. *I hardly ever opened it. The only reason I take it to church is out of mere habit from my childhood.* The edges of each page were accented with shiny gold trim, making the book appear even more valuable. He thumbed through the pages several times as he listened to the crisp papers flap together. *What is this book anyway? It was written by a bunch of guys thousands of years ago. Who's to say they weren't just making up all these stories just to pass on to their kids? And here we are today retelling the same bed time stories they told! Even if it were true, how could I know it was translated correctly? Hasn't this thing been copied over and over again? It's bound to be full of errors and contradictions by now.*

He stopped fanning through the pages and opened it up to the first chapter of Genesis. A glistening image caught his eye. The image, about the size of a half-dollar coin and positioned in the middle of the page, was centered above the *Genesis* heading. It was a picture of a tree with thick branches, leaves, and long, winding roots protruding from its trunk. Various shades of gold coloring made the image sparkle as the light from the late morning sun shone through the upper window behind him. *That looks like the tree I saw in my strange dream the other day. Why would the publisher put a tree here? Shouldn't it be a cross or something a bit churchier?*

Jeff read over the text of the first page. Samson joined him on the couch, and Jeff scratched Samson on the head while he continued reading, but for reasons unknown, his feline companion wasn't purring as he usually did. After finishing the first chapter, Jeff smiled to himself and laughed aloud. "I can't believe so many people actually buy into this idea that God—whoever God is—made everything like the Bible says," he said out loud. *Science has disproven all of this nonsense.*

He turned to the next chapter. After reading it, he said out loud, "And right here, just one page over, there is a blatant contradiction. Chapters one and two go against each other in the order of creation. Why didn't I ever see this before?" He read on to the third chapter about the serpent tempting Eve. "This is some crazy *hisssstory*!" Jeff laughed at his quick pun. "A talking snake? Who would ever believe that? No snake fossil with a voice box has ever been found. Besides, animals don't talk. Right, Samson?" Samson twitched his ears and repositioned himself on the couch's backrest.

He thumbed through a few more pages and found Chapter Six. He said out loud again, "Oh, the flood—the story of an old man hoarding animals on a big boat!" Jeff laughed as he read the text. He felt shame for having been as gullible as a child to believe all the Bible stories. He read all three chapters about the flood and then came to Chapter Eleven. "Ah, yes, the Tower of Babel: Where our primitive, illiterate, sheep-herding ancestors were so technologically advanced they built a tower up to heaven! And then God got mad at them so He gave them all different languages? This is just ridiculous. Linguists have proven how language evolved, and they didn't need a god to intervene."

The perceived absurdities prevented Jeff from finishing the chapter. He slammed the book shut, looked at the cover again, and angrily tossed the book across the room where it landed open in the hallway, knocking over the pictures he had just stacked up.

"What is true!" Jeff yelled, He buried his face into his hands as he was overcome with confusion. "Everything those Sunday School teachers told me could never be backed up with evidence. If the creation stories aren't true, then what about the history and the prophecies and the gospels?" He paused and slowly lifted his face out of his hands. "What about...Jesus?"

Samson jumped up from his nap. He stared at something in the corner of the room as his fur stood on end. He arched his back and hissed.

"What's gotten into you?" Jeff asked.

Samson jumped down from the couch, ran around the far perimeter of the room as he stared fearfully at the corner, and then scurried into the bedroom as he made a low, rumbling growl. A hot breeze blew out from the same corner, and the air in the room became thicker. Feeling the temperature rise, Jeff flipped the ceiling fan on to create some circulation.

A car door slammed shut outside, and Jeff realized he had been talking to himself this entire time. Kate came inside with her hair in disarray and her face in an angry grimace. "I could just scream. I cannot believe how difficult one little lady can be. She doesn't understand anything and just talks out of her head."

"What happened this time?" Jeff asked.

"I helped her inside the house and then brought in her clothes and money. I was going to put the money back in the dresser, but she jerked it out of my hand and gave me a cursing that would make a sailor blush. I'm mentally exhausted now.

Your mother needs a nursing home or something because I'm done trying to help her!"

"I agree something needs to be done. The nursing home is out of the question though. They will take everything she has and I'll get nothing in her will."

Kate agreed, "Normally, I would complain about how selfish that was for you to say, but right now I just don't care. I need a break from it all." She collapsed on the couch next to him. "Why is it so hot in here?"

"I don't know. It just came all of a sudden. I turned the fan on."

"That's strange. Have you checked the thermostat?"

"No, not yet. We need to cut back on our air conditioning anyway. I can't afford the luxury."

"Where's your 'couch-mate'?"

"Samson?" Jeff asked. "He was here just a minute ago. Something spooked him and he ran back to the bedroom."

"Typical cat stuff, I guess," Kate commented. "But still, something doesn't feel right in here. Something feels…evil." Looking at the Bible in the hallway, she asked, "What's that doing over there?"

"Eh, I threw it and that's where it landed," he casually replied.

Kate gasped, "Why did you throw your Bible?"

"It's just a book, Kate. It's not like it has any value."

"You didn't answer me. Why did you throw it? Your mother gave it to you as a gift. Besides, this is the Bible. You don't just throw a Bible around!" Kate was already upset, and now an argument was on the horizon.

"I don't know what is true anymore," Jeff said as he sighed. Pointing at the Bible, he added, "If the beginning of that book is not true, then what about the rest of it?"

"What are you saying, Jeff?"

"Well, think about it. I'm a scientist with eight years of college under my belt. Science has provided tons of evidence to support evolution, yet the Bible says that science has gotten it all wrong. How can I, a doctoral level biologist, believe something that is in complete contradiction to the scientific evidence? Even Pastor Bill said Sunday that the stories in Genesis are just moral lessons and can't be relied on as true history."

"But, what about God? Didn't He write the Bible? Isn't it God's Word?" Kate asked, hoping to prevent Jeff from losing his faith.

"People say He wrote the Bible, and I used to believe that myself. But think about it— all cultures have a god or goddess of some sort. Christianity is not the oldest religion, you know. There are several others religions out there. How do we know this God of the Bible is the right one? What if we have been worshipping the wrong god all this time? What if the people who wrote the Bible got it all wrong? I am seriously doubting everything in that book. As far as I can see, it's just a collection of stories and fables the Jewish people told each other. None of it applies to me now."

Kate remained silent for a few moments as she tried to think of an answer for Jeff. "Are you giving up on your faith?"

"I don't know. Science has answered my questions. None of my Sunday School teachers helped me build a firm foundation on what I learned back then. Instead, they just told me to have faith."

"We are supposed to have faith," Kate said, repeating the cliché she had heard many times at church.

"Faith may work for some, but for me, I need to see evidence," Jeff said. "If God is real, wouldn't He have prevented me from getting demoted, especially since I tried to defend Him? Why do all of these bad things happen? Where is God in the midst of tragedy, sickness, and death?"

Again, Kate was at a loss for words. After a few moments, she humbly replied, "I don't have all the answers you are looking for. I didn't grow up in church like you did, but ever since I was saved I have felt a significant change in my life. I do believe in Jesus and that His death saved me. I can't answer the questions about creation or the Bible. Maybe

God used evolution to create the world. Who knows? I'll admit I don't understand the majority of that book, but I do know my life has changed, and you can't deny that."

Jeff listened but didn't show much acknowledgement to what his wife said. "Look at yourself, Kate. You're tired and worn out from dealing with my mother. Don't get me wrong—I'm thankful you have helped me with her. But consider this: What kind of God would allow a good woman like my mom to lose her mind like she has? She's way out there now and will never get better. I thought God was all powerful and able to do anything, so why did He allow this? What did Mom ever do wrong?" Jeff had her cornered. He knew she would not be able to give a good answer.

Kate looked down at the floor and sighed. "I…I don't know. I mean, we all get old. This is just part of life. I don't like it any more than you do."

Jeff replied, "With God, His plan is for all to die, regardless of how good or bad you have been. Then He sends you to heaven or hell. But in evolution, which has the supporting evidence, only the weaker ones die and the stronger survive. It's every man for himself; the survival of the fittest."

Kate's eyes widened as she stared at Jeff. "What are you saying?"

"The more I think about it, I believe what Dr. Farris said is true. Mom just isn't the strong one anymore. Evolution will soon take over and she will die. She lived a good life, but as they say, 'all good things must come to an end.'"

"I can't believe you just said that, Jeff! She's your mother!"

Jeff looked away for a moment. He didn't want to argue, but it had begun. The heat in the room continued to increase. Forcing himself to stay calm, he replied, "I'm not being callous, honey. Death is a part of the cycle of life. We are born, raised, get an education and career, get a family, contribute to society, and then we are done. Really the only thing that matters is we pass on our genes so that life will go on. Mom has served her time, and she passed her genes onto me. She has no further purpose in life. You and me Kate, we are the stronger ones and still have yet to pass on our genes. But if we keep up with the stress of taking care of Mom, we will become the weaker of the species and die out before our time."

Although he made a valid logical conclusion, Kate valued human life and did not want to think of Evelyn as a useless person. She knew there was more to life than what Jeff had said, but she had become too fatigued and emotionally drained to argue, and the heat was making her more aggravated. "I'm done talking about this for now. I believe in Jesus and the Bible regardless of your opinion. I don't know what's come over you, but I want no part in causing any harm to your mother. And I don't want you trying to get her money! Yes, it was tempting to use it for ourselves, but all along I knew it was wrong. You've become greedy, Jeff. You are not the person I married. I have faith in my God that He will get us through this financial crisis. That's more than evolution could ever do!" Kate felt good about her final remark. Before Jeff could answer, she turned, went into the bedroom, and slammed the door. That was her trademark way of ending arguments.

Jeff stayed on the couch and just sighed. *Was it wrong to talk about Mom no longer having any purpose?* Jeff knew Evelyn would never get better. Physically, she could still do a lot on her own, but mentally, her mind was quickly disappearing. *Could she ever have a meaningful life again?*

Jeff picked up the phone and called Dr. Norman's office. Through a series of transfers, he was connected to Nurse Melinda.

"How can I help you?" she asked.

"My name is Jeff Duncan. I'm calling about my mother, Evelyn Duncan. Dr. Norman said she would not be safe living on her own. I've tried to move her in with me, but she doesn't even recognize me now. She has called the police on me twice and accused me of stealing from her."

"That's awful," Melinda said sadly. Jeff could hear the authentic concern in her voice. "I don't have her chart with me right now. What is her diagnosis?"

"She's been diagnosed with a very progressive form of Alzheimer's disease, and just a few days ago she fell and injured her head. She's taken a turn for the worse. Today she got violent and threw stuff in our home. Do you have anything I can give her to calm her down?"

Melinda responded, "Let me go ask the doctor right now and see what can be done for her."

While waiting on hold, he looked down the hallway at the bedroom door where Kate had gone and was reminded of the many fights they had during their first few years of marriage. They had a crazy cycle of arguments—he would tell her what he thought, and she would do the same. Then, he would vegetate in front of the television; she would go to the bedroom and bawl.

Soft instrumental music played over the phone as he waited on hold. The chorus of the song began to play, and immediately Jeff recognized it as the old hymn, *Turn your eyes upon Jesus.* He unknowingly started to hum along, and just as he begun, the heat coming from the corner of the room immediately changed into a refreshing breeze.

As he continued to wait, his mind wandered back again to his childhood faith. Everlasting Glory was a "prim and proper" church. There was no talking during service and Jeff was terrified of accidently making a noise among the silenced crowd during the morning sermons. *If they were so good during church, what were they like at home?* He recalled a time when Evelyn asked him to take a casserole dish back to their car after a potluck. On the way back inside, he saw one of the deacons smoking a cigarette behind the church's storage shed. When their eyes met, the deacon quickly threw the cigarette off into the distance. Jeff didn't think it was right for the man to smoke because his mother told him it was a sin. That incident bothered him for many months, and the deacon went out of his way to avoid making contact with Jeff. It was an eye-opening incident, though, because from then on Jeff realized the church was full of people putting on a pretty face every Sunday morning, but during the week they were struggling with their own problems.

Melinda's voice came back on the phone. "Okay, Mr. Duncan. The doctor has written a prescription for some anxiety medication. These are capsules Ms. Duncan can take every six hours as needed to help calm her down. The pharmacy should have them ready in an hour."

"Okay. I'll go get them this afternoon. Thank you for your help," Jeff replied. He went into the kitchen to warm up some leftover pizza for lunch. As the pizza reheated, he went back into the hallway and retrieved the Bible. After picking it up, he saw it had landed open to the fourteenth chapter of Psalms. Out of curiosity, Jeff read the first verse.

The fool says in his heart, "There is no God."

Talking to himself again, he muttered, "If you are a fool for not believing in God, then what are you if your faith is faltering, like mine?" Closing the book and placing it back on the coffee table, he whispered desperately, "Where are you, God?"

The microwave beeped, and Jeff went back into the kitchen to get his lunch. He took his time eating as he was in no hurry to see his mother and have another battle with her. Jeff attempted to watch daytime television while he ate. *There is nothing on television these days.* He turned it to the local news, hoping to find something of interest.

The noon news aired a commercial before the broadcast to let its viewers know what the top story was. "A house fire took the lives of a local family of five this morning. No word yet on the cause of the fire, but it is under investigation by the fire marshal and Grayson City Police." The television showed live footage of what was left of the home. All of the walls had burned down and the roof collapsed in. The fire had long since been put out, but smoke still wafted up from hot spots hidden deep inside the heap of rubble. Firefighters continued spraying down the charred remains.

"That's tragic," Jeff said out loud. "Burning alive is the one way I don't want to die." *What happens at death? What if there really is a heaven and a hell...and where would I end up?* Jeff brushed his lingering thoughts aside and finished his lunch. He walked down the hallway toward the bedroom, put his face close to the door, and told Kate he was going to the pharmacy. She never opened the door, but Jeff could hear her reply with a muffled "okay." There was no need at this time to take the conversation any further because they would just start to fight again. *Wait for her to admit she is wrong and then you can get on with your life.*

CHAPTER SEVENTEEN

JEFF DROVE into town to Golden's Pharmacy, a locally owned business that had been in operation ever since Jeff was a child. He hadn't been to the pharmacy since Kate got sick with the flu a few months prior. He walked in and headed toward the back of the building where the prescriptions were filled. A teenage girl came to the counter. "Can I help you?" she asked.

Jeff glanced at her name tag—Brittany. "Yes, Brittany, I need to pick up a prescription for my mother, Evelyn Duncan."

Brittany turned around and rummaged through an alphabetized box of medicines waiting to be picked up. "Here it is," she said as she came back to the counter with a small white paper bag.

"How much is it?" Jeff asked as he reached for his wallet.

"Hmm," Brittany said as she studied the computer screen. "We don't have any updated information on Evelyn. She hasn't filled a prescription here in years. We don't even have an insurance card on file. Does she have insurance?"

Jeff's dwindling patience had now completely emptied. "I'm not sure. Shouldn't she have some type of insurance for being a senior citizen?" he gruffly asked.

"Yes, she should if she is a senior, but I'm not finding it in our computer. Without insurance this prescription will cost three-hundred and twenty-five dollars."

"What!" yelled Jeff, glaring at the helpless clerk. Other employees at the pharmacy stopped what they were doing and stared at him. An awkward hush fell across the entire building as other customers stopped and turned to see the commotion at the pharmacy counter. Jeff didn't realize he had yelled so loudly, but he wasn't expecting the medicine to be so expensive, either. "How can it cost so much?"

"I'm sorry, sir, but that is the price set by the manufacturer," Brittany replied, clearly shaken by Jeff's anger. Her quivering hands reached for a small card. "Here, this is a free discount card we give to people who don't have insurance. It's provided by the pharmaceutical companies and usually takes a generous percentage off the price."

"How much will it be with the discount?" Jeff asked, embarrassed at his outburst.

"Let me see," Brittany said as she turned back to the computer and typed in some numbers. "With the discount, this prescription will cost two-hundred dollars. That's a bigger discount than most medicines get." Her worried eyes looked back at Jeff as she hoped he would not yell at her again.

"I guess that will have to do," he muttered. He opened his wallet and gave Brittany his credit card. *I haven't even gotten paid yet, and now this senile old woman has put me in more debt!*

Brittany hastily processed the transaction and gave Jeff the receipt and paper bag. An angry scowl formed over his face as he stormed out of the pharmacy. He got back in his car and drove to Evelyn's house. While driving, he fumed over the cost of the medicine. He grimaced at the small bag in the passenger seat next to him, trying to understand how something so small could cost so much. Then, the thought suddenly occurred to Jeff: *How am I going to get her to take this medicine? She doesn't even know who I am! I'm such an idiot!* Jeff screamed and cursed out loud. No one could hear him of course, but screaming had always been a good stress reliever. He slapped his leg in anger for using his own money to get the medicine that Evelyn probably wouldn't take anyway. *I should have planned this out better.*

Jeff arrived at her house and approached the door with the bag in hand. He raised his hand up to knock, but stopped himself, for he had to first devise a way to get his mother to take the medicine. *It cost me two-hundred dollars. She's going to take it one way or another.* Jeff went ahead and knocked on the door without a plan in place. Inside, he overheard Evelyn talking. He put his ear next to the door to listen closer.

"I don't know who it is," Evelyn said worriedly. "I'm not sure what to do. Someone knocked at the door, but I'm not expecting any guests." She paused for a minute. "Should I answer the door? I'm so confused! What do you think I should do?" His curiosity got the best of him. The curtain on the window next to the front door was slightly pulled away from the wall, so he stepped to the side and peered through the small gap. In the living room, Evelyn paced back and forth, looking up at the holes in the ceiling as she talked. *Who is she talking to?*

Jeff stepped back to the door and knocked a second time while saying, "Hey, Mom, it's your son, Jeff. May I come in?"

He listened again and heard Evelyn say, "They are still knocking. He said something about my son. I'm going to answer it this time. I'll let you know what they wanted."

Evelyn unlocked the deadbolt and slowly opened the door. Her blue eyes stared suspiciously at the tall stranger. "Can I help you?"

Jeff sighed to himself. *Great, she doesn't recognize me again. I'm not going to get anywhere with her now.* "Hi, Mom, I'm Jeff, your son. Remember?"

Evelyn smiled politely. "I don't know who you are, but you're not my son. He's just a little boy. You must have the wrong house."

Without waiting for a response, Evelyn slammed the door shut, making the metallic clicking sound as she hastily turned the deadbolt. *Now what am I going to do? I've got all this medicine, and it is not going to waste.* Jeff ran his hands through his thick hair as he took a deep breath. Then, he overheard Evelyn talking again.

"That was some man thinking he was my son. He must've been lost." Jeff looked through the window again. Evelyn stood directly under the ceiling holes and continued her conversation.

Running out of options, he desperately wanted to call Kate for advice, but they still weren't on talking terms. Truthfully, he had hoped she could convince him the Bible was true during their recent argument, but instead she got mad and walked away.

Jeff decided to go to the back door and knock. *Maybe I will look different to her in a new setting.* He went around to the side of the house, opened the wooden gate, and walked over to the small back porch that led up to a sliding glass door. The bags of trash he had dumped on the grass were stinking now more than when they were inside the home.

Looking through the door, he saw past the kitchen and into the living room where Evelyn's shadow on the floor confirmed that she was still in the same place and talking to the ceiling.

Jeff knocked on the door again, hoping for a different result. Evelyn's animated shadow stopped moving. *Did I scare her?* He listened closer.

"Now what was that?" Evelyn asked. "I've never heard that sound before?" He knocked again and called Evelyn's name. She peered around the living room wall and fixed her eyes on Jeff. Cautiously, she walked through the kitchen toward the glass door, staring through worried eyes at the man on the other side.

"What do you want?" Evelyn asked through the door.

Jeff started to say that he was her son, but then tried a different approach. "I'm Jeff...from Golden's Pharmacy. I have your medication ready." He then held up the bag of anxiety pills, hoping it would not look suspicious.

"Oh, okay. Let me unlock the door," Evelyn said as she fumbled with the lock and tried to get the door opened. *Twenty seconds later and she has already forgotten what I look like.* To Jeff's surprise, Evelyn opened the door with minimal effort, unlike the struggle she had had at his house earlier that morning. She slid it open halfway and reached her hand out to grab the bag. Jeff let go of it without thinking. Evelyn quickly said "thank you" and closed the door.

I need to make sure she takes it. "Wait, I, uh, need you to sign for the package," Jeff added, well aware that he sounded very unprofessional and may have blown his cover.

"What?" Evelyn said as she turned around.

"Yes, uh, I need you to sign to show proof that you received the medicine. May I come in?"

"Well, make it quick because I have things to do." Evelyn opened the door again and let Jeff come inside. *I can't believe it worked!*

"Now, where do I sign?" Evelyn asked hastily.

"It's in here; let me get it," he said as he took the bag from Evelyn's hand. He reached inside for the receipt.

"Okay," Jeff said. "Sign this paper showing that I delivered the medicine to you. And before I go, I'm supposed to tell you when to take the pill and watch you take the first dose."

"What?" Evelyn said. "I don't need your help. I can do it myself. Come to think of it, my doctor hasn't even ordered any medicine for me. Who are you anyway?"

She's too smart for this. Jeff began to worry. He remembered a piece of notebook paper he tucked into his pants pocket earlier. He pulled it out and acted as if he were reading from it. "According to my, uh, Dr. Norman's orders, you were recently in the hospital, and he wants you to take this medicine." Jeff grabbed the bottle out of the bag. "You are supposed to take one capsule every six hours." He noticed the pill bottle said "take as needed," but he didn't think Evelyn

146

would ever believe she needed medicine. *She is oblivious to her condition.* He looked back at his paper. "The doctor wants me to watch you take one pill while I'm here, and then you are to take the rest on your own. Remember: one pill every six hours." Jeff folded his paper and quickly stuffed it back into his pants pocket.

"Let me see that!" Evelyn snapped. "I don't believe you."

Why is she being so defiant? Jeff had to think fast. "Ma'am, I can't allow others to see the doctor's notes. It's confidential."

Evelyn reached out her hand and grabbed the bottle from Jeff. She adjusted her glasses to examine the bottle more closely. "Well, it has my name on it, and that's my doctor's name. Let's see…it says to take one capsule by mouth every six hours as needed."

She'll never take it now!

"This says 'as needed,' but you said it was every six hours," Evelyn said angrily. "You lied to me! I don't need any medicine. I'm doing just fine without it."

Jeff grew more frantic. *I should have called Kate.* "Ma'am, I'm just telling you what the note said. Will you please take the pill now? Dr. Norman wanted me to make sure you took it."

"Now, you listen here. I don't often take medicine, but when I do, I take it just the way it says on the bottle. And it says here to take it 'as needed.' What's this medicine for anyway?"

Clever old woman. "The doctor told me it was to help you, uh, not fall again. He said you were in the hospital because you fell, and this is to keep you from falling again."

"I didn't fall! No medicine would keep me from falling anyway. I'll just watch my step from now on," Evelyn said. She gave Jeff the medicine bottle back. "You tell the doctor I said 'thank you,' but I can take care of myself."

Jeff finally had had enough. He raised his voice and stared directly at his mother. "Mom, it's me, your son. I am

Jeffery! Why don't you recognize me? I'm your only son! You raised me! I used to live here with you when I was a small boy, but now I'm a grown man! I'm trying to help you take care of yourself, but you don't even recognize me!" Jeff slammed the pill bottle on the kitchen table. The cheap plastic container shattered, causing all one-hundred and twenty capsules to spill onto the table and floor.

Evelyn's mouth gaped open and her body trembled in fear. She backed up toward the kitchen wall and yelled at Jeff, "You are not going to come in my house and talk to me that way." Her long, bony finger rose up and pointed threateningly at him. "You are not my son. I've never seen you before. And I'm not taking any of these pills. I don't care if they came from you, the doctor, or some dope head off the street. I'm calling the police right now!"

"No, you're not!" Jeff declared as he stomped past Evelyn and grabbed the cordless phone hanging on the kitchen wall. He yanked the battery pack out of the back side, turned, and threw it toward the far wall in the living room. He turned and went back to the glass door in the kitchen and locked it. "Listen to me, Mother. You are going to sit down and take one of these pills. You need them. You have Alzheimer's disease. You are not well. You have to take these pills in order to feel better!"

Evelyn screamed, "Help!" as tears welled up in the corner of her eye.

Did she hear anything I just said? He walked behind her and pulled out one of the chairs from the dining room table. He placed the chair behind his mother and then put both hands on her shoulders as he forced her down onto it. Evelyn screamed again as she landed hard on the seat. Fearing that others would hear her yell, Jeff forced his hand over Evelyn's mouth. "Don't yell! We don't need anyone else involved in this. I'm here to help you, but you won't let me!" Jeff grabbed a capsule and handed it to Evelyn. "Now take it, Mom! Take this pill!"

148

Fear had taken over, causing Evelyn to come to a degree of compliance. She reached out her quivering hand and grabbed the pill. Jeff moved his hand from her mouth so she could swallow it. Taking advantage of the opportunity, she screamed again, "Help me! Help me, somebody please!" and dropped the pill back on the table.

Jeff slammed his fist down on the wooden tabletop, and a few more pills rolled around until they fell to the floor. He quickly put his hand over her mouth again to keep her quiet. Her raspy scream left warm, sticky moisture on his palm. He stood behind her with his hand still in place as he thought about his next move. Seeing the expensive pills on the floor made him angrier. *Two-hundred dollars!* Evelyn whimpered, and although the sound was heart wrenching, he couldn't let it deter him from trying to help her.

Growing more desperate and worrying that someone would hear Evelyn screaming, Jeff took his intervention to the next level. He reached down, wrapped both arms around her waist, and hoisted her up. She screamed louder than ever. Jeff knew Evelyn would not be heavy because of her recent weight loss, but he didn't expect her to be so easy to carry either. An unpleasant feeling came over him as he carried his own mother away from the kitchen. Her greying hair tickled his chin, and it was obvious she hadn't bathed herself in a while. The noon sun cast enough light through the living room window to allow Jeff to see into the bedroom. He carried her over to her bed positioned in the rear of the room and set her down. He tried to be gentle so he wouldn't hurt her or worse, break a bone, but despite his efforts, Evelyn had a rough landing on the squeaky mattress.

"Stay here and don't move!" Jeff barked at Evelyn. She continued crying and screaming. Jeff closed the door to muffle the pitiful sound. He went back to the kitchen and kneeled down on the floor as he scooped up all of the spilled capsules. He put the pills back on the table and went to the cupboard. He grabbed a glass, filled it with tap water, walked back to the kitchen table, and grabbed one of the capsules. By now his hands were sweating and shaking, making it difficult to grasp the small pills. He managed to break one open over the glass of water. The particles slowly descended into the bottom of the glass. Jeff stuck his finger in and stirred the mixture. As he got up from the table and started to walk back to the bedroom, Evelyn's cries grew even louder. *These are anxiety pills. She's too anxious now for just one to calm her down.*

Jeff went back to the kitchen table and sat the glass of water down. He grabbed another capsule and broke it open over the glass. *It doesn't look like much. Maybe a few more should do the trick.* Jeff opened up three more capsules and poured them into the glass. He stuck his finger in the water again and stirred it, creating a liquid tornado of red crystals. *That should calm her down.* He hurried back to the bedroom with the glass in hand. He opened the door and approached Evelyn, who had now curled up in a fetal position.

"No, go away! Go away! Somebody help me!" Evelyn whimpered, still with the frightened tone in her voice. She was a miserable sight with her hair disheveled, congested nose, and face covered in tears. He could leave, but then she would put the battery back in the phone and call the police. She had to calm down somehow.

"Okay, you want me to leave? I'll leave after you drink this." Jeff raised his arm with the glass in it and put it closer to Evelyn.

"What? Why? What is it?" Evelyn asked worriedly as the tears continued to stream down her wrinkled face. The stress caused from years of grief over her husband's abandonment, raising a child by herself, and working two jobs caused her to physically age faster than others.

"It's just...it's just water. All this crying makes a person thirsty. If you drink it all down, I promise I'll leave and never return." *Someone else can deal with her.*

"Oh, please leave. I'll do anything if you just leave!" Evelyn said.

Jeff handed the glass to her. "Drink it all down and I'll be gone."

Evelyn paused for a moment, but then reached out with her quivering left hand.

"Here, let me help you sit up," Jeff said. He put the glass on the nearby night stand so he would have his hands free.

"Don't you touch me," Evelyn snapped. "You really hurt me. I don't know you, I don't trust you, and I don't like you. I want you to leave. Give me that glass and I'll drink, but don't hurt me anymore!"

I never wanted to hurt you. Jeff handed Evelyn the glass and she slowly began to drink. Her body shook from fear as she drank, causing a trickle of water to flow down the side of her mouth. She tipped her head back to get the last few drops.

"There, I drank it. Now get out of here!" Evelyn demanded. She pointed her shaky finger at the door as she stared at Jeff through hurt, sorrowful eyes.

"I'm gone," Jeff replied. His anger became more than he could handle, and he didn't want to stay for another minute. *Of all the things I try to do for her and she treats me like this. At least she took the medicine.*

Jeff exited the bedroom and left the door open. He went to the kitchen, and as he walked he noticed that his head hurt, his heart pounded, and his breathing was labored. The stress had finally overtaken him, and he couldn't safely drive under this much tension. The remaining pills sat in a pile on the table. *These pills are for anxiety.* Jeff decided if the pills could calm his mother down, then they could do something good for him as well. He grabbed one of the pills, brushed it off on his shirt, and popped it into his mouth. The stress had left his mouth dry, so he got a glass from the cupboard, filled it with water, and washed the pill down. He grabbed another glass and put the remaining pills in it for storage and then set the glass on the counter. Jeff unlocked the back door to leave but suddenly stopped. *She owes me for that medicine.* He marched back into the bedroom.

"No, you said you would leave! Go away!" Evelyn cried.

"Listen, I just spent two-hundred dollars of my money for your medicine, and you owe me," Jeff said hatefully, forgetting that Evelyn probably didn't understand half of what he said anyway. He went over to the dresser, opened the middle drawer, and found the two shoe boxes tucked in the back.

"What are you doing?"

"I told you, Mom, you owe me for that medicine!"

He reached down, opened one of the lids, and grabbed one of the bundles of money. With a stack in hand, he turned back to face her.

"Watch me," Jeff explained. "Your medicine cost two-hundred dollars. I'm going to take two one-hundred dollar bills from here."

"No! Don't take my money!" she screamed. "That's all I have to live on. I didn't want any medicine in the first place!"

Jeff removed the two bills from the stack, but as he pulled them out, three other bills were stuck to one another, and they came off the stack also. *I guess I deserve a little something extra for this.*

"Alright, I got what I need. I'm leaving now," Jeff said angrily as he put the lid back on the shoebox and closed the drawer. He left the house, slamming the door as he closed it. When he opened the gate, Jeff worried that the neighbors may have heard Evelyn screaming even though he had tried to suppress her voice. He walked causally to his car, hoping no one would see him or get suspicious ideas, and also hoping no one heard his mom scream. He sat in his car and turned the ignition, all the while looking around to make sure no one was watching him. He turned to his left, and staring directly at him was Evelyn's neighbor, Martha Mansfield—one of Jeff's least favorite people. Martha was the typical gossipy neighbor who always had her nose in other people's business and was well known for stirring the pot of delicious rumor stew. Many friendships were destroyed because of Martha and her unbridled tongue.

Martha got up from her porch swing, waved her arm at Jeff, and walked across her yard to his car. *What does this busy-body want?* Martha approached Jeff's window. He begrudgingly rolled it down as she leaned over and stared at him through condescending eyes.

"Hi, Martha, I haven't seen you in a while," Jeff said with a broad, fake smile.

"No, it's been quite a few years. You know you should check on your mother more often. I worry about her," Martha nagged in her nasally voice.

If you had any idea. "I have been checking on her, Martha. My wife and I have been spending quite a bit of time with her lately."

"Why? Is something wrong with her?" Martha asked, reminding Jeff once again that she was too nosy. He admired her skill of being able to pull information out of people, but today he had no time for her games of manipulation.

"Ah, you know. The same old Evelyn," Jeff said, not wanting to give away any details of the past week.

"Jeff, I heard someone screaming and came outside. Was it her? Is she okay?"

Jeff could feel the blood drain from his face. "Uh, yeah, she fell just a few minutes ago when I was helping her. She's okay now, just a little sore."

"She fell? You need to get her to a hospital! Jeff, when older people fall, they can break a bone or have some other serious injury! If she were my mother, I'd take her to the hospital."

Is it lonely there at the top? "Martha, she is fine. She just…she was sitting in her recliner and stood up but lost her balance and fell back into the chair. She had a soft landing. It scared her more than anything. That's all that happened."

153

Martha looked doubtfully at Jeff. "Well, like I said, you need to check on her more often. The poor thing is in there by herself all day."

"I heard you the first time, Martha. Thanks for the concern." Jeff rolled his window up, showing that he was finished with the conversation. He backed out of the driveway, and as he drove away from Evelyn's home, he looked up at the rearview mirror to see Martha still standing in the driveway with her hands on her hips and glaring back at him. *She better mind her own business.*

CHAPTER EIGHTEEN

"THIS IS 9-1-1. Please state your emergency."

"Yes, my name is Martha Mansfield. I am neighbors with Evelyn Duncan. I came to check on her today and found her passed out on the bed."

"Is she breathing?" asked the dispatcher.

"Yes, but I cannot wake her up," Martha replied, her voice becoming more frantic.

"Do you know if she has any medical conditions?"

"I'm not sure. I think she has dementia or something. I came to her house after her son left. The back door was unlocked, and when I entered I found some pills in the kitchen and a pharmacy receipt dated for today. I don't know if Evelyn took too many pills or what. I didn't think she took any medicine at all."

"Okay, we will send an ambulance to her residence. Please wait there until they arrive. If Evelyn stops breathing, are you able to perform CPR?"

"I don't know how. I used to, but it's been years since I had a class."

"I will walk you through the steps if she stops breathing."

"Okay," Martha replied. "I don't trust that son of hers. He hasn't been by to see her lately, but today he was here and look what happens."

"What is the son's name?" the dispatcher asked.

"Jeffrey Duncan. I've known him all my life. He used to be a good kid when he lived here with Evelyn. I don't care too much for his attitude, and now he is neglecting his mother."

"Ma'am, do you think Jeffrey might have done something to Evelyn?" the dispatcher asked.

"It was odd to see him visit today. I saw him leaving the house shortly after I heard Evelyn screaming from inside. He was very rude to me but all I did was try to have a conversation with him. He said that Evelyn fell, but I'm not so sure about that."

"Just in case, I will send a police officer to the house as well," replied the dispatcher.

The ambulance arrived within five minutes. "Okay, the ambulance is here," Martha said to the dispatcher. "I'm going to hang up. Thank you for your help."

"Okay, thank you," the dispatcher said.

Martha went to the front door and waved at the two paramedics. One of them, Troy Fisher, ran up to the house while the other one stayed by the ambulance, waiting for orders to bring in the gurney or any other medical supplies.

"What is the problem, ma'am?" Troy asked.

Martha repeated everything she told the 9-1-1 dispatcher.

"Where is Ms. Evelyn?" Troy asked.

"She's over there in her bedroom," Martha said as she pointed toward the bedroom and stepped aside to let the paramedic into the home. Troy used his stethoscope to listen to her respirations and heart rate. He put a blood pressure cuff on her arm and began to pump it. Martha stood over Troy's shoulder, watching him as he worked. "Her breathing is slow." Troy paused for a moment as he measured the blood pressure. "Her pulse is low, and her blood pressure is even lower. Martha, do you have the pills?"

"They are in the kitchen. I'll get them." Martha left and returned in a short time with the drinking glass that contained the pills. "I'm not sure how many are here. Do you want me to count them for you?" she asked.

"Well, if you don't mind," Troy replied. "You mentioned a receipt?"

"Here it is," Martha said as she handed Troy the paper. "I just now found this broken bottle on the floor under the table. It has the name of the medicine on it." Troy took the bottle from her and examined the label.

Martha poured the pills out on top of the dresser so she could count them. Meanwhile, Troy radioed the other paramedic. Shortly after, his partner, Rex Mahoney, came into the house with the gurney. Officer Tom Baker, who had just arrived, came inside with Rex as Martha finished counting the capsules.

"There are one-hundred and fourteen pills here," Martha announced to Troy as she began to scoop them back into the glass.

"One-hundred and fourteen?" Troy asked. "The label here says there were one-hundred and twenty when the prescription was filled. If Ms. Evelyn got her pills today, it appears she has already taken six of them."

"What's going on now?" Tom asked Troy.

"Hey, Tom. I can't figure out for sure what has happened, but it appears to be a medication overdose," Troy said.

Tony handed the broken pill bottle to Rex. "Hey, I took one of these before," Rex said. "I needed something to help me with test anxiety. I just took one, but it knocked me out and I slept through the entire test. I can't imagine what six of these pills would do!"

"We may never know what really happened," Troy said. "Regardless, her vitals are not looking good; we need to get her to the hospital."

Rex wheeled the gurney into the bedroom and positioned it near Evelyn's bed where she remained oblivious in her deep slumber. Rex locked the wheels in place; then he and Troy lifted Evelyn's limp body onto the gurney.

"Do you think she might have misread the dosage or something?" Tom asked as the paramedic's strapped her onto the gurney.

"Who knows? Martha said Ms. Evelyn might have dementia. It's quite possible she got confused and took too much," replied Troy. "That happens sometimes."

Martha turned to Tom. "Officer," she said, "Ms. Duncan's son was here right before I came over today. I don't know if he had anything to do with this or not. I have been checking on Ms. Duncan because that no-good son wasn't helping her, and I never recall seeing any medicine over here in the past, except maybe a couple of times when she was sick. I wonder if he made her take the pills."

"When did her son leave?"

"It was no more than twenty minutes ago. He left, and then I went inside to check on her. When I found her unresponsive, I called for help."

"Do you know where he was going?"

Martha replied, "He was heading east toward downtown."

Tom updated his dispatcher and then said to the paramedics, "I need to leave and see if I can find this man. I would like to think he didn't overdose her." He got back into his police cruiser, did a U-turn, and drove toward the downtown business district.

CHAPTER NINETEEN

"WHY DOES that lady have to stick her nose in other people's business?" Jeff yelled aloud in his car, fuming over his encounter with Martha. "I'm just trying to take care of my mother!"

He didn't want to go home yet. If Kate was still mad, he would probably take his anger out on her, especially if she found out what he had done to calm his mother. He decided to drive through the downtown business district and visit one of his favorite bargain hunter stores. It was a pastime he had grown to love ever since Evelyn had taken him to yard sales as a child. She taught him how to find bargains, how to barter for lower prices, and when and where to go for the best deals. Had it not been for those yard sale clothes, Jeff would have had nothing to wear to elementary school. Evelyn did what she could on their tight budget to help Jeff have his basic needs met. *No thanks to Dad.*

He drove a few blocks into town to "Bargain Basement." The business had been around for many years as it attracted a wide variety of customers due to the ongoing economic crisis that had caused even the wealthy to pinch their pennies. This store carried a little bit of everything— books, cosmetics, electronics, scratch-and-dent furniture, clothes—and the prices were unbeatable if you didn't mind being caught with off brand or outdated products.

The mid-day crowd was about average for people browsing on their lunch break. Jeff strolled through the book section but found nothing of interest among the assortment of recipe books. He was in no hurry to leave so he took his time perusing different dump bins full of assorted junk, most of which was archaic. At the back of the store was the electronics department, albeit scarce of name brand items. He walked toward the back and browsed through a few more dump bins along the way that had caught his attention. One contained an assortment of computer and electrical wires. Another one contained VHS and DVD movies. Jeff sorted through the various titles, most of which were old or unheard of films. None of them sounded interesting. Regardless, this helped Jeff calm down and stop thinking about all the recent stressful events.

The televisions on the nearby wall were set to the local news channel, and the hour-long news program was about to go off the air when suddenly the head anchor announced a breaking-news story. Upbeat music started playing to add to the urgency in the anchor's voice. Jeff turned to the screens to see what had happened.

"A local woman was found unconscious today at her home. Grayson City Police and paramedics arrived at the home of Evelyn Duncan, and the authorities believe someone broke into her home and drugged her. The police are looking for a certain person of interest. If you have any information, please call the Grayson City Police."

Jeff stared blankly at the television as his body stiffened. His heart thumped in his chest and every muscle became tense. There before him was his mother's house displayed on multiple television screens. Video footage showed the ambulance leaving her residence as the siren wailed and red emergency lights flashed.

Another man in the electronics department who had been studying the features on the different televisions had watched the breaking news story. When it ended and another show started, he turned to Jeff. *He knows it was me!*

"It must be a slow day for that to be considered breaking news. Still, that's awful what people do to the elderly, isn't it?" the man commented. *Wait, he was just making a statement. Or was he?* A nauseous feeling came over him. He cautiously looked back at the man and slightly nodded his head in agreement.

"Say, buddy, you don't look so good. Are you okay?" asked the man.

Jeff fumbled for words. He wanted to say he was fine, but even though his mouth moved, words would not come out. He nodded his head again awkwardly, turned around, and started walking to the front of the store to leave. The man stared curiously as Jeff hurried away and then shrugged his shoulders as he turned back to the televisions.

Jeff felt as if every eye was watching him. He picked up his pace as he left the store and went to the parking lot. All he could think about was the newscast, his mother, the police, "person of interest"….Jeff jumped into his car and quickly pulled onto the road. He didn't realize how fast he stepped on the gas until the tires squealed, causing the strong smell of burning rubber to fill the car. His forehead and armpits became moist from sweat, and his heart continued to pound. To make matters worse, he began to feel the effects of the anxiety medication, although he had not anticipated what any of those effects would be. Dizziness and an overpowering fatigue crept in. The cell phone in his pocket started to ring.

"Hello!" Jeff yelled, not realizing how frazzled he sounded.

"Jeff, where are you?" Kate asked. "I've been worried sick. Have you seen the news? Something happened to your mom!"

Jeff paused. *Now she knows. It was on the local news! Everyone knows!* "Uh, what happened?" He tried to sound ignorant.

"It's terrible," Kate replied with a quiver in her voice. "The news said someone broke into Evelyn's home and drugged her! We need to go to the hospital to see her. Come home, please!"

"I'll be home in a minute," Jeff replied and then abruptly hung up. Kate may have been frustrated with her mother-in-law, but she still loved and cared for her. Jeff cared for her too, but right now he had to take care of himself. He pulled his car onto the main highway that led out of town and toward his home. Jeff focused intently on the road and traffic, but he felt his attention dwindling, and the dizziness grew more intense. Regardless, Jeff increased in speed. He was in a hurry but didn't know why. *No one is chasing me. Or are they?*

"I've got to get out of here. If I go home, I'll get caught. If I go to the hospital, the police will be there to interrogate me. Where can I go!" Jeff screamed aloud in his car. He approached an intersection, and although he had the right-of-way, he carelessly sped through without making sure it was safe first. A yellow light at the next intersection turned red, and the traffic forced him to stop. He angrily hit his fist on the steering wheel. *I'm in a hurry!*

When the light turned green, Jeff continued driving until he approached the newly built four-lane bypass. Using this route, he would be home in less than ten minutes. *But why am I going home?* Jeff began to increase in speed as the traffic spaced out farther. *I'm in a hurry, but where am I going?*

His eyes became heavy and his vision began to blur, making it difficult for him to focus on the road. *Why did I take that pill!* The mid-afternoon sun sent bright reflections off the street signs toward him, adding more limitations to his visibility. *Go away, sun! I have to focus so I can escape!* He kept speeding to gain enough distance from the cars behind him. Jeff sped past a billboard positioned close to the road, and as he flew past, he never had the chance to see the police car hiding behind it. Immediately, the officer turned on his blue lights, pulled out from behind the sign, and began pursuing Jeff. Seeing the flashing lights in his rearview mirror, Jeff cursed out loud. He faintly remembered someone in the past telling him the police hide out behind that particular sign, but today, he had not remembered it soon enough.

"No! This can't be happening. They know it was me!" Jeff yelled. "They are after me now. They are going to catch me; and I'll be put in jail! I can't let this happen!" He put his foot to the floor, and his car approached ninety miles per hour.

* * *

"Dispatch, this is Unit 641," Officer Alex Carlton said. "I'm in pursuit of a blue hatchback. License plate is VL5-582. Suspect is speeding forty miles over. Suspect is swerving over the road, increasing in speed, and refusing to pull over. I need back up. Location, Route 401 North."

Seconds later, Officer Tom Baker responded, "Unit 143, copy. Blue hatchback on Route 401 North. ETA two minutes."

Alex quickly sped up to Jeff's car but maintained a safe distance of three car lengths behind. The lights continued flashing as the siren wailed, but Jeff stayed at ninety miles per hour. He continued to swerve over into the right lane but then jerk his steering wheel back to the left side. At one hundred yards ahead, Jeff saw a flashing red light at a fast approaching intersection.

"No, not a stop light! I can't stop. He'll arrest me for sure if I do." Jeff envisioned himself in jail with a bunch of gang members and drug abusers taking turns attacking him. "I can't go to jail. I have a Ph.D. for crying out loud!"

A semi-tractor trailer carrying a fuel tanker approached the intersection from the left. "Slow down, guy! I can't stop!" Jeff yelled. He increased his speed to ninety-five. *Maybe I can get through the intersection before that trucker does. I have to make this!*

Jeff kept pushing down on the gas as his engine roared and strained. Both vehicles were less than fifty feet away from the intersection, and neither slowed down. Jeff refused to yield, thinking he would be able to go through the intersection

163

before the semi arrived. As he got closer, the man driving the semi sounded his air horn. *Why isn't he slowing down?* Jeff suddenly remembered the trucker was on the primary road and had the right-of-way. *This isn't a four-way stop! He doesn't have a red light! We're going to crash!*

CHAPTER TWENTY

IT WAS too late to stop. The trucker tried to slow down, but the momentum only caused him to skid through the intersection at a high speed. Jeff never took his foot off the gas.

The small hatchback violently slammed directly into the tanker and lodged into its underside. Together as one unit, both vehicles skidded at an angle through the intersection, knocking out every utility pole and street sign in their path.

During his hasty departure from the discount store, Jeff had forgotten to buckle his seatbelt, and his entire body shot up out of the driver's seat and landed horizontally on the dashboard. His head banged onto the already shattered windshield and his body lay wedged in-between the windshield and the cracked dashboard. The tattered leftovers of the hood of the car poked some holes into the tanker, and fuel started leaking out.

"This is 641," Alex announced. "We have a two-vehicle collision at the intersection of Highway 401 North and Florence City Bypass. There is a tanker leaking petroleum. We need two ambulances, the fire department, and the HAZ-MAT team now!"

Alex stopped his car at the intersection and backed up several yards in case the tanker exploded. He got out of his car as Tom arrived to the scene. Alex ran toward Jeff's car but remained cautious, fearing that in any second the leaking fuel would send everyone into a fiery death. Jeff's engine caught fire, and the flame grew closer to the leaking tanker. Alex looked into the car and saw Jeff's motionless body lying on the cracked dashboard. Blood had splattered all over the window, and now it dripped to the floor mats and formed small pools.

Tom immediately rushed to the car. He went to the passenger side and opened the door to see Jeff's mangled body. "I know this guy," he said to Alex. "I've been out looking for him. Help me get him out! I'll grab his legs and pull. You support his head. This tanker is going to blow any second now!"

Both officers were skilled in rescue. They were usually the ones who beat the fire department to the scene and had to do all the dirty work when it came to car accidents. Typically they would leave the people in the car, but when there was a fire risk, they had to act fast.

The collision caused the semi to tip over onto its side. Earl Robertson, the middle-aged truck driver, managed to force his passenger door open, climb out to the top, slide down to the pavement, and limp over to the officers. "I swear I tried to stop, but he kept coming! I had the right-of-way—it wasn't my fault!" Earl exclaimed, trying to declare his innocence.

Tom barked, "Get away. It's going to blow!"

"Can I help?" Earl asked eagerly.

"Here, support his legs while I pull the rest of his body out of the car. We are going to carry him back to the other side of the intersection behind the police car. Can you do that?" Tom asked frantically.

"Uh, yes, sir" Earl said as he tried to grab onto Jeff's legs. After grabbing them, they lay limp in his hands for the bones had shattered from the impact. To keep from dropping him, Earl grabbed onto Jeff's blood-soaked pants instead. Earl slowly backed away from the door with Jeff's legs in his hands as Tom reached into the car, grabbed onto Jeff's upper chest, and picked him up. The flames under the car's crumpled hood continued to grow, and the leaking fuel formed several small puddles on the hot asphalt.

"Hurry up! Take him over there behind the car!" Tom yelled. Both men walked as fast as they could as they carried Jeff's body to the designated area, and Alex joined them and held onto Jeff's mid-section. The trio managed to arrive behind the police car and gently placed Jeff's body on the grass near the shoulder of the pavement. The sirens from two fire trucks and two ambulances sounded from several hundred yards down the road.

"I'll check for vitals," Tom stated.

A small piece of plastic used to house some of the electrical components in Jeff's car caught fire. The heat caused it to melt and fall to the ground. Inches away, a small trail of fuel trickled out from an overflowing puddle toward the plastic piece just before the flame died out.

BOOM!

The dying flame on the small plastic piece formed an explosive chain reaction as the fuel and flame joined together. The three men covered their ears and ducked down to the grass. Across the intersection, amidst a pile of destroyed power lines, street signs, and utility poles, a giant ball of bright, yellow fire shot high into the air. The explosion sent a forceful wave of heat and energy in all directions, and the three men trying to help Jeff felt it move over their cowered bodies as they lay low, protecting themselves from the erupted gas tanker. The force slammed the doors on the police cars shut. Violent black smoke fumed upwards from the tanker as the fuel supply burned away.

"That was too close!" Tom exclaimed while trying to catch his breath. All three men stared in awe at the fiery scene less than thirty yards away. "That could have been us."

Tom knelt down next to Jeff and attempted to check his vital signs again. "Hey, buddy. Are you okay? Can you hear me?" He put his fingertips on Jeff's neck. "He's got a pulse, but it's very weak." He put his ear next to Jeff's mouth and listened. "He's barely breathing." He took his handkerchief out and wiped some of the blood off of Jeff's forehead. Blood poured out from lacerations on his head, neck, chest, arms, and legs, in addition to the multitude of puncture holes made by the shattered windshield.

The Grayson City Ambulance pulled up and two paramedics jumped out. One hurried to the police car where Jeff's body lay. The other paramedic soon joined him and brought along the gurney.

"We meet again," Troy, the paramedic, said to Tom. "Have you guys checked his vitals yet?"

"Yeah, he's barely hanging on," Tom said. "We need to get him out of here before civilians start gathering around. They don't need to see this mess."

"Sure thing," Troy replied. He and Rex, the other paramedic who had responded to Evelyn's house less than an hour ago, quickly placed Jeff on the stretcher. Meanwhile, the Grayson City Fire & Rescue Squad arrived and sprayed blankets of foam onto the burning vehicles.

"He's all set. Let's roll out!" Troy said as both paramedics hurried Jeff to the ambulance. Rex rode in the back with Jeff as Troy drove to the hospital. Troy was a veteran with the ambulance service and the most experienced driver, especially in emergency situations. Rex had some experience with trauma victims, but most of the ambulance calls he went on were for minor injuries or medical transports.

"Uhhh," Jeff groaned.

"Are you okay, buddy?" Rex asked, surprised that Jeff was even alive.

"Ahhh!" Jeff groaned again, much louder this time. "Ahhh!" His eyes fluttered open.

"Hey, there you are!" Rex said, happy to see Jeff's eyes were open and there was still a chance for survival. "We're on the way to the hospital right now to get you some help. You're going to be okay." Rex was used to giving generic, positive affirmations to his patients, although he knew in the back of his head that severe trauma victims like Jeff had a poor chance of survival, and even if they did live, they would face a long and painful road to recovery before ever having a normal life again.

"Ahhh! Don't let me die! I'm not ready! Please! Save me!" Jeff screamed in a raspy voice. His eyes were wide open now and staring straight at Rex, who was surprised to see the sudden response from his patient. He'd never seen any of his trauma victims have enough energy to scream at him or have so much fear.

"Wha... we won't let you die. We are almost at the hospital, sir, just hang in there," Rex comforted.

"I'm going to die!"

Knowing he would violate the policies of Grayson Ambulance Services, Rex did the only thing he could to calm his patient down. "Sir, do you know Jesus Christ?"

Darting his eyes back and forth, and then again fixing his gaze on Rex, Jeff whispered, "I'm not sure." Then, just as if a switch had been flipped, Jeff's eyes closed shut.

CHAPTER TWENTY-ONE

A COLD, tingling sensation began to form over his body, starting first in the lower parts of his abdomen and then gradually spreading outward to his extremities. Suddenly, his eyes opened wide without any effort, and Jeff was able to see everything in the ambulance more vividly. The swirling images caused by his dizziness had subsided, and the throbbing pain all over his body disappeared. The afternoon sun shone through the back window of the ambulance. Jeff knew he was in route to the hospital, but didn't know his exact location, and he really didn't care anymore.

As though every pound of flesh and bone disappeared, Jeff felt the sensation of weightlessness spread throughout his body. He had been feeling the soft padding on the gurney below him, but now felt as though he was hovering above it.

"We're losing him, Troy! Step on it!" Rex yelled to the driver.

"ETA five minutes. I'm going as fast as I can," Troy replied.

Slowly, his body rose a couple inches per second until he was completely off the gurney. Something in Jeff's peripheral vision caught his attention. The cabinets on both sides of the wall of the ambulance began to draw closer to him, and the light in the ceiling became brighter as it, too, drew closer. Jeff moved his head from left to right and verified for sure that he was elevating. *What is going on here?* He turned his head farther to the right and his whole body turned with him. Now he faced the gurney where he had been laying, and he hovered one foot above it while continuing to rise.

There before him lay his body. *How can I see me?* Bruises and lacerations covered skin. Smeared blood covered his face, hair, and ears. The clothes were torn around the shoulders, and blood had splattered onto his shirt. Both of his arms were broken in several places. Each of his pants legs was ripped, and Jeff could see that his legs were broken in multiple places. Some pieces of bone poked out of the open wounds, and in other areas where bones had shattered, the skin had sunken inwards.

Jeff's body slightly increased in speed as it continued to rise up. Suddenly, a long and steady beep sounded from a machine near the gurney. Rex stood up and grabbed the defibrillator. Jeff watched the entire scene, feeling both helpless and worried. It immediately disappeared as Jeff found himself floating through the ceiling of the ambulance and now hovering outside on top, staring at its white, metal roof with the flashing red lights and loud, wailing siren.

Outside, Jeff continued to ascend at an even faster speed. As the top of the ambulance disappeared from his view, Jeff could see other cars on the road. He moved his head to the left, and his body turned with him so he was now facing the heavens. He raised his head and looked toward his feet, causing his entire body to rise to an upright standing position. He now had a better view of his surroundings. Off in the distance he saw more flashing red lights where his car accident had taken place. Below him, the ambulance and other cars drove off far into the distance as Jeff made his ascent. The weightless sensation allowed him freedom to move in any direction without any effort.

The speed of his ascent had exponentially increased as Jeff went higher into the sky. He looked down and saw the highway becoming just a small, gray stripe with occasional dots of cars driving along. His altitude now equaled that of the Appalachian Mountains, and from this vantage point Jeff could see far out into the horizon.

He ascended higher and higher into the atmosphere, allowing full view of the entire North American continent as though he were looking at a globe. To his left was the Pacific Ocean and to his right, the Atlantic. Jeff had been so awestruck by his weightless ascent that he never took the time to try to understand why he was in this situation to begin with, but it didn't matter to him either. Nothing mattered anymore.

*   *   *

"May I please speak with Kate Duncan," Tom Baker asked in a firm voice.

"Speaking," answered Kate, adjusting the phone between her ear and shoulder as she continued getting ready to leave to go see Evelyn at the hospital.

"This is Officer Baker. I believe we have met?"

"Yes, sir. You came to my house a few times because of my mother-in-law." Having seen the news story about Evelyn, Kate feared the worst. "Is everything okay?"

"Ma'am, I have some bad news."

Kate paused as a swarm of butterflies flapped about in her gut. "What's wrong? Is she okay?"

"Who? Your mother-in-law?"

"Yes. I saw what happened to her on the news."

"I'm not sure about her," Tom replied. "She was taken to the hospital and I haven't had a chance to follow up with her yet."

"...then what's the bad news?"

"It's your husband, Jeff Duncan," Tom said solemnly. "He was in a very serious car accident a few minutes ago. He left in the ambulance as soon as they arrived, and by now he should be in the emergency room."

Her face turned pale white. *Jeff?* "Wha...what happened?" she asked nervously.

172

Instead of going into the gory details, Tom simply replied, "It's still under investigation."

"But what about Jeff? Is he going to be okay?

"After we pulled him out of the car, I checked his vitals, and he was still breathing and had a pulse."

Thank you, Jesus! "So he is still alive?"

"I can only tell you what I saw when he was with me. He did experience a lot of trauma. You will need to hurry to the emergency room."

Oh please don't die, Jeff! Without saying another word, Kate hung the phone up and dropped to her knees on the hard tile in the kitchen where she had been standing. "Jesus," she prayed, "please save Jeff. Don't let him die…"

CHAPTER TWENTY-TWO

DARKNESS. The fast ascent into the heavens came to an abrupt end as the earth below disappeared into a thick, opaque cloud. No longer could he determine if he was up or down, nor did he have any concept of time or location.

A blinding flash of light chased away the darkness that had surrounded him. He shielded his eyes from the bright light. Gradually, the light's intensity faded, and Jeff removed his hands from his eyes. A feeling of pressure touched his feet. He looked down and saw that he was now standing on a black and white checkered floor. A glowing, golden stripe bordered each of the square tiles below his feet. Jeff raised his head up to determine his location. The checkered floor extended for miles in all directions around him. Above him was a checkered ceiling, and into the horizon, a large ball of pulsating bright light beckoned Jeff to approach. *What is this place?*

Cautiously, he walked toward the distant light. He called out "Hello?" into the silence, but his echo was the only response. He continued walking, yet he could never get any closer to the light.

"Why did you doubt?" asked a reverberating voice coming from behind him.

Startled, Jeff turned around in the direction of the voice, but he saw no one.

"Where is your faith?" asked the same voice from the opposite direction.

Jeff turned back around, but still there was no one in view. "Who's there?" he asked worriedly. The pulsating light came closer to him.

"You have always known me. I elected you before the foundations of the earth were laid. I have always been there with you, during both the good times and the bad. But now you question my very existence?" The voice asked from behind.

Jeff quickly turned around again. A tall man stood before him. He wore a long, white robe. A blue sash wrapped around his left shoulder and draped to his right hip, and a golden belt encircled his waist. He had short black hair and wore a beard. The man stretched his arms out. Looking at his hands, Jeff saw a quarter-sized puncture wound on each of the man's palms.

Jesus? Immediately, Jeff fell to his face and worshipped, weeping uncontrollably.

"Arise, Jeffery Duncan," Jesus commanded.

Wiping away his tears, Jeff struggled to stand up from the floor. He gazed in awe at his savior. *He is real! I knew it all along!* Tears continued to pour out. All of the questions he had about Jesus came back to him, and he was overcome with guilt for having doubts. Full of shame, he lowered his head as he continued to cry.

Jesus approached Jeff and embraced him. Jeff wrapped his arms around Jesus and buried his head into his shoulder. The soft cloth of his robe soaked his tears up.

"I brought you here for a reason, Jeff," Jesus said as he loosened his embrace. "You were so dedicated to me as a child and a youth. That curious mind of yours that I created had many questions about me that were never answered. How I love it when people want to learn more about God! However, your teachers in church could never answer your questions. Because of that, your faith in the Bible dwindled away to the point that you doubted everything you had been taught—Creation, Heaven, Hell, and even my existence."

Jeff stood in silence as he gazed at Jesus. God knew everything about him; even his doubts. "I never stopped believing in you although there were many times, especially recently, when I almost abandoned my faith altogether."

Jesus said. "There are billions of people on this earth who are just like you, Jeff. They have so many questions but get so few answers. Some simply live off of faith and do very well in life, but others, like you, desire to back up their faith with evidence. Some leave the faith altogether when they don't receive the answers they are looking for. I have chosen this time in your life to show you the fate of those who fall away from the faith and never return."

"But, why me? Who am I?" Jeff asked.

"Take my hand," Jesus said. "You will understand in time." He stretched his right hand out and Jeff grabbed it, feeling the scabbed wound on his hand.

* * *

The emergency room doors swung open with a great speed as both paramedics rushed Jeff into an operating room. Nurses and doctors stood nearby prepped with gowns, masks, and gloves. As soon as the stretcher entered the room, several nurses gathered around and carefully lifted his body onto the operating table. One nurse hooked up an IV drip while others cut off the tattered remains of his clothes and changed out his bloody bandages with fresh dressings. The room that had moments ago been quiet as the medical personnel stood by was now ripe with action as doctors examined Jeff's body from head to toe, barking orders for tests, splints, and pain medicine.

"You have your hands full with this one," Rex told Renee, the charge nurse.

"We will do all we can to save him," she replied in a dry tone. Her years of experience in emergency medicine had been full of trauma and sudden, tragic deaths. She and the medical team were required to do everything they could to save one more life, but death sometimes had a way of changing those plans.

Rex signed his name on some standard paperwork and then he and Tony wheeled the stretcher back to their ambulance and left the hospital. Just as they pulled onto the highway, Kate slammed her brakes as she made a sharp turn into the emergency room parking lot, barely missing the side of the ambulance.

"Watch it, woman!" Troy yelled.

Tunnel vision had prevented Kate from noticing much of anything. Since leaving her home, her only thoughts were of losing Jeff, and she fervently prayed that he wouldn't die. She parked her car and rushed into the hospital. "Where's Jeff! I have to see him! Where did they take him!"

The security guard posted at a desk near the entrance stood up. "Ma'am, please calm down. Who are you looking for?"

"My husband! Jeff! Where is he?" she yelled. Fear and worry had caused her heart to pound, and she struggled to breathe.

Jamie, an intake nurse, overheard Kate's emphatic screams and rushed over to offer assistance. "Ma'am, please tell us his full name so we can help you."

"Plea...se," Kate gasped for air. "I need...to see...Jeff Duncan." Overcome by anxiety, Kate's knees gave way and she fell backward. The security guard caught her in his arms just before she hit the floor. With the help of the nurse, they sat her down in a nearby chair in the waiting room.

CHAPTER TWENTY-THREE

THE LIGHT in the room grew dim. The checkered floor dissolved away, and Jeff felt his body descending. Holding onto his savior's hand, together they fell at lightning speed toward the earth. Jeff looked down at the blue and green planet fast approaching. *We are going to crash!* When they came to a mile above the land, a long, swirling tornado snaked out from the earth. Jeff's bird's eye view of the top of the tornado allowed him to see a thick blackness inside the whirling funnel.

They descended into the tornado. Strong winds blew all around him, but he and Jesus remained in the center of the tornado and weren't tossed about by the gale. The air grew hotter as they descended. When they came to the bottom of the tornado, the winds dissipated and a light from an unknown source shone upon a red, rocky wall that now surrounded them. The heat coming from below intensified, causing Jeff's skin to sting.

Far below them into the darkness, Jeff heard a multitude of voices wailing and crying. He could not see anyone for the light did not shine far enough, but he identified the pitiful voices belonging to both men and women.

The descent came to an end as Jeff and Jesus placed their feet on a floor full of jagged, uneven rocks. The screams continued at a deafening decibel, and the heat came from all directions, sucking the energy out of Jeff as he struggled to get a full breath.

"What…is…this…place?" Jeff asked Jesus as he gasped for air.

"The fate of the unforgiven; the abode of the damned; the final destination of those who follow the well-beaten path—Hell," Jesus declared.

It really exists? Why didn't they ever talk about this in church? "Why did… you bring… me here?"

"I have chosen you to carry a message to a lost and dying world," Jesus said. "Your pastor, your college professors, and the recent problems you had with your boss have all resulted in you casting doubt on your childhood faith. Those who abandon their faith come here after death and never leave. They face an eternity of torment for unforgiven sins."

"I can't… take the… heat!" Jeff cried. The penetrating heat burned his skin and dried his mouth, yet he could not see where the heat came from.

Jesus blew air toward Jeff and immediately all of the heat left his body as it was replaced with a cool breeze. "I wanted you to have a brief feeling of the fires of Hell. The people here experience heat far worse than that at all times. They never have relief or comfort."

Jesus raised his hand, and a light shot out from his palm. The light encircled them, allowing them to see about twenty feet in all directions. Jeff surmised that they were standing in a cave; the same jagged red and brown rocks seen earlier also adorned the walls except for a large, primitive gate in the distance. The agonizing screams from unseen people continued at an ear-piercing volume. *Where are the screams coming from?*

"Follow me," Jesus said. Jeff reached out and grabbed onto Jesus' hand as they walked toward the large gate in the distance. Similar to those used in medieval castles, the gate was made of a dark, heavy metal. As if the gate had a mind of its own, both of the broad doors creaked open. As the next room came into view, a bright light forced Jeff to close his eyes, and a hot wind blew onto his face.

Jeff gradually opened his eyes and saw a large lake of fire in the room. *There really is a lake of fire!* The lake was miles wide, and there was no bottom in sight. Several thousand feet in the distance sat another wall where the lake came to an end. On the sides of the lake were rock walls and a ledge. Perched on the ledges were scores of large, hideous, unearthly creatures, each more grotesque than the other. Their asymmetrical bodies resembled neither humans nor animals. Some had multiple arms, legs, or heads, and they all had a pair of wings on their backs, but the wings were bent and misshapen. *These are...demons!*

Jesus walked toward the ledge of the lake, and Jeff followed close behind. His body shook from fear, yet still, he felt secure as long as he held onto Jesus' hand. Thick columns of fire in the lake were positioned every eight to ten feet. Some of the columns were stationary while others shot up from the depths at random times. Deafening screams echoed from the depths of the lake.

As he watched the raging columns of fire in the lake, Bible verses flashed in his mind. Jeff had never been one to memorize Scripture, but out of nowhere unfamiliar verses came to him:

"...This is the second death, the lake of fire." (Revelation 20:14, ESV);

"And he seized the dragon, that ancient serpent, who is the devil and Satan, and bound him for a thousand years, and threw him into the bottomless pit..." (Revelation 20:2-3, ESV);

"And cast the worthless servant into the outer darkness. In that place there will be weeping and gnashing of teeth." (Matthew 25:30, ESV);

"They will suffer the punishment of eternal destruction..." (2 Thessalonians 1:9, ESV);

"And if your hand causes you to sin, cut it off. It is better for you to enter life crippled than with two hands to go to hell, to the unquenchable fire." (Mark 9:43, ESV).

Turning to Jeff, who continued staring in horror at the sight before him, Jesus said, "They were warned of their fate by My Word."

CHAPTER TWENTY-FOUR

"HELL WAS created for Satan and the one-third of angels who followed him at the great rebellion thousands of years ago," Jesus said. "It was made for them; they deserve this torture for their rebellion and the countless problems they have caused on earth. The people of earth that I created were never meant to come here, but everyone is a descendant of the first man, Adam, and because of his sin, all are born into sin. There are none who are righteous, but forgiveness is available to mankind. Those who die unforgiven end up here."

"But," Jeff asked, "Is Hell necessary? Do people have to suffer for an eternity?"

"A sin committed against an infinitely holy God requires an infinite punishment," Jesus answered. "Although God is loving, He is also just and cannot let unrepentant sin go unpunished."

Hearing the mournful screams coming from far below, Jeff pleaded with Jesus, "I want to leave. It's just too painful for me to hear all these people crying."

"Peace, be still," Jesus commanded. An overwhelming sense of peace immediately came over Jeff, and he then became fearless. "I want to show you this room." Jeff looked around but could only see the large gate they entered through and solid rock walls surrounding the exterior. Jeff suddenly felt himself descending. He looked down and saw his feet sinking into the rock, yet he did not feel anything. He turned to Jesus, and He too was descending into the rock with him. Although he didn't understand what was going on, Jeff felt reassured that he would be okay as long as Jesus was with him.

Jesus didn't say anything as they went through the floor and exited through the ceiling of a room below them. They floated down into a dimly lit room where they were greeted with a loud chorus of sorrowful moans.

When they arrived at ground level, Jeff got a better view of his surroundings. This room had the resemblance of a long and wide hallway. The familiar stone floor and walls were present, and crosses lined the walls on both sides stretching far into the darkness. Almost every cross had a person hanging from it, and they all cried and moaned in pain.

"What is this place?" Jeff asked as he continued surveying the room and looking up at the people who hung from the crosses.

"This is a sad place, Jeff," Jesus replied quietly. "Some of the people you see on these crosses have been here for days while others have been here for just a few hours. They will eventually be taken down and experience a new torment. There are several types of punishments in Hell based on how people spent their time on earth. Most of the people you see on the crosses lived relatively good lives. They gave to the poor, took care of the sick, and volunteered their time. Some even served in churches as pastors, elders, deacons, and members of the choir. They were good by their own standards but still had unrepentant sin in their lives.

Jeff looked perplexed at Jesus. "If they lived good lives, then why are they here?"

"These people on the crosses before you—they thought they could enter into Heaven based on their own merits. But as I said through my servant Isaiah, 'Their works are as filthy rags.' All sin causes a separation between God and man, but there is no sin so severe that God won't forgive when a person repents. Jeff, the reason I made the ultimate sacrifice for people was so they would not have to earn their own salvation. It is impossible to please God based on good deeds alone. It is faith that saves you.

"The heart of man is desperately wicked, and no one can trust it. Because of Adam's rebellion in the Garden of Eden, and since every human on earth is a descendant from Adam, all are born into sin. Regardless of the amount of good works people do in their life, everyone is still affected by sin, and death is the penalty for sin. I came to earth to make the ultimate sacrifice that paid the penalty for sin thereby opening the door to eternal life, but many have rejected my free gift, and Hell is their fate.

"Jeff, all of the people in this room, and everyone else in Hell, have heard the saving message of the gospel. I have appeared to people in dreams and visions. I've sent missionaries all over the world through centuries past. And now through technology, the gospel has spread to all parts of the world. Had the world not heard the gospel, they still would have known me through my creation. All who come to Hell have done so because they rejected the gospel. They all understood that they needed to be forgiven, but they refused to repent of their sins. Sin cannot enter into the Kingdom of Heaven."

Jeff stood amazed at how simple it was for a person to get to Heaven, yet all of the people on the crosses before him, and all of those he had heard wailing in the fiery lake, had come here because they would not repent.

"Come, I want to show you something," Jesus said as they began walking to the left. Jeff held onto Jesus' hand as he looked up at the men and women hanging on the crosses. They were a wretched and woeful sight. Their hands were nailed into blood stained beams of wood, and their feet were nailed together on vertical wooden beams. Their bodies would slide down, causing intense pain in their arms. Each person struggled to push themselves back up to relieve the pressure. They cried out in agony and tried to reason with one another as to why they had been sent to Hell.

As the two kept walking, strange voices were heard in the distance. The language was unfamiliar, and the voices were deep and had a gurgling sound. Jeff also heard a woman screaming and speaking in English. There was some movement a few yards ahead of them.

"No! Let me go! I don't belong here!" cried the woman.

Five demons appeared in the distance. Without thinking, he stopped walking, and Jesus also stopped as they watched the scene unfold in front of them. The demons were large in stature and had heads that resembled cattle skulls. They walked with a hunch in their back, and their arms lazily drug behind them. Two of the demons were on both sides of the woman holding her arms. The three others fastened a nearby chain around an empty cross. All three of them pulled down on the chain, causing the cross to come crashing to the floor. The demons then picked up the cross and flipped it over so that it would be right-side up.

"What are you going to do to me!" the woman cried again.

The two demons holding onto the woman dragged her to the cross. One picked her feet up and the other grabbed her head and shoulders. They carelessly dropped her down upon the center of the two beams. The three demons who had prepared the cross came over to the woman. A demon kneeled on either side of her, grabbing her hands and holding it in place on the horizontal beam. The third demon held her feet together on the vertical beam.

The woman screamed at the demons to let her go. She turned her head to the left and right and pulled her arms in hopes of breaking loose from their grip. She continued to fight, but her efforts were no match for the demons holding her down. The demons on both sides of the cross grabbed a stone mallet and a long, metal nail. Each one placed a nail on both her hands, raised the mallet up, and beat down on the nail. A wet, smacking sound was made as the nails drove deeper into the woman's flesh. The clanging of the nail and mallet echoed throughout the cavernous room. She screamed louder and louder as the nailing continued. She begged the demons to stop, but they ignored her. The demon near her feet used a much longer nail and drove it deep into both of the woman's ankles. The entire crucifixion took less than a minute to complete, and Jeff was impressed at the teamwork and efficiency of the demons albeit a very macabre sight.

When they finished hammering, all five demons worked together to lift the cross up with a chain and archaic pulley system. They placed the vertical beam into an already-existing hole, fastened the chain onto a hook in the wall, and then walked away in silence.

The woman screamed at them, "Don't leave me here alone!" Take me down this instant, you monsters! I don't deserve to be here!"

Jesus pulled his hand away from Jeff's grip. Looking at both of the wounds in his hands, he began to cry. "I do not like to watch these crucifixions, Jeff, but I wanted you to see for yourself what I had to go through for you and everyone else. I was beaten by the Roman guards prior to my execution and that alone could have ended my life, but I knew that in order to fully pay the ransom for sins, I would have to live until the crucifixion was completed. Cursed is any man who hangs on a tree, but I chose to take that curse for the sake of mankind. Despite the suffering I endured for My creation, people rejected it and now they are here in Hell paying the price that I already paid for them."

Jesus walked toward the woman, and Jeff followed close behind. The woman looked away from the demons that had walked out of sight and turned toward Jesus. "Thank you! Thank you for coming to save me, Jesus!" she said eagerly.

"I have not come to save you," Jesus said in a calm and sad voice.

"What?" the woman said with fear and panic in her voice. "You have to save me! I am a good person and I lived a good life! I raised three children. I volunteered at a nursing home. I gave to charities at Christmas. I don't belong here!"

Jesus listened to the woman's plea until she finished. "Although you did good things in your life, you never accepted my free gift of salvation. There was unforgiven sin in your life, and although it may have been minor in your eyes, it still caused a separation between you and me."

"What sin are you talking about? I've done more good than bad! Doesn't that count for something?" the woman yelled at Jesus.

"You committed adultery. While you were married, you had an ongoing, intimate relationship with a man and kept it hidden from your husband for years. The man with whom you committed adultery carried a contagious, deadly disease, and after you became intimate with him, you acquired that disease and passed it on to your husband. When you found out he had the disease, you accused him of having an affair and then divorced him, although it was you who had the affair and spread the disease. Your sin finally took your life away, and now you are here.

"I would have forgiven you for that, but you never accepted my forgiveness. You thought you could earn your way to Heaven by doing good deeds. I sent many people to tell you about my forgiveness, but you just ignored them. You became agitated with those I sent to you, and finally you told them all to leave you alone. You had a fair chance just like the others who are here with you now."

Jesus then walked away. Jeff looked back at the woman as he followed closely behind. She kept watching Jesus and yelled, "You're not going to leave me here, are you?" Jesus didn't answer. She yelled again, "I'm sorry for what I did to my husband. I really am! I believe in you now, Jesus! I really do! Come take me with you! Get me out of here!"

Jesus stopped, and with a mournful face, turned back to the woman, "You had your chance while you were alive on earth, but now it is too late." Jeff felt himself start to sink into the floor again. "Come with me, Jeff," Jesus said, turning away from the woman. "There is more I want to show you."

Jeff strengthened his grip on Jesus's hand as they again descended farther into the depths of Hell. Feeling the crucifixion wound on His hand, Jeff now had a greater appreciation for what his savior did for him on the cross.

CHAPTER TWENTY-FIVE

"MA'AM? Can you hear me?" asked a nurse.

Kate fluttered her eyes. A bright light from the ceiling forced her to squint as she came to. "Where...where am I?" she asked.

"You are at Grayson Regional Hospital, ma'am," the nurse said.

She turned her head to the side. A heart monitor and other medical equipment were in the room making a chorus of beeps as they measured her vitals. The bed rails had been locked in place, and she had a blanket pulled up to her shoulders.

"Why?"

"You passed out in the waiting room almost an hour ago," the nurse answered. "The doctor said he could find nothing wrong with you, but we brought you into a room to keep you safe until you came to."

Kate paused for a moment. Her head spun, and she had developed a throbbing headache. "Why did I come to the hospital?"

"The security guard said you had come to see your husband," the nurse replied. "What is his name?"

"Jeff Duncan."

"There is a Jeff Duncan here. He is in surgery right now," the nurse replied. "There is also an Evelyn Duncan. Are you related to either of them?"

As though a fast-forward button had been pushed, everything came into focus and Kate remembered the events leading up to her driving to the hospital. "What about Jeff? I need to see him!"

"You cannot see him now. He has been in surgery for over an hour and the doctors cannot be disturbed," the nurse answered.

Please don't die, Jeff! "Evelyn is my mother-in-law. Is she okay?"

"I'm not sure. She was moved to an observation room. When you are feeling better, you may go visit her."

"Can I go see her now?" Kate asked.

"Yes, she is in room 526."

Slowly, Kate sat up. Her head continued to spin and she struggled to stand to her feet. "I better rest here for a minute. I don't think I can walk yet."

* * *

After a short descent, Jesus and Jeff stood before a metal-barred door. Jesus waved His hand across the bars and the door opened. They walked a few feet into the room and stopped. "Jeff, this is the prison. People have been in here anywhere from a few days to thousands of years. They have no hope, no relief, no rest, and no chance of escape."

Jeff scanned the room. The ceiling could not be seen for it was thousands of yards above them. Lengthwise, the room extended far out of Jeff's view, and he could not see an end. Millions of small, individual cells were built into the rock walls on either side of the room, and countless rows of cells extended up toward the ceiling. Each row of cells above the first floor had a small ledge, and demons paced back and forth on the ledges as they kept guard.

Jesus led Jeff over to a cell on the left side of the wall. Jeff looked inside and saw an elderly woman lying on the floor.

"Jeff, this woman has been in here for almost fifty years now. She has been sent here because ever since she was a child, she has been rebellious and evil. During her life, she created heartache and grief for a multitude of people. She would marry men for money and then quickly divorce them, allowing her to accumulate wealth through the divorce settlements. Later in life, she befriended widowed men in nursing homes, gained their trust, and eventually married them and moved them into her home. Through manipulation and deception, she had the men change their wills and life insurance policies so she would benefit from them after their death. After gaining their trust, she would deprive the men of their life-saving medication and physically abuse them until their ultimate death. After their death, she collected the insurance money and fled to another region to start over with another victim.

"Throughout her life I sent people to witness to her. Church leaders, righteous women, and neighbors all presented the gospel to her, yet she refused to listen. She would never admit that she had taken part in the schemes. I allowed her to live for ninety-eight years, which gave her ample time to seek forgiveness, but her pride never allowed her to repent, and she died alone from a heart attack.

"I wanted to forgive her for all of her numerous sins, but she would never take responsibility and repent. She never sought after me and only wanted to please herself. All of her life she took away from others and never faced an earthly punishment for it because she was never caught. But now, she has to suffer for eternity."

She's a black widow. Jeff gazed at the disheveled woman on the floor. She had no hair and her body was burned, lacerated, and covered in blisters and bite marks. She turned her head and looked up at Jesus.

"Lord, please forgive me! I have changed now. I know what I did was wrong. I'm sorry, Lord! Get me out of here!" the woman begged. Immediately, black spiders fell from the ceiling above her and covered her body.

"You know why you are here," Jesus told her. "It is too late." He turned to walk down the corridor of cells, and Jeff grabbed tightly onto Jesus' hand. As they walked away, muffled screams came from the woman. *What were those spiders going to do to her?* Jeff knew better than to look back and see for himself.

They walked for about an hour and passed by hundreds of cells. Jeff glanced into the cells and saw all sorts of people inside. There were both men and women ranging in age from adolescent to the elderly. Some of the prisoners were experiencing torture as they passed by. A man was held upside down by a demon and repeatedly dipped into a cauldron filled with fire. One demon carved skin off a woman's shin bone with a rusty blade. Another one poured a hot acidic chemical down an elderly man's throat. One woman had been strapped to a mattress full of spikes while a demon hammered on her body with a stone mallet. An adolescent girl had both arms and legs tied as demons pulled on her from opposite ends. Cries of agony and sorrow from the numerous destructive tortures echoed throughout the cavernous room.

"The people you see in Hell led lives of abuse, selfishness, laziness, apathy, and indulgence. They are liars, thieves, drunkards, and murderers. They did not care for their fellow man and only served themselves. Had they repented, they would not be here now," Jesus said as they stopped at a cell where they were both eagerly greeted.

"Hallelujah! I knew you'd come for me. Thank you, Jesus! Let's get out of here!" a man inside the cell exclaimed enthusiastically.

Jesus turned to Jeff. "This man has been here for sixty years because of the evil he did in his life. He grew up in church and was taught the true gospel. His parents raised him to work and earn a living, but he rebelled, and as he grew up, he became a sloth. He never wanted to work and always borrowed from others or cheated to get what he wanted. He did this for several years until finally his friends and family stopped giving to him. This man then decided to start preaching. He lied to his friends, saying he had a revelation from me and that he was to deliver my message. The problem is that I never called him to preach. He did not deliver my message but instead deceived others. He formed a church and preached many false things about me and also taught that people can become gods themselves. He convinced his church members that they can earn their way to Heaven by giving money to him. He was so persuasive that people in the church gave him millions of dollars over the course of his career as a charlatan. He told his congregation that he gave the money to charities, but in reality, he used it all for himself. Despite the money coming to him, he was never satisfied. He then moved his church into a big arena and televised his sermons throughout the world. He could have reached billions of lost people with the gospel, but instead he only told them more lies and filled them with a sense of false hope. Some people even referred to this man as 'God' and worshipped him.

"Jeff, so many people who were part of his congregation died as false converts; they died believing they were saved. Since they were unforgiven, they were sent here forever. I sent my servants to this man and his congregation, and some of his followers repented before they died, and now they are in Heaven. But the majority refused to listen to my servants and instead followed his deceptive lies."

Jeff stared at the man. He wore a broad smile—the same smile he used to win the trust of others while on earth. The floor below him glowed with hot coals, and constantly the man had to move his feet to bring relief from the burning. His naked, burned body was full of deep puncture wounds. He begged Jesus to end the torment and take him to Heaven. "I am so tired, Jesus. I don't deserve this punishment. I was a pastor! I told people about you! You have to set me free!"

"You know why you are here," Jesus said with a stern voice. "You served yourself. You purposefully lied about me and the gospel. You lead thousands of people astray."

193

Out of the walls on either side of him, sharp, rusty spikes started to poke through. The man in the cell heard the metal screeching against the rock wall. He turned his head to see the spikes growing closer to him.

"No!" He cried out. "No more! I can't take any more of this!"

Turning to Jeff, Jesus said, "This is the fate of Pastor Bill and his father, Larry, if they do not repent."

Jeff quickly turned to Jesus. "What!"

"It is true," Jesus said. "They have knowingly misled many people away from the true gospel. Neither of them confronts sin nor even teaches repentance. Even you questioned your faith, especially after hearing Pastor Bill cast doubt on the trustworthiness of My Word. I stopped Larry by silencing his voice, and the same will happen to Bill if he doesn't stop."

That's why Larry got esophageal cancer! "But, they are good people. They are preachers!" Jeff pleaded. "They don't deserve what this man is getting."

"If they repent and come back to the truth, they will not experience this. But there is more to the problem, Jeff," Jesus said.

"What?"

Jesus then lifted his hand up, and a ball of light emitted from his palm. Within the light, Jeff saw what looked like a movie playing. He saw his pastor in his office at the church. Before him on his desk was the Sunday morning offering. Bill counted the money and stacked it into piles according to denomination. Jeff estimated that there was at least ten thousand dollars on his desk. Bill then pulled out the church accounting book, wrote "$5,000" under a column entitled "Offering" and then put five-thousand dollars into a bank bag. He took the rest of the money and bundled it together. He walked over to his door and locked it, and then went back to his desk. Behind his desk, a picture hung on the wall. He removed the picture from the wall, exposing a hidden safe. Bill unlocked the safe and put the bundle of remaining money

194

inside among other piles of money. He locked the safe and hung the picture back up. He then put the accounting book and bank bag in his desk drawer so the church treasurer would take it to the bank on the next day.

"This can't be," Jeff said quietly. "He's embezzling money from the church!"

"It is true," Jesus said. "He stores it in the safe and uses it for himself. He has been doing this for quite some time, but no one, not even his wife nor his father, knows about it."

Something has to be done about this.

Thinking about his pastor, Jeff glanced back inside the cell. The spikes had now crept within a few inches from the charlatan's body. He tried to move away from them, but no matter where he stood, he would be stabbed multiple times by the spikes. Jesus covered Jeff's eyes with his robe as they walked away to the sounds of the charlatan letting out a blood curdling scream.

CHAPTER TWENTY-SIX

SEVERAL MINUTES passed as Kate lay on the hospital bed with her eyes closed, trying to stop her head from spinning. She opened her eyes once again and slowly sat up on the bed. She put her left foot down on the floor, and then her right. Bracing herself on the bed rail, she stood up and took a step forward. Feeling that her headache had subsided, and she no longer felt dizzy, Kate told the nurse that she felt better and then went to check on Evelyn since Jeff was still in surgery.

Evelyn lay in her hospital bed asleep. Kate didn't want to awaken her, but still, she needed to know that her mother-in-law was okay. She placed her arm on her shoulder.

"Evelyn?" Kate asked, lightly shaking her. "Evelyn, can you hear me?"

Her eyes fluttered and then opened up fully. She turned to Kate and said, "They have been quiet. I hope they stay that way."

Kate smiled, happy to see a sign of life. "Who are you talking about?"

She gently lifted her index finger and pointed up to the ceiling. "The young family up there," Evelyn replied. "They like to talk a lot, but so far they have been really quiet, and I've been able to get some rest."

Kate slowly turned her head to look up. Sheet rock, hooks for the privacy curtain, two fluorescent lights—nothing she saw appeared to be causing Evelyn any problems. "I don't understand. Who are you talking about?" she asked.

"You can't see them. I haven't seen them, but they are there," Evelyn replied mysteriously, still looking up at the ceiling.

Kate looked back up. "Who is there?"

"I guess you could say they are my neighbors, but most neighbors live next door or across the street."

Kate paused as she tried to understand the riddle. "Your neighbors? Are your neighbors in the hospital also?"

"I guess so," Evelyn replied. "I've heard them talking a lot, but right now they are quiet."

"You must have good hearing," Kate said. "I don't know how you can hear them on the floor above us over all the noise."

"They aren't on the floor above us," Evelyn said. Her calm face turned to a frown. "They are living in the ceiling, and they won't leave. I need you to do something about the people up there. Just make them stop talking, please."

Living in the ceiling? Trying to clarify, yet knowing something wasn't right, Kate asked, "When did they get into the ceiling?"

"It wasn't that long ago," Evelyn replied. "I never saw them move into my house, but one morning I woke up and heard them talking. I looked all over the house but couldn't find anyone. The only place I couldn't get to was the attic, so that has to be where they are living."

"But you are in the hospital. You aren't at home."

"I guess they followed me," Evelyn said. "Wait, why am I in the hospital? I'm not sick!"

"But I saw on the news…" Kate stopped. Evelyn didn't know where she was at, and it would upset her to hear what the news report said earlier. She put her purse down and pulled a chair closer to the bed so she could keep Evelyn company.

Still trying to understand, Kate asked, "Are you sure people are living in the attic?"

"Yes!" Evelyn snapped. "That is where they live. They have a baby up there, too. I hear it crying at night. I have told them to leave, but with it being so hot outside I couldn't just throw them out, especially if they have a baby. I did put some air holes in the ceiling so they could get some fresh air."

That's what those holes were for! "Maybe those people will move when it's cooler outside," Kate said, playing along.

"Please help me. I can't afford to feed them anymore." Evelyn said as she laid her head down on the pillow. Her brief anger had subsided, and her eyes started to flutter. She soon fell asleep, so Kate brushed the graying black hair out of Evelyn's eyes and tucked the sheet around her to make her more comfortable.

* * *

"I have one more person I want to show you," Jesus said as they walked away from the cell.

"I've seen enough, Lord. Can we please leave this place? I hate it here!" Jeff replied.

"I want you to see this last person, and then we will leave," Jesus said calmly. "The reason I am showing you these things is because people don't believe in Hell anymore. Many churches are not teaching about it. Even some seminaries don't teach it anymore, yet during my earthly ministry, I taught more about Hell than I did about Heaven. Jeff, Hell is real, and I want you to let others know about it. Many are on their way here now, and several hundred have arrived just as I've been speaking. I don't want people to come here. I want them to repent of their sins and join me in Heaven."

Jeff felt his body begin to rise, and he saw that Jesus was also levitating. "There is a person near the top I want you to see," Jesus said.

They rose for several minutes, passing by thousands of cells filled with tortured souls. Jeff forced his eyes shut to avoid seeing any further punishment. They arrived at the very top row of cells, which were positioned at about ten-thousand feet above the floor. Jeff looked down and was suddenly reminded of his fear of heights. "Do not fear, for I am with you," Jesus said in a comforting voice.

They walked along the ledge of the cells, passing by many lost souls within the confines begging to be set free. As they walked, Jeff again heard Jesus cry. "Jeff, I have told you that I hate this place. I never wanted anyone to come here. I did not create people as robots where they were programmed to love me. What joy would that be? I gave people the ability to choose to love me, and I offered them a home in the Kingdom of Heaven. Some who are here used to love, worship, and live for me, but the devil deceived them, and they began to love their own lives and fulfill their own desires instead. I had blessed them with homes, cars, wealth, and other worldly goods, but they used those things to only satisfy themselves. They didn't give their possessions to those in need but instead wasted it on their own lusts. In the end, their selfish lives led to the ultimate rejection of my gift of salvation."

After their long walk, Jesus arrived to a particular cell. It looked the same as all of the others, but something was not right about this cell and its occupant. Although Hell had an overbearing presence of evil, the malevolence coming from this cell was far more powerful. On the floor sat a glass box resembling a kitchen oven. Inside the box lay a man and a bright, hot fire. The heat could be felt coming from the box, and an ear piercing scream came from the inside.

Jesus turned to Jeff and said, "This is a very sad story. The man before you had a violent childhood. He was abused by both his parents. They beat him and took turns sexually abusing him. His parents were both severely abused when they were younger, and when they abused this man, they only did what they thought was right. Of course, that didn't mean it was the right thing to do, but because of sin, many families struggle from violence and abuse, and the cycle goes from one generation to the next.

"This man endured these torments until he became a teenager, at which point he was removed from his home and put in foster care. The new family he lived with was very faithful servants of mine. They gained this man's trust and provided him with true love and care. Until he started living with this new family, he did poorly in school, was malnourished, and was not even developing correctly due to the abuses he had received. With his new family, though, the man started to improve in his overall health. He even graduated from high school, went to college, and landed a successful career.

"As this man grew older, he began to build up a harsh bitterness toward his biological family. Although he had received therapy to help overcome his painful childhood, he swore that he would never forgive his parents. Unforgiveness ate away at this man's soul, and he entered an ongoing state of depression. I sent my messengers to his parents, and they repented and turned their lives over to me. They became my servants and spent the rest of their lives building my kingdom. However, this man's foster family presented him with the gospel many times, but he never repented of his sins. One day, he was introduced to the dark powers of the occult, and soon he became a priest in Satanism. He did everything from performing rituals, casting spells, and sacrificing animals and humans.

"Jeff, I sent many of my servants to this man to lead him to me, but he refused and hardened his heart toward me. He knew I was real, but he believed he would receive better power through dark forces. After many years of his servitude toward Satan, he began to receive direct messages from the devil and soon had various demons at his command. The forces of evil allowed him to perform miracles, and he became famous for his feats. Things were going well for him until one day the demons told him his powers would fade away if he did not offer the blood sacrifice of his biological parents. Afraid of losing his power, this man obeyed.

"Satan told him that if he killed his parents, he would be a co-ruler of Hell. The man brutally murdered both his parents as he conducted a ritual sacrifice with other Satanists. After the murders took place, all the other worshippers participating in the ritual turned on this man and destroyed him. They chopped up his body into several pieces, burned it, and then ate his body with hopes of gaining the powers he had.

"There are many out there who are just like this man. They seek power from the evil one. They practice occult rituals, magic, and sorcery, which are promoted in popular movies and books as harmless entertainment, but they lead to destruction, and there is no place for such evil in my kingdom. Remember that Satan is the father of lies and a master of deception."

Jesus then held up his left hand and produced another ball of light. Jeff stepped closer to the light to get a better look at a scene unfolding within. "Watch what happened to this man after he was murdered," Jesus said.

Jeff saw the grisly aftermath of the man being slaughtered and eaten by his fellow Satanists. The scene changed to the moment the man died and fell into Hell. He landed in an ornate, stone room. A giant throne decorated with human skulls sat in the center of the room, and seated on the throne was a large, hideous beast. Six-foot long curved horns stuck out of the top of its head. A broad, black face with powerful jaws and yellow teeth sat atop a muscular body. The arms and legs were like thick tree trunks. Above the throne, a sign read "Prince of Darkness."

"You have done well, my servant," Satan said to the man. "You served me during your life and killed your Christian parents. They were destroying my kingdom, and I have you to thank for stopping them."

"You are welcome, great master!" the man said to Satan as he bowed down. "May I now have my share of the kingdom?"

With a loud, thunderous laugh, Satan yelled at the man, "No one shares in my kingdom! This is all mine and you will have no rule over any of it!"

"But…master? You promised I would rule with you in return for my servitude!"

Satan laughed again, "Fool! You were my pawn on earth and that was all I needed. You get nothing but the punishment due all of us!" Jeff watched as Satan grew larger in stature and morphed into a tall, hideous beast, similar to the dragons Jeff had seen in Chinese folklore.

The dragon stood up and exhaled a long, hot flame of fire toward the man. The fire clung to the man's body and he screamed in pain. Then the dragon reached forward and grabbed the man with its piercing teeth. Out from behind the throne, a scaly demon brought a glass box to the center of the room. The box was about the size of an oven, and with it opened up, the dragon spit the broken body into the box. It had been mangled beyond recognition. The dragon then exhaled fire into the box, and the man became engulfed in red hot flames. The demon standing nearby closed the lid of the box as the man inside writhed about in utter misery. He tried to escape, but the glass lid was locked shut.

Jesus closed his hand and the violent scene disappeared. "He remains in that box to this day. Although he has been burning for forty years now, he will never get used to the agony. His body was destroyed so long ago, but he still feels every flame, every broken bone, and every wound caused by the devil's teeth. This man knows why he is here."

Jeff asked, "Can't you stop it? Forty years is long enough!"

Jesus turned toward the box. "He chose this life. I gave him many chances to repent, but in his sin he believed the lies of Satan instead of my truth." Jesus then blew air toward the box, and instantly the fire went out and the box unlocked and opened by itself. Black smoke billowed out of the box and a putrid stench of death and decay filled the room, causing Jeff to gag and cough.

Slowly, the charred, pitiful man lifted his head up and looked outside of his cell. "Jesus?" he weakly whispered. His entire body quivered and was as black as coal. Many of the bones were exposed amidst patches of red, bubbling skin.

The man spoke up again. "Jesus? Have you come to rescue me? I am sorry. I served the wrong god. It should have been you who I served. I rejected all of those who came to me with the gospel. I didn't want to hear it because I wanted the power that Satan offered. Now I am here for an eternity. Jesus, will you please release me from here?"

With a mournful voice, Jesus replied, "It is too late. Everyone has ample time on earth to choose life over death. You had many opportunities to turn away from your evil life, but you chose not to. I would have forgiven you, even up until the moment before you died, but you did not seek me. You listened to the lies of the evil one and chose to come here. You now have to pay for the unrepentant evil you have done."

The man, with as much strength as he could muster, yelled out a string of blasphemies at Jesus. He cursed and blamed Him for being sent to Hell. Jesus did not respond to the man's words. Jeff again tightened his grip on Jesus' hand as Jesus turned and walked away. Before they were out of the cell's sight, Jeff heard a noise coming from within it. He looked back and saw that a demon had entered the cell. It breathed fire into the box and closed the lid, locking the man inside the inferno. He began screaming in agony again. Amidst the screams, Jeff thought he could hear the man apologizing to Jesus.

He burns forever. "Can we please leave now? I have seen too much," Jeff pleaded.

"Yes, we shall leave now," Jesus replied. "It is time for you to go back to your body and begin your mission."

Jeff grabbed onto Jesus, and they ascended through the ceiling above, passing through several layers of red rock. Jeff felt protected by Jesus and was in awe of his Savior's ability to go anywhere and do anything. *All powerful, all knowing, and in all places at all times.*

Their ascension out of Hell came to a sudden halt as they stopped in a dimly lit room. People all around were crying. "Why are we stopping?" Jeff asked, thinking they would be out of Hell by now.

Jeff heard more reverberating screams as people on fire began falling through a hole in the ceiling. They landed on the rocky ground with a bone crushing thud. Hundreds of people fell from above and landed in a growing pile of bodies on the jagged, rocky floor.

"What is going on?" Jeff asked.

"An earthquake just occurred," Jesus said mournfully. "Many people were crushed by buildings or trapped underground in coal mines. Hundreds of lives were lost just now. My faithful ones entered into Heaven, but the rest came here."

Jeff was speechless. *They never saw it coming.*

"Those who just now died from the earthquake thought they still had time left to repent. No one knows when they will die. It is imperative that people hear the gospel and repent of their sins before their time is up. That is why the Father is sending you. You will be used to further my kingdom."

"How will I further Your kingdom? What can I do?"

"The foundations have been destroyed. You, Jeff, will restore them," Jesus said confidently. Without another word, they ascended farther up through the rocks as more people fell into the growing heap of flaming bodies below. Their departure from Hell soon ended when they shot up through the ground of the earth and entered into the atmosphere at warp speed. The refreshing cool night air brushed over them. City lights far below lit up the sky and stars dotted the heavens above.

"My child, it is time for you to go back to your body," Jesus said.

Jeff felt his body descending to the earth. "My Lord, may I ask you just one question before I go?" Jeff asked.

"Yes, you may."

His body stopped descending as he fumbled for words. "I don't understand why we suffer. Why does my mom have Alzheimer's disease? She is in pitiful shape. She doesn't recognize people, she's become stubborn, she gets angry...Jesus, she didn't do anything to deserve this. She's a good person. Why does she have to suffer like this?"

Jesus answered, "Philosophers and theologians have pondered that very question for centuries. It has been quite a stumbling block, causing many people to question my existence and ultimately abandon their faith. Everyone suffers in one way or another. Maybe they were born with a physical disability, or they grow up in an unstable home. It is how they respond to their suffering that determines their outlook on life. The reason people suffer is very simple, and the answer can be found in the Book of Genesis. Let me show you."

Jesus spread out his hands, and the sky and earth beneath them turned pitch black.

CHAPTER TWENTY-SEVEN

"I CREATED the world to be very good," declared the Lord. "I will show you how it once was perfect, but due to the choice of your forefather, Adam—that is, his ability to choose to be disobedient—all perfection fell apart. Understanding this will explain why there is suffering."

Out of Jesus' hands came flashes of rainbow colored lights. Jeff squinted from the brightness, yet he kept his eyes opened just enough to see the spectacle. Beautiful colors shot out in all directions and then collected together into a swirling formation. It reminded Jeff of the colorful lollipops his Sunday school teacher used to give out as rewards for bringing a friend to church. The swirling grew exponentially in size and soon filled the blackness. A distant rumbling sound came from the center, and it grew louder until it exploded with a powerful *boom.*

The collaboration of the colors and sound created picturesque scenery. It was as if Jeff was watching a movie on a large screen, but this was more lifelike. Before him he saw lush, green vegetation covering the ground. Large, ripe fruits hung from an assortment of trees and plants. Small hills decorated the land, and four meandering rivers flowed through it. A cool breeze lightly tossed the grasses and leaves about. In the distance, Jeff heard a stomping sound increasingly getting louder. Coming up from a small valley to his left were two large, sauropod dinosaurs. Their long, graceful necks hung outward as they walked, occasionally stopping to munch on some fruit hanging from the trees.

Deep within the thick branches of the trees from which the dinosaurs were eating, there was some movement and a loud racket. Suddenly, two eagles flew out of the tree and soared across the sky. They were painted in unusual colors of red, yellow, and orange. The two graceful birds stayed in Jeff's view, flying from his left to his right. He watched as they effortlessly soared over the rivers and toward some distant hills. Then, something moving along those hills caught his eye. A large assortment of animals—wolves, elephants, monkeys, giraffes, and even other kinds of dinosaurs— approached, and although Jeff could identify them, they did not look like the animals he had seen at zoos and in his textbooks. They had different body types, colorations, and were much larger in size.

"This is my creation, Jeff," Jesus said fondly.

"Even the dinosaurs?" Jeff asked, perplexed to see something he had never considered being a part of God's creation.

"Of course! How else would they have gotten here?" Jesus replied with a laugh.

"Why does everything look so much…better?" Jeff asked.

"Just keep watching," Jesus said.

More animals appeared from all directions, and Jeff was still able to identify them although they, too, looked much different. Everything about the earth, plants, and animals was so unlike what Jeff was familiar with as all forms of life had a much healthier appearance. The fur on the animals was fuller and alive with color. Their statures were more robust and there were no signs of disease or struggle for survival. *Everything is so much better here.*

Nearby, he heard two people talking. Jeff turned back to his left and saw a man and woman walking amongst some trees. They were naked and holding hands, and they showed no shame for being uncovered. Jeff did not recognize the language they spoke, yet somehow he understood everything they were saying.

"God has created such a beautiful garden for us, Eve," said the man.

"He has, Adam. It is truly remarkable what our Creator can do," Eve replied.

"Look over there!" Adam pointed and smiled. Under a hedge of shrubs, two raccoons playfully wrestled with each other. A pair of turtles hopped into the river for an afternoon swim. Around a tree filled with fruit, giraffes ate from the top while monkeys climbed to the inside and searched for food. Two lions rested below in the shade of the tree, and next to them, sleeping peacefully, lay a pair of sheep. A pair of pterodactyls flew above, gracefully soaring over the garden. The atmosphere was filled with serenity, and instead of fighting for survival, all the animals shared their space and food supply with each other.

Adam and Eve walked along after taking a few moments to admire the animals. The couple was clearly in love and had mutual respect for one another. Jeff saw they were not light skinned as they had been portrayed in the book illustrations he saw as a child. Instead, both adults had a medium-brown complexion. Adam had thick, brown hair, and Eve had long, blonde hair.

Eve approached a large tree nearby. Hanging from its limbs were red and orange colored fruits. Jeff could not identify the tree, but the fruit was very appealing. A serpent slithered out from a limb next to Eve.

"You should try some of this fruit," the serpent suggested.

Eve replied, "No, I can't. We aren't supposed to eat from this tree. Our Creator gave us permission to eat from everything in this garden except for this tree."

The serpent replied, "What will happen if you eat this fruit? It's just food, isn't it?"

"If we eat or touch the fruit, then we will die," Eve said plainly. "That's what God said."

The serpent laughed. "No, you are not going to die just from eating a piece of fruit! God meant that if you eat it, then you will become like Him, knowing good and evil. Don't you want to be more like Him?"

Adam stood nearby overhearing what was being said, but he didn't interrupt. Eve, having been convinced of an alternative meaning to God's mandate, grabbed one of the pieces of fruit, snapped it off of the branch, and took a bite from it. She licked her lips to keep the juices from flowing down her chin.

"This is really good, Adam," Eve said, turning to her husband. "It tastes different from all the others we've tried so far. Here, have some."

Eve handed the fruit to Adam. He grabbed it and admired the texture. Its smooth outer skin looked tasty, and the fragrant aroma emitting from the inside smelled just as sweet as the other fruits in the garden. Still, God had told him to not eat from this tree. Adam looked over at Eve to see if anything had happened to her. She continued to chew the fruit, and there were no obvious changes or ill effects, and she didn't die. Adam turned the fruit around and took a bite from the other side. He chewed and swallowed the fruit along with its seed.

Immediately after Adam swallowed it, a breeze blew against his skin, and he looked down and realized he was naked. Although he had always been naked, it never posed a problem until now. He dropped the fruit, and when it hit the ground, it started to smoke and rot away into the dirt. He used both hands to cover his private area. Eve, also realizing she was naked, did the same to cover her nudity. They looked away from each other, embarrassed.

"Adam? Where are you?" a male voice called out from a short distance away.

Adam and Eve ran to a nearby assortment of tall bushes and hid. He turned to Eve and whispered, "God doesn't need to see us naked." A few fig trees had grown behind the bush. "Here, let's use some of these leaves and cover ourselves."

They both quickly tied together some vines and leaves and produced an itchy, shabby outfit. Jesus, God incarnate, approached the bushes and leaned over, looking at Adam and Eve.

"Why are you hiding?" Jesus asked, smiling.

"Because we heard you walking in the garden and didn't want you to see us naked," Adam responded shamefully.

"Who said you were naked?" Jesus paused and looked behind him toward the Tree of the Knowledge of Good and Evil. "Did you eat from that tree? Didn't I command you not to eat from it?" His smile faded away into disappointment.

Pointing his finger at Eve, Adam quickly replied, "Eve gave it to me! She gave me the fruit and I ate it."

Eve replied angrily, "That serpent over there tricked me into eating it!"

Jesus turned around and quickly walked over to the forbidden tree where the serpent hung on the branches and laughed menacingly. "What have you done?!" Jesus yelled at the serpent. The snake lowered its head. "From this day forward, you are cursed above all other animals. You will forever move on your belly and eat the dust from the ground. You have deceived my people, and now the world is cursed!" Still talking to Satan but pointing his finger at Eve, Jesus proclaimed, "There will forever be hostility between you and this woman for all generations to come!"

The serpent scurried away into the tree, slithered down the trunk toward the ground, and hurried off into the distance. Other animals nearby swatted at the serpent and tried to bite it. Jesus went back to the bushes. Adam and Eve came out from the bush and hung their heads like scolded children.

Jesus said to Eve, "Because of your disobedience, I will greatly multiply your sorrow, and you will endure hardship and many struggles. You were created to produce children, but now you will have more pain during childbirth. You will also desire to rule over your husband and be in charge of him, but it will be he who rules over you."

Eve hung her head down and wept. Jesus turned to Adam. "Up until now, your work in the garden has been simple. But because of your disobedience, I will curse this very ground. Work will become much more difficult and unpleasant for you. Thorns and thistles will grow, causing you to get cuts and scrapes when you sow and when you harvest. The hot sun will beat down on you as you work, causing fatigue and discomfort. Adam, I created you out of the dust of the ground, and you and Eve were going to live forever here in the garden, but now, because of your rebellion, your life will one day come to an end, and you will return to the very dust from which I created you."

Jesus raised his hands, and two, twelve-foot tall muscular angels appeared with a flaming sword in hand. They turned around to face Adam and Eve with an angry grimace. One angel thrust the sword outwards and said, "You must leave the garden! Go now!"

Adam and Eve turned and quickly ran away from the angels, never to return to their earthly paradise.

As they ran into the distance, Jesus turned to Jeff. "Now, watch what happens."

Jeff looked back at the vision. Out of the ground, long, sharp thorns began to grow onto different types of foliage. Animals that had once shared the fruits and vegetation together now started to have vicious fights with one another over the food supply. Adam and Eve, who once had a healthy glow, started to show signs of aging.

Jesus continued. "Man was my greatest creation, and my plans were for him to live with me forever in this paradise, but man also came with the ability to make choices, and because of Adam's decision to disobey me, all creation now suffers. You see how the animals are fighting now, the earth is changing in appearance, and the people are aging. Adam and Eve will eventually die, as will all animals and plants.

These are the effects of sin. Since Adam is the father of all people, including you, he has passed down the harmful results of sin through his genes. Adam and Eve had healthy DNA, but sin caused their DNA to form mutations and errors that have caused disease, birth defects, and other health problems, like Evelyn's Alzheimer's disease. Generation after generation passes down these harmful traits, and they are getting worse as all creation groans. The effects of sin are not biased—both good and bad people are affected.

"I had to ban Adam and Eve from the garden because otherwise they would have eventually eaten from the Tree of Life and lived forever in a cursed, decrepit body. Adam's sin resulted in death, and it caused a separation between God and His creation. All people die and suffer from the effects of sin because of Adam. I was sent to earth to redeem my creation and restore their separation from God. All people can have eternal life through me. The Father loves His creation so much that He sent me to redeem it for Him. My sacrifice provided a way for one to avoid Hell and enter into eternal life in Heaven."

Jeff took some time to absorb all Jesus had said. "Because of Adam, we all die. But through You, we can have eternal life?"

"That is correct," Jesus affirmed. "Repent of your sins and believe in me as the risen King of Kings." Jesus then lowered His opened right hand and closed it shut. Immediately, the vision they had been watching disappeared before them, and the city lights below lit up the night sky. "It is time for you to go back. You are on a mission now. Tell everyone your witness of Hell. Find your student, Jordyn Monroe. She will teach you the truth about creation, which you have never been fully taught. I will have more in store for you then."

Jeff had forgotten about Jordyn. Jesus said, "I sent her to your school so she could bring you back to the truth. Did you know she had a full scholarship to a bigger and more prestigious university? Jordyn has always submitted to my will, and she chose to attend Grogan University because she knew I had a mission for her there. Jeff, you were her mission. When I send you back, I want you to talk to her. She will know what to say."

"Yes, my Lord," Jeff humbly replied. He was overcome with shame as he thought about how he had mistreated Jordyn and upset her. *I was so foolish.*

"Although you have been spiritually healed," Jesus added, "your physical body has suffered much damage from the car accident. You will find your body awaiting you in the hospital."

* * *

A nurse came into Evelyn's room where Kate had been waiting. "Mrs. Duncan, your husband has been moved to room 223. He is unconscious, but you may go see him."

"He's...okay?" Kate asked.

"Yes, he made it through the surgery."

Thank you, Jesus! Evelyn had fallen asleep hours ago, so Kate grabbed her purse and hurried down the hallway to the elevators. She pressed the "down" button repeatedly, but the elevator took too long to arrive, so she turned and rushed down the stairs to the second floor. She pushed the stairwell door open and sprinted to Jeff's room.

CHAPTER TWENTY-EIGHT

JEFF FELT himself descend down through the night sky at a fast speed. The city lights showed him the familiar landmarks, and he felt himself being drawn to the hospital. The descent continued, and his body slowed down as it entered through the hospital roof. He floated through several floors and patients' rooms. Most of the patients were awake. *Can they see me?* An elderly man in one hospital room had a visitor, and the visitor had brought the man's small dog to see his sick owner. As Jeff descended through the ceiling, the dog looked directly at Jeff and excitedly barked and wagged its tail. The elderly man, not being able to see Jeff's ethereal appearance, told the dog to be quiet. Jeff just laughed.

His descent came to an end as he entered through the ceiling of his hospital room. He looked down and saw his body lying on the bed, covered in bruises and scrapes. His legs had casts on the shin bones and thighs, both arms were covered in thick casts, and he had bandages on his head. He heard a steady *beep...beep...beep* coming from a machine on the left side of his bed near the window. On the right side sat his beloved wife, Kate. *What a sight for sore eyes!* Tears fell down her face as she whispered prayers for her critically injured husband.

Like snapping two puzzle pieces together, Jeff felt his soul rejoin with his body. Soon after the two entities

214

connected, a strong shooting pain throbbed throughout his body. All of his muscles ached, and pain shot out from his broken bones. He also had an immeasurable thirst for water.

"Lord, please save Jeff. Heal his broken body. Deliver him from this coma. Please, Lord, don't let him die." Kate prayed while wiping away a tear with a tissue.

Jeff opened his eyes and slowly turned his head to the right. He was afraid to move anything because he didn't know if his neck was broken. A smile formed over his face as his eyes fixated on his faithful wife. The last time he saw her, they were at odds with one another. Now, he didn't even remember what they had been fighting about.

Kate stopped praying and sniffed her nose. She glanced over at the clock on the wall, cleared her throat, and turned back to Jeff.

"…Jeff?" Kate asked with a hushed but excited voice. "Jeff, are you awake? Can you say anything?" She reached out her hand and touched his exposed fingers.

"Uhhhg," Jeff moaned. He wanted his first words to be more intelligible but he could only make incoherent vocalizations.

Kate quickly stood up and, without even considering Jeff's level of pain, wrapped both of her arms around his neck and kissed his cheek.

"Uhhhg," Jeff said again as he winced. "Wa…wa…wa-er"

"Huh?" Kate asked. "What did you say? War? Water? Yes, water!" She walked around to the other side of his bed and grabbed a bottle of water that had been sitting on the table. She poured it into a hospital mug, grabbed a nearby straw, and dropped it into the mug. Kate then leaned over the bed and carefully held the straw up to his mouth. Jeff fumbled with his lips and tongue until he finally grasped onto the straw. He drank as fast as he could.

"Slow down, honey, you don't want to drink too much at one time!" she said.

Jeff ignored her warning and consumed the entire glass. "Mo…more," Jeff said, forcing the words out.

"I don't have anymore. Let me call a nurse. I need to let her know you've awakened." She put the mug down, ran into the hallway, and yelled in the direction of the nurse's station. "Hey! Somebody! He's awake! Jeff is awake!"

Jeff turned his head toward the door to watch. He had always found it funny when Kate became overly excited. She waved her arms wildly until someone at the nurse's station noticed her. Shortly after, the sound of rubber shoes was heard rushing toward his room. He was eager to see someone come and help him with his pain, and, hopefully, bring him more water. Two nurses ran into the room and stood on either side of him.

"You check his vitals and I'll do a neuro-check," one nurse said to the other.

"Okay," the other nurse said.

Jeff estimated that they were in their mid-forties. They wore name tags with big red letters that said "R.N." The nurse on his right named Linda examined the monitor next to his bed and wrote down his vitals. Deborah, the nurse on his left, pulled out a clip board and began asking him questions.

"Sir, my name is Deborah, and I'm one of your nurses. I need to ask you some questions. Do you know what your name is?"

Jeff attempted to give a response, "Ye…Ye…" but he could not get the full "yes" off of his tongue.

"What is your name?" she asked.

"Je…Je…Jeff…Du…Duncan."

"Very good," she replied as she made a check mark on the form. "Okay, next question: What year were you born?"

"Nine…nineteen…seven…seventy-eight."

"Very good. Next question: Do you know where you are?"

"Hos…hospital."

"That's right. You are doing well, Mr. Duncan. Let me ask you a few more: Do you know why you are here?"

216

Jeff pondered that question. Was it the right question to ask a patient? *I don't deserve to be here. I should be in Hell because I am a sinner. I was on a path to eternal damnation, but my savior stepped in and turned me around.* Jeff mustered up enough energy and said, "I'm here…because Jesus…saved me…from Hell."

Silence filled the room except for the incessant beeping coming from the nearby monitor. The nurses exchanged confused glances to one another. Kate, who had been standing nearby, stared at Jeff in amazement.

"What did you say? Why did you say you were here?" Kate asked.

"I need some wa…water," Jeff said. Deborah then put her clipboard down and left the room. She came back a few moments later with two bottles of water. She grabbed Jeff's mug and poured one of the bottles in it and then put the straw up to his lips. He drank the entire bottle in a matter of seconds.

"I went to Hell." Jeff said after wetting his tongue. The cool liquid helped him speak more clearly. He turned to Kate. "I met Jesus and he showed me what Hell is like. There were so many people there, and they were all in terrible agony."

Linda looked at Deborah and said in a hushed voice. "He must have some brain damage. His vitals are stable, but he's talking out of his head."

Jeff was offended that Linda talked about him as though he couldn't hear her. Even more so, he was upset that she didn't believe him.

"Do you know Jesus?" Jeff asked, turning to Linda.

Linda looked at Jeff and stared for a moment. Distracting herself, she unstrapped the blood pressure cuff. "I…well, that's a rather personal question, Mr. Duncan. I'd rather not discuss it here."

"Ma'am, if you don't know Jesus, then you will go to Hell. It's a terrible place! I was with Jesus just a few minutes ago. He loves you, Linda. He wants to forgive you of your sins so you can live with Him forever in Heaven."

"Sir," Linda said with agitation growing in her voice. "This is neither the time nor place to be preaching to me about your Jesus. I'm trying to help you get better, and I need to focus on my work."

Jeff did not respond. The thought of Linda, or any person, suffering an eternity in torment made him shudder. *Please save her, Jesus.* Jeff turned to Deborah. "Do you believe in Jesus?"

Deborah had been hanging on to every word he said. "Yes I do as a matter of fact! He is my savior and my source of hope."

"Isn't He wonderful?" Jeff said with a smile. He paused for a moment and said, "I was losing my faith in Him, but He showed me His truth. You and I need to help Linda find Jesus."

Kate spoke up, "Jeff, what has gotten into you? You've never talked about religion like this in the past, especially around complete strangers!"

"Now that I've seen Jesus and the fate of the damned, I have to tell everyone!"

"Before you go out preaching, you better get some rest," Linda said sarcastically. "You took quite a beating from that car accident."

Jeff turned to Linda. "Wha...what happened to me?"

"Well, let's see," Linda answered bluntly. "You were in an accident with a fuel tanker. Apparently you drove straight into it. Both of your thighs and shins are fractured in multiple places, your right ankle is shattered, you have fractures in both of your arms, there is some damage to your spinal cord, and you have a minor skull fracture. There may be brain damage, but we haven't done a test on that yet. A few of your organs have minor injuries, but they should heal on their own."

Jeff tried to soak in everything she said, but it was too much. Pain shot up from his legs and both arms, and his head throbbed. "Am I going to be okay? Will I ever walk again?"

For the first time since he came back to his body, anxiety and despair crept in. "Will I ever be able to teach again?"

Linda grabbed Jeff's chart at the end of the bed and thumbed through it. She was happy to do anything to avoid conversations about Jesus. "I'm looking at the doctor's notes. The fractures are severe, but we have them set in casts. You still have some other surgeries that need to be done, but the doctors just wanted to stabilize you first. You should expect a full recovery although you will need a lot of physical therapy before you can walk again. The doctor hasn't said anything about that yet; I'm just letting you know what to expect. I'd rather him tell you about your prognosis. We still have to do the tests on your head to see if there is any brain damage. Honestly, we didn't think you would even come out of the coma."

"You should talk to my Healer about that," Jeff said assuredly. Linda didn't respond but instead busied herself with paperwork.

Jeff was thrilled to be alive and back on earth with his wife. He was given a second chance at life, but the long road to recovery filled him with doubt. Still, there was nothing better than seeing Jesus and getting out of Hell.

The nurses finished their paperwork and assessments. "I will call the doctor's office and leave a message with them that you are back with us. He will come see you sometime today," Deborah said.

When they left, Jeff turned to Kate. "How long was I in the coma?"

"You had the accident Thursday afternoon, and it's just now turning seven o'clock on Friday morning," she replied. "I don't know how you survived this, much less come out of a coma so quickly. I came to the hospital as soon as the police called me about the wreck. I couldn't see you while you were in surgery, so I stayed with Evelyn."

Jeff suddenly remembered everything that took place before the car accident. The frustration with his mother, the pill overdose, the breaking news report, the police...*I deserve Hell.* "Is Mom okay?" he asked worriedly.

"Yes. She is as confused as always, but she is stable. The nurse said she will probably go home this morning after the doctor sees her." Kate went on to tell Jeff about the "attic people."

"So that's who she's been talking to all this time! I wonder where she got that idea from."

"I don't know. I guess it is part of the Alzheimer's," Kate said.

She doesn't know what I did to Mom. "What did they find wrong with her?" he asked.

"They did all kinds of tests but only found a high level of her anxiety medicine in her blood system. The doctor said she may have overdosed on her medicine, but he said it would have taken hundreds of pills to really cause serious damage. The amount she had in her system was just enough to knock her out for a few hours."

Jeff breathed a sigh of relief, thankful he did not cause permanent harm to his dear mother. *Why couldn't I have been more patient with her?*

"What did you sigh for, honey?" Kate asked.

"I have to confess my guilt, Kate. So much happened this week that affected my faith. Pastor Bill denied the literal account of creation and casted doubt on the reliability of the Bible. Mom injured her head and that made her dementia even worse. I got demoted at work because of my stance on academic freedom, and Dr. Farris challenged my beliefs and belittled me. All of that cumulated in me seriously doubting my faith. I was fooled into thinking there was nothing more to life than survival, and because of Mom's illness, it's as though she became a second-class citizen.

"After you and I argued on Thursday, I called Evelyn's doctor and he prescribed some medicine to help her calm down. I went to her home to give it to her, but she didn't know who I was. I got so frustrated with her that I mixed up several of the pills in a glass of water and made her drink it."

"You did what!" Kate exclaimed. Her expression of joy quickly transformed to anger. "How could you!"

"Please, I was so stressed. I tried to help her. You tried to help her. Nothing worked, and I was concerned about her being home alone. I…did what I thought was best to calm her down. I feel terrible."

"That was an awful thing to do," Kate concluded. "At least she's okay now."

"After I forced her to take the pills, I took some of her money. Part of it was to pay for the medicine; the rest I outright stole. I guess it got destroyed in the car accident. I even tried to steal her life savings and spend it on myself. How could I have turned so bad? I'm a terrible son."

Kate reached over and patted Jeff on the shoulder.

"No," Jeff said. "I don't need pity. I have done some awful things. I should be locked away forever. Jesus showed me Hell, but by the way I acted, I deserved to stay there."

"Jesus was being merciful to you," Kate acknowledged.

"His grace gave me something I don't deserve—a second chance."

"Before the car accident, that police officer that had come to our house—Baker, I think—came by again looking for you. He came over right before I saw the news report about Evelyn. I told him I didn't know anything, and truthfully, I didn't. The officer asked how he could contact you, so I gave him your cell phone number.

"He may try to call you," Kate continued. "This could be something serious. I hope not, though. You've already been through enough so maybe they will let you off the hook. Besides, the police have been busy trying to find an arsonist. A house in our neighborhood burned yesterday, and another one burned across town this morning."

Jeff sighed again. "Things are different now. I have to fess up to what I did. I deserve to be punished, but I guess we will have to burn that bridge when we get there."

221

Linda came back into the room. "I have a cocktail of sleeping and pain medication for you. This should help you rest for several hours and ease the pain."

She proceeded to inject the concoction into Jeff's IV port. "Ma'am, I'd really like to talk to you about Jesus. Will you please let me do that?" Jeff pleaded.

When finished, Linda pulled the syringe out and dropped it into a red biohazard container hanging behind her on the wall. She sighed and turned back to Jeff. "Maybe some other time. I don't see any need for a god, but if I get sick or something, maybe then I'll start to think about it. A lot of my patients become 'holy rollers' when they come here; but when they go home they change back to normal. You'll do the same thing."

"But what if you were to die suddenly, like in a car wreck or earthquake?" Jeff asked, thinking about the last thing he saw in Hell.

"I don't like to play the 'what-if game,' Mr. Duncan," Linda said as she hurried to finish her paperwork and leave the room. She went to the door and turned back to Jeff. "And I really don't care for religion."

"I don't like religion, either," he replied. "Religion is man coming to God; Christianity is God coming to man." Linda gave Jeff a funny look, and then he closed his eyes and drifted off to sleep as the medication kicked in.

CHAPTER TWENTY-NINE

THE LATE summer sun shone through the window as Jeff woke up late Friday evening. Kate sat in a chair by his bedside holding a cup of coffee and watching the last half of the local evening news.

"How'd you sleep?" she asked, putting her coffee down and readying her hands in case he needed something.

"That was the best sleep ever. I didn't feel any pain at all. We need to get that recipe before I leave," he replied with a laugh.

"It must have been really effective because you've been asleep since early this morning," Kate replied. "They discharged your mother so I took her home. Of course, I had to tell her I was with the taxi company, otherwise she wouldn't have listened to me. It was quite an ordeal, but she is home now."

"That's good. I'm thankful she is okay. Still, we need someone to check on her."

"Yes, we do," Kate said. "By the way, when I came back here after lunch the nurses said you were crying in your sleep. I meant to ask you about that."

"I was?"

"That's what they said. Were you dreaming about something?"

223

"I don't really recall, but if I was dreaming, then it had to have been about what I saw in Hell," Jeff said. "There were millions of people suffering. And it was unbearably hot. The screams, the cries, the wailing, the agony…" Jeff started to cry. Never before had he encountered such misery, such despair. "They rejected God's free gift of salvation, and now they suffer forever."

"I just can't imagine what you experienced," she said consolingly.

"Before sending me back to my body, Jesus told me I have two things to do. One of them was to tell others about my experience in Hell, and the other one was…that reminds me—will you run to the house and get my laptop?"

"Sure. I was going to check on Evelyn anyway. I'll run by the house first." She kissed him on the cheek and left the room. The evening news continued, and Jeff watched to see if he had missed any important events during his unexpected departure from this world.

A news story showed footage of a devastating earthquake in Europe where thousands had died. *That earthquake caught so many people off guard. They thought they had more time on earth, but now they are dead.* The female news anchor faced the camera from a different angle and continued talking. "In local news, several arsons have been keeping the police and fire department of one community busy during the past week. The Grogan City Police are asking for your help. If you can provide any information about these fires, please call the number listed on the screen."

The television then showed a picture of a house engulfed in flames. Fire shot through the busted windows and spread quickly around the exterior of the home. A family of four stood outside, watching their home burn while several fire crews worked to extinguish the blaze.

Jeff's eyes were fixed on the fiery images, all the while having flashbacks to the columns of fire he had seen in Hell. He watched as the fire destroyed the family's home. Dark smoke billowed up into the air and filled the sky. The camera zoomed in closer to the fire and the flames became brighter and more intense as the image filled up the entire screen.

At the top of the television, a flame leaped out and latched onto the black plastic that housed the screen. Jeff began to panic and breathe heavy. He clenched his teeth as he watched the flames begin shooting out of the television and reaching up toward the suspended ceiling in his room. The fire spread over the ceiling tiles and quickly reached the wall in front of him. *This can't be happening! I'm going to get burned!*

The flames moved down and across the walls and spread to the wall behind him. The ceiling and all four walls had become engulfed in flames. The heat penetrated his skin and he started to sweat. Smoke filled the room as the hungry fire roared. A flaming ceiling tile above his bed fell and landed on his sheets, and they caught fire. His bed was quickly engulfed, and the flames started burning his legs. He tried to move but couldn't. He could wiggle his fingers, but his arms and legs were covered in thick casts that prevented any other form of movement.

"Ahhh! Help me!" Jeff screamed, causing his throat to burn from his loud shriek.

Within seconds, a young nurse named Morgan ran into the room. She braved the leaping flames and hurried toward Jeff's bed side. "What's the matter?" she asked worriedly.

"What do you think! I'm on fire! Put it out! Get me out of here!" Jeff yelled at the nurse. Flames from the floor climbed onto her clothes, but she ignored it as she tried to help him. "I'm burning up! You have to get me out of here!"

Two other nurses overheard his screaming and came into the room. Jeff saw that they, too, had run through the growing fire but ignored the flames attaching to their scrubs. They stood next to Morgan, and the flames engulfed all three of them.

The charge nurse looked intently at Jeff, "Sir, what can we do to help you?"

225

"Lady, I'm on fire! Put it out! Do something! Get me out of this room! The smoke is too thick and I can't breathe." Jeff grew impatient and started to cough from the smoke.

"Do you want us to take you into the hallway?" the charge nurse asked.

"Yes, do something! Please!" Jeff yelled. The charge nurse moved to the head of Jeff's bed while the other two unlocked the bed wheels. She pushed Jeff's bed out into the hall while Morgan held onto his IV stand and walked alongside the bed. Within seconds, the burning trio of nurses escorted Jeff into the hallway and out of the flames.

"Is this any better, sir?" the charge nurse asked.

Jeff could hear the flames roaring in his room behind him as the heat pulsated through the door. There was no fire in the hallway so he felt safe. His bed sheets were still flaming, and he began to blow air in hopes of extinguishing the flames.

"What is he doing?" Morgan whispered to her supervisor.

The charge nurse replied, "He must be hallucinating. He evidently thinks he is on fire and is trying to blow the flames out. I've seen some wild things during my career as a nurse, but this one is going to the top of my list."

Jeff had overheard the conversation while he was busy blowing out the flames. "Do you not see this?" he asked angrily. "All three of you are on fire! Why aren't you doing anything about it?"

"Sir, we don't see or feel any fire," replied the charge nurse as politely as she could.

Jeff looked at the sheets. The flames began to die down quickly, and he no longer heard the crackling flames in the room behind him. His charred sheets turned back to white, and the heat on his legs disappeared. *What is going on here?* Jeff looked quizzically at the three nurses. Everything had turned back to normal, and the nurses were no longer on fire. "Where did the fire go? You didn't see it?"

"No, Mr. Duncan," the charge nurse said. "Sir, you were in a very bad car accident. You just had a hallucination. These things happen to those who have experienced trauma. Although the fire seemed to be very real, it was only in your mind."

I saw the flames. I even sweated from the heat! "Let me see. Are the flames gone?"

The nurses turned his bed around and showed him his room. There was neither flame, heat, smoke, nor any fire damage at all. His blood rose and his face turn red. "Well, I'm embarrassed."

"Don't worry about it. It's common with trauma patients," the charge nurse said with a warm smile. "Do you want to go back into your room now?"

"Yes, please." Jeff looked back toward his sheets to make sure they weren't on fire. The nurses pushed him back into the room. He surveyed the walls and ceiling but still found no evidence of the fire ever being there. They pushed his bed back in place and locked the wheels. "Is there anything else I can do for you?" Morgan asked as the other nurses left the room.

The news played a recap of the ongoing arson investigation. "Would you mind turning that thing off? I don't want to hear anything else about fire." *The flames of Hell will haunt me forever.*

"Sure," she replied. She reached over Jeff's bed and pushed the power button on the remote. "This is a call button." Morgan put a small cylindrical device in Jeff's hand. "Push the red button here if you need any help."

"Okay," he said. He looked at the table next to his bed and saw a Gideon Bible. He began to reach for it, but then remembered he couldn't move his arms.

"Was there something else you wanted?" Morgan asked, seeing Jeff trying to move.

"Well," Jeff said. "I'd like to read the Bible, but I keep forgetting I can't use my arms yet. Could you just put it here on my chest?"

"Sure," she said as she walked back into the room. She grabbed the Bible and asked, "Do you want me to open it for you?"

"Yes, please. Will you open it to Genesis?" Jeff asked.

"Okay," she replied as she opened it and turned the pages. "Here you go." She placed the open book on his chest where he could see it. "Will this work?"

"Yes. I can read it from here. Thank you," he said.

"I like the Bible," Morgan said. "It gives me a lot of hope and comfort, but sometimes I just don't understand it."

"What do you mean?" Jeff asked, eager to talk about his re-discovered faith.

Morgan looked off into the distance. "Well, when I was in nursing school, I had to take several biology classes, and they taught about evolution. It never applied to the field of nursing nor have I ever had to think about evolution when helping a patient. But still, it was taught as fact. It caused me more confusion than anything else. I mean, the Bible says that God created everything, but evolution says it all happened without God. I don't know what to believe."

Jeff was overcome with excitement. *A chance to defend my faith!* "I'm a biology professor at Grogan. Did you know I used to teach evolution as fact? I went through the same feelings you have, but since my accident, I have come to understand that I was wrong about everything. I've now realized that when I learned evolution, it was taught dogmatically and filled with half-truths, assumptions, and just-so stories. I never really took the time to critically think for myself, so I became one of the deceived."

"It's strange to hear that coming from a biology professor," Morgan replied with a laugh.

"I will no longer teach evolution as a fact," Jeff affirmed. "Evolution in and of itself means change, and of course change does occur in living things. The theory of evolution is different, though. That is where the deception lies. It proposes that all life came from a common ancestor

228

millions of years ago, and you and I came about through natural selection and random, unguided mutations. Nature doesn't select anything outside of what already exists in the DNA, and I know of no mutation that has ever added information to the DNA. I don't have enough faith to believe the evolution theory anymore. It is simply a naturalistic philosophy." *Why couldn't I see this before?*

"I never thought of that," Morgan replied. "I was never taught that there was a difference between the two."

"It makes all the difference, Morgan," Jeff said. "Some professors and textbooks use convincing word play, and many students don't catch it so they become deceived. For example, they will say that evolution is true because evolution is observed. But what they really mean is evolution, that is, change, does occur and is observable, but evolution theory, which states that we all have a common ancestor, is not observable—it's based on faith. They base their evidence on the observed changes within the species, and then extrapolate backwards. The evolutionary theory is full of gaps that are filled with faith. You've studied biology and anatomy, right? Have you ever wondered how such complex organisms could ever evolve on their own?"

"I have thought about it but I was too afraid to ask my professors for fear of ridicule," Morgan replied. "I've seen the complexity of cells in the microscopes. These little things inside us function like an entire city! I just can't figure out how they could have evolved without some intelligent force guiding the process." Jeff heard a buzzing sound. Morgan glanced at a pager attached to her hip. "I'd love to stay and chat more, but another patient is calling for me."

"Come back any time!" Jeff replied as Morgan left the room. Helping others understand their faith filled him with joy. *God has really opened my eyes!* He looked down at the Bible on his chest and started to read from Genesis. *Last time I read this, I made a mockery of it.* He focused on each word and letter of the text and found that he had a higher level of understanding now, as though the Holy Spirit had given him the ability to comprehend. Just as he was finishing the first chapter and starting the second, Kate walked in.

"I brought your laptop," she said as she sat next to Jeff. "What are you reading?"

"I'm reading the Bible again. Now that I've experienced God first hand, I want to know more about Him," Jeff replied with enthusiasm. "Was Mom okay?"

"She wouldn't let me in the house, but when she came to the door, she had a jar of peanut butter in her hand, and there was a little dab smeared on the side of her mouth, so at least she is eating something."

Jeff grinned at the imagery. "I'm glad she is okay. She's been functioning on her own for a while, so I guess she is safe for now."

"We will figure out some way to help her."

"I sure hope so," Jeff said. "Will you turn my laptop on?"

"Sure," Kate said. After the operating system loaded, the computer automatically connected to the hospital's free Internet service.

A middle-aged doctor with graying hair entered the room. "Hello, I'm Dr. Wallace," he announced. "I've come by to see how you are doing now that you are out of your coma."

Jeff looked up at the doctor. "I'm better than I have been," he replied. "I'd very much like to get out of here and go home. Do you know when I can leave?"

"You were pretty beat up in that wreck," Dr. Wallace replied. "We thought we were going to lose you, but you kept hanging on." He opened up Jeff's medical chart and turned a few pages. "Your legs and arms have serious fractures in them, and it will take some time for them to heal."

Jeff didn't want to hear any bad news. "So, maybe in a few days?" he pleaded.

"It takes a while for bones to heal, and it will not be safe for you to go home until you can walk on your own and use your arms. It may be a few weeks. Besides, you are scheduled for some additional surgeries." Dr. Wallace had a caring look on his face, and he knew Jeff wasn't happy with that response, but he had to be honest. "On the bright side, since you are young and in good health, your body should heal quicker, so maybe you will get out of here sooner than expected. How is your pain level?"

"Both of my legs are throbbing. This morning's medicine helped me sleep and it took away the pain, but I could use something right now because it's wearing off."

"Okay, I'll have one of the nurses bring you some more pain medicine." He scribbled a few notes in the chart and left.

Although grateful to have a second chance at life, a cloud of depression came over Jeff as the news sunk in. "I want to go home, Kate. I can't stay in here."

"Honey, you can't move. Everything is bandaged up."

"How am I going to fulfill the mission God gave me if I'm stuck in this bed? People are going to Hell as we speak!"

Nurse Morgan came back into the room with another cocktail of pain medicine. "This will help you sleep and take away your pain," she said as she injected the liquid into his IV port. Seeing Jeff's sad countenance, she asked, "Is something wrong?"

He let out a sarcastic laugh. "Yes. I'm stuck here. That's what is wrong."

Morgan put the syringe into the biohazard box, went to the door, and closed it. She came back to Jeff's bed side. "I'd get in trouble for doing this, so I closed the door so no one would see me. Do you want me to pray for you?"

Kate looked up at Morgan with a surprised expression. Jeff grinned. "Yes, please," he said. Morgan took Kate's hand and placed her other hand on Jeff's unbandaged fingers. "Heavenly Father, we thank you for saving Mr. Duncan after his car accident. We ask that you heal his body soon so he can be healthy enough to go back home. In Jesus' name we pray, amen."

CHAPTER THIRTY

JEFF WOKE up Saturday afternoon. His pain was temporarily gone, but still he had the nagging depression from the thoughts of having to be stuck in the hospital for weeks. *I have to fulfill my duties to God.*

"Why did you want me to bring your laptop?" Kate asked after he aroused.

"I completely forgot about that," Jeff said. The prognosis his doctor gave him last night had interrupted his plans.

"Did you want me to look up something for you?" She asked, knowing that Jeff would not be able to use the keyboard yet.

"Yes," Jeff replied. "Before Jesus sent me back to my body, he told me to contact one of my students. I have to find her and see what this is all about." He then went on to instruct Kate how to access the university's website, and then directed her to a page that only the faculty had access to.

"Scroll down until you see my name, and then click my picture there," Jeff said.

Kate found Jeff's picture and clicked the link. "Now what?"

"To the left is a link that says 'Student Roster.' It should show each of the students signed up for my class. You can click on their name, and a box will appear displaying their email address and phone number."

Kate clicked on the link and found a list of over fifty names. "Okay, who are you looking for?"

"Her name is Jordyn Monroe," Jeff said. He had not had a chance to personally talk to any other student yet, so Jordyn's name was fresh in his memory.

Kate scrolled down until she found Jordyn's name and then clicked on it. Her email address and cell phone number appeared.

"Okay, great," Jeff said. "Will you dial the number and put the phone up to my ear?"

"Are you sure about this?" Kate asked. "She's a student and you're her teacher. It might look weird."

"I don't see a problem with it. The university wants us to have good relationships with the students. It helps them learn better, supposedly."

Kate picked up the hospital phone and dialed Jordyn's number. "It's ringing," she said as she put the phone up to his ear.

"Hello?" a female voice answered.

"Uh, hi. Is this Jordyn?"

"Yes, it is. Who is this?"

"This is your biology professor, Jeff...er, uh Dr. Duncan."

There was a brief pause. "Oh, uh, okay," Jordyn sounded confused and uncomfortable.

Jeff cut to the chase. "Listen, I know it sounds strange for me to call you, but it is very important that we talk."

She paused. "Are you going to mock me again?" she snapped.

"No, not at all," Jeff apologetically replied. "You were right, Jordyn, I did misrepresent your beliefs and ridicule you in front of everyone. I was wrong to have done that, and I'm sorry. I really need to talk to you."

"About what?" she asked

"Jesus said He had sent you to me. You had scholarships to other schools but chose to come to Grogan because you felt God's calling to go there."

Silence. "How did you know that?"

"Jesus told me," Jeff said matter-of-factly.

"What are you talking about?"

"Did you hear what happened to me?"

"Yes, everyone at school is talking about your wreck," Jordyn replied. "It was sent out as a mass email. They didn't give many details except to say that you were in critical condition."

"Well, I am," Jeff said with a sigh. "But, I'm out of my coma at least. Is there any way you can come to the hospital today? I'm in room 223."

"Are you okay?" she asked.

"Now that I'm not in Hell, I'm doing great!"

"I'm sorry but I can't come today. I can tomorrow after church," she replied, and they ended the phone call.

Thank you, Jesus!

Jeff turned to Kate, "I want out of here. God has sent me on a mission to tell others what I experienced in Hell and the fate of the unforgiven, and He wants me to somehow restore the foundations of the Bible. There is so much I have to do now, and I don't want to be stuck here while people are perishing."

Kate smiled fondly. "Something has definitely happened to you, Jeff. You used to never talk about God, but now you are completely focused on Him. You were even reading the Bible when I came back last night. I've never seen you do that before."

"I've been given a second chance and have to make the most of it."

Nurse Morgan came back into the room. "It's time for you pain medicine again."

"I've had quite a bit. I'm not going to get addicted, am I?" Jeff asked, acknowledging the growing problem of pain pill abuse throughout the United States.

"We are regulating it and only giving you the required dosage," Morgan replied. "You shouldn't worry about that right now, anyway. You've experienced a lot of trauma."

"I am in pain, but I know my Healer will take care of me." His vision became fuzzy as the medication kicked in, and he soon fell asleep.

CHAPTER THIRTY-ONE

"I HAVE sent you on a mission, Jeff. Jordyn will teach you about God's creation, and then you are to teach others about creation and warn them about Hell," The Voice sounded from a blazing blue light hovering above Jeff's bed.

"I can't go on a mission if I'm stuck here in the hospital," Jeff said to the Light. "I'm not supposed to get out of here for weeks.

"Do you believe I can heal you?" the Voice asked.

"Yes. Will you heal me?" Jeff asked.

"Go!" yelled the Voice. A bolt of lightning shot out from the center of the blue light and struck Jeff's chest. The bolt then transformed into four separate bolts, and they each moved away from his chest and toward his arms and legs. The light created a mild, tingling sensation throughout his body, yet it was very comforting. When the four bolts reached the end of his fingertips and toes, they moved back toward his chest and formed again into a single, larger bolt again. The light grew brighter until it exploded in a flash, filling the room with a blinding illumination.

Jeff suddenly woke up in his hospital bed. Kate sat next to him reading the Gideon Bible. A new nurse was writing her name, "Carla," on a whiteboard in the room. The wall calendar had changed to Sunday, and the early afternoon sun shone through the window. Jordyn sat in a chair in the

236

corner of the room working on a homework assignment. *What just happened?*

"Welcome back," Kate said. "Did you sleep well?"

Jeff scanned the room. *Where did the light go? And that voice? It was all just right here with me?* "Yeah, I slept really well, and all of my pain is gone. I feel much better...one-hundred percent better!"

Carla turned to Jeff. "That's quite an improvement, but you still have a ways to go before you are fully recovered."

Kate looked over at the nurse, "He's a bit upset because the doctor said he will have to be here for a few weeks."

"No," Jeff said with a surprising calmness. "I'm completely healed now. Watch me." Jeff began to slowly lift his right arm. "See, I couldn't do that before!"

Carla was startled. "Sir, you don't need to do that! You will make the fracture worse!"

"The fracture is gone," Jeff said, smiling. He lifted his left arm up. "It doesn't hurt anymore. All the pain is gone!"

Kate and Jordyn's mouth fell open as they watched Jeff. "You aren't supposed to be able to move anything! What's going on?" Kate asked, visibly shaken.

Without answering, Jeff sat upright in the bed. "Sir, please stop. You will make things worse!" Carla ordered, now more harshly. Jeff put his arms down and turned his body to face the door. Slowly, he moved his right leg off the bed and onto the floor. He did the same with his left leg.

"I'm going to stand up now. I've got work to do." The casts covered his thighs and shins, but the knees were exposed, allowing him to have some degree of flexibility. His arms could bend also because the elbows weren't bandaged.

"Jeff, don't do this! You cannot walk yet!" his wife yelled.

Carla left the room to get her charge nurse. While she was gone, Jeff told Kate, "While I was asleep, Jesus healed me completely. You saw how immobilized I was earlier, didn't you? Well, look at me now! This is proof that I am healed and ready to go home."

He pushed himself up off the bed and stood straight up. He wobbled slightly as his body became erect, but he quickly regained his balance. As he stood up, Jeff felt a rush of heat flow throughout his body, causing another tingling sensation.

Carla and her supervisor came back into the room. "Sir, please listen to me," ordered the charge nurse. "Your body has not healed yet. You are going to hurt yourself! This is not…" On Jeff's cut face, bruised eyes, and exposed chest, which had its fair share of bruises and lacerations, the injuries disappeared just like water drops evaporating from a hot stove. His flesh turned back to its normal color as new skin rapidly grew over the open wounds. Silence filled the room.

Ignoring their reprimands, Jeff focused on adapting to his newly healed legs and establishing his balance. The heat moved down to his toes, healing all of the wounds caused from the accident. He turned to greet Jordyn. "Thank you for coming by, but it looks like we will need to have our meeting elsewhere. I'm going home now," Jeff said confidently. "Nurse, will you please begin preparing the discharge papers?"

"Uh," Carla said, paralyzed in astonishment. "Uh, I have to get the doctor." She stared at Jeff's body, amazed at the complete healing that had taken place before her eyes. She ran out of the room and called for Dr. Wallace.

Jeff smiled as the nurse left. He grabbed his IV stand and wheeled it along beside him as he took a few steps toward the door. Both Kate and Jordyn instinctively stood on both sides of him to make sure he wouldn't fall.

"Why is this happening? You aren't supposed to be able to walk!" Kate asked, bewildered. "And your bruises and wounds disappeared right in front of us!"

"Jesus came to heal me while I slept. He told me I had a mission to complete, so now He's prepared me for it. Start packing your bags, we're going home!"

Jeff walked back and forth through the room, laughing as he relished in the miracle of his recovery. Due to the casts on his legs, he had limited flexibility, but that didn't stop him from moving about. "This is great! Whoever said Jesus isn't healing anymore was badly mistaken!" He giggled like a little child.

The nurse came back into the room with several other nurses. "Sir, the doctor has already left for the day, and I'll have to ask one of the other's to sign you out, but he probably won't do it. You cannot be discharged until he signs the order." She paused while she watched Jeff walking back and forth in the room. "We don't know why you are healed, but it's clear something has happened to you."

"Don't bother the other doctor," Jeff said politely. "I don't need him or anyone else to tell me I'm healed. I'll just go home." He turned to his wife. "Kate, is everything packed?"

"I'm working on it," she said, turning back to a suitcase she brought.

"Sir, you can't just leave a hospital. Your insurance won't cover the costs if you leave against medical advice."

"What insurance?" Jeff replied with a laugh. *I lost my insurance because I stood up for what I believe in.* "Just mail me the bill; I'll pay for it in full somehow."

The nurses all looked at each other, hoping that one of the others would have something to say. Instead, they all left the room, and ten minutes later, the charge nurse returned with a clipboard. "Sir, I need you to sign this form stating that you are of sound mind and have decided to leave the hospital against our advice."

The nurse kept the clipboard closer to her chest, hoping Jeff would change his mind. Without hesitation, he strolled over to the nurse and reached for the clipboard. Reluctantly, she gave it to him. He scanned over the form, signed his name at the bottom, and then handed the clipboard back to the nurse.

"I need to get your IV unhooked before you do anything," the nurse said. She turned off the machine and pulled the needle out of his arm. She cleaned off the area with some antiseptic and put a bandage over the small hole.

"Alright, time to go!" Jeff announced. "Jordyn, will you come home with us?"

"I…yeah I can come over," she replied. "I had other plans, but God is doing something miraculous today and I want to be a part of it."

"Great!" Jeff then realized he didn't have any clothes to wear home. "I'll just wear this fancy hospital gown outside."

Kate and Jordyn looked at each other and laughed. "You don't need to be exposing yourself to the public," Kate said.

"Don't worry, I'll be modest," Jeff said dryly. "Time to go! C'mon!"

Jeff walked out of the room feeling better than ever. It was hard to walk with the casts on, but they would be removed as soon as he got home. *Nothing hurts me! This is wonderful!* Kate gathered the other bag and some other unpacked belongings in her arms and hurried out. Jordyn put the laptop back in the case and slung it over her shoulder as she followed behind Kate.

Jeff held his head up high and a broad smile filled his face as he led the trio out of the room while all of the medical staff stood in the hallway watching Jeff in silent awe. Not all of the employees had talked to Jeff or seen the extent of his injuries, but everyone knew about the terrible car accident and how he had been hanging on for his life. It had even made the local news. Many thought Jeff would die, but now a walking miracle was leaving the hospital right before their eyes.

"Thank you all for your help," Jeff said to everyone as he passed by. "Jesus loves you! Trust in Him alone!" The nurses and other medical staff continued to stare at him without responding. The scene resembled those cheesy movies Jeff used to watch where, as the protagonist marched

240

through a village to fight off the evil dragon, a few of the townspeople would slowly clap in unison until everyone joined in applause. This was different, though. In reality, people were simply too shocked to even move.

Jeff entered the parking garage as Kate and Jordyn tried to keep up with his pace. "I've never felt better. Who cares if I'm wearing this gown and still have these casts on?"

"I'm driving," Kate said with that familiar tone that let Jeff quickly understand she was serious and there would be no questioning of her authority.

"That's a good idea. Last time I drove I nearly killed myself."

CHAPTER THIRTY-TWO

THEY ARRIVED home Sunday evening. Samson eagerly greeted them at the door, happy to see his two servants come home. Jeff went to the utility closet, got out a box cutter, and carefully removed the casts from his arms and legs. After removing them, he flexed his arms and legs back and forth, enjoying the full range of motion. There was no sign of injury anywhere.

"Can you believe how He healed me!" Jeff exclaimed, showing his flawless arms and legs to the two women.

"I thought you were off your rocker earlier," Kate said, "but now I see it with my own eyes."

"It's truly a miracle," Jordyn added.

"Kate, do you want to order pizza for our guest?"

"We are tight on money, and now the hospital bills are going to start coming in. I have some hamburger meat."

"Okay, let's have some burgers," Jeff said. He was glad Kate could keep him in check with their budget, or in this case, the lack thereof.

He offered Jordyn a seat on the couch, and he sat down in his recliner. He wanted to relax some, but Jordyn was here on her time, and he didn't want to waste any of it.

"It seems weird being here, I'm sure," Jeff casually remarked to Jordyn.

"I'll admit I've never been to a professor's house before, but then again this is my first experience in a college setting. I was homeschooled ever since I was five, so my parents were my teachers," Jordyn replied.

"Tell me, Jordyn. Why is it you were homeschooled?"

"My parents didn't trust the public education system. They said that the states mandate curriculum that go against our Christian beliefs."

"What do you mean?"

"Well, for one, my church and my family teach that God created the world just as the Bible says. But in the schools, they teach evolution as a fact, and there is no room for exploring other ideas or even challenging the problems in evolution without risk of ridicule and chastisement. They don't promote critical thinking or the free exchange of ideas. Some of the curricula are full of propaganda that even the teachers fail to notice."

Jeff thought back to his years of public education and graduate school. "I see what you are saying. We were never given neutral and honest information about other theories on origins, especially at college. Evolution was taught dogmatically. There was not one student in my graduate class that believed any other theory, including myself."

"Academic freedom just isn't allowed in the public system," Jordyn continued. "When I was homeschooled, my parents taught me all about evolution, intelligent design, and Biblical creation. They showed me the strengths and weaknesses in all of the theories, and it was I who made the decision to agree with Biblical creation. I was not forced one way or the other."

Jeff grinned, "You sound as though you are quite intelligent."

Jordyn blushed at the compliment. "Thank you, Dr. uh, I mean, Jeff."

"So what are you studying? Have you selected a major?"

243

"I love to work with the elderly," Jordyn said. "I'm majoring in psychology and minoring in gerontology. I hope I can get a job counseling seniors one day."

"What is it that attracts you to the elderly?" Jeff asked.

"I feel so sorry for them. Many are isolated in their homes, or their families abandon them in nursing homes. They don't get many visitors so I spend my weekends keeping them company at the nursing homes here in Grayson. Some of them refer to me as their granddaughter."

After hearing her authenticity, Jeff didn't hesitate to make an offer. "My mother has severe Alzheimer's disease. Her doctor wanted her to live with us, and we tried it, but she doesn't even know who I am anymore so she refuses to stay with us. This seems kind of sudden, but would you be willing to help us take care of her? I can pay you a little bit."

Jordyn thought for a moment and then said, "I could use some extra cash. When can I meet her?"

"It's too late in the day now. Let's try a visit tomorrow," Jeff said. "We are really concerned for her safety as the Alzheimer's gets worse, not to mention a recent head injury."

He smiled warmly and then paused. "Jordyn, I want to be honest with you." She looked at him intently. "I was wrong to make fun of you in front of those students. It was such a terrible, immature thing to do. Will you accept my apology?"

Jordyn turned and looked out the window for a moment. Turning back to Jeff, she smiled and said, "Of course, I forgive you. Jesus teaches us to forgive. There is no use in harboring bitterness."

"You are wise beyond your years," Jeff replied. Jordyn blushed again. "I'm sure you remember the bizarre conversation I had with you on the phone?" She nodded. "While I was out, Jesus told me that He sent you to Grogan University and you agreed to enroll there even though you had an opportunity to go to other colleges."

Jordyn paused for a moment. "There is no way you could have known that, but yes, it's true. I felt like I was supposed to go there. I never understood why, but it's what I call 'one of those God things.' It's when you know God has a plan for you, and although you aren't sure what it is, you just take a leap of faith and go with it.

"Wayne, my dad, just started working with the Tennessee Department of Education. He had suggested several other schools for me to go to, but I told him God was sending me to Grogan, so Dad let me follow God's will."

Surprised to hear about her father and his job, Jeff remarked, "He must be an important man to work at such a high level. What does he do there?"

"My dad was frustrated with how the school systems—from elementary to the university level—were indoctrinating the students instead of teaching them how to learn and think for themselves. The test grades were low and the students weren't absorbing the material, so he wanted to make a change in the system. Of course, he has a lot of opposition. Most of his co-workers don't see his side of the problem. They are the ones pushing toward more indoctrination instead of academic freedom.

"He directly reports to the governor about changes needed in the education system. He just recently started his job so he may not have much power right now, but he and the governor do get along quite well."

Jeff said, "We need more people like your dad in the government. I believe in academic freedom, but doing so costs me a great deal. Do you remember our first day of class, and I told you that you could keep your beliefs on creation, but you had to learn the material I was teaching in order to pass the class?"

"Yes, I remember."

"Well, apparently it wasn't the right thing to say. I got into huge trouble with the dean, Dr. Robert Farris. He removed me from all my other classes and demoted me to part-time status. I lost my insurance benefits and a huge chunk of my salary."

"That is awful!" Jordyn exclaimed. "He did that just because of what you said to me?"

"Yep, and he was quite insulting about it, too. I talked to one of my colleagues and found out he's been doing this for years. Dr. Farris has a lot of pull at the university and can get away with anything. I was so mad about the demotion and how he treated me that I took it out on you at our next class meeting. Please forgive me!"

"I already have, Jeff," Jordyn said with a laugh. "I didn't know that happened, but it has to stop."

"If he finds out I reported him, I'll lose my job for good and never work again. He just has too much power."

"I understand your concern," Jordyn replied. "If you want me to talk to my dad about it, I will. He's just a phone call away."

"Okay, that's good to know," Jeff replied. "Jordyn, the reason I wanted you to come over was because Jesus said you would know what to say. I'm...not sure what He meant though."

"Jesus said that?" Jordyn giggled and blushed. "I'm not exactly sure what He meant either, but I do love to talk about creation."

"Perhaps that is what He wanted you to talk about?"

"Great! Ask me anything; I've studied this topic all my life."

"Hold on, let me get some paper first," Jeff said as he got up and went to his bedroom. He hollered back to her, "It's funny—the student becomes the teacher!" Jordyn laughed. Jeff returned with a yellow legal pad and a pen and sat down on the edge of his recliner. Kate remained within earshot in the kitchen as she prepared supper.

"Okay," Jeff began. "Here is my first question: How do we even know the Bible can be trusted? Wasn't it written by ordinary men and copied over and over again? It's bound to have lost its true meaning."

"That's a good question, and a lot of people wonder the same thing," Jordyn replied. "The Bible is a very unique book in and of itself. It consists of sixty-six separate books written by about forty different authors. The different books were written over a span of about fifteen hundred years. It consists of history, laws, prophecies, narratives, and letters. But what sets the Bible apart from the other historical writings is the fact that many of its authors did not know each other, live on the same continent, or even live during the same time frame, but the Bible tells of one consistent theme all throughout. How could the authors have done that? I haven't even mentioned Bible prophecies yet."

"What do you mean?" asked Jeff.

"There are hundreds and hundreds of prophecies in the Bible, some of which have been fulfilled and others that won't be fulfilled until the end times. All of the prophecies of Jesus were fulfilled. Some critics say, since Jesus knew what the prophecies were, he purposely fulfilled them so as to make himself *look* like the Messiah. But there are problems with that claim. See, if Jesus was just a mere man trying to fulfill the prophecies, how could He control when, where, and how He was born, and then fulfill those prophecies? How could He have known how He would die, that the Roman guards would cast lots for His clothes, and that He would be buried in someone else's tomb? Jeff, all of these prophecies were written before they were fulfilled, but Jesus could not have purposely fulfilled them because those events were out of His control as a man, and it was definitely not a coincidence.

"Even His crucifixion was prophesied in the twenty-second chapter of Psalms. Not only was it written about a thousand years before Jesus' birth, but crucifixion hadn't even been invented yet! When Jesus died on the cross, he said 'My God, my God, why have you forsaken me?' In doing so, He actually quoted the first verse of that very Psalm."

"That is just...miraculous," Jeff replied as he stared out the window trying to absorb all the information. "They never taught me that in Sunday School."

"I haven't even answered your question yet. You had asked if the Bible is still accurate after all these years. Let me explain how we got the Bible." Jordyn went on to tell Jeff how the Jewish scribes meticulously recorded the words of God on different writing materials. These texts were then copied by the Masoretic scribes who used an intricate counting system to ensure they were copying the text verbatim.

"It was all hand written," Jordyn continued. "Once the copy was finished, it had to be reviewed. If there were errors in it, the scribe had to throw it away and start all over. They had a high level of reverence for God's word and did not want it to get distorted. Things changed for the better when the printing press came around. Translators were able to make copies of the Bible at a faster speed without having to worry about copying errors." She then explained the process of how the canon of Scripture was determined by church leaders under God's direction.

"One of the greatest archaeological finds was the Dead Sea Scrolls," she continued. "These scrolls were dated to be at least one-thousand years older than the oldest copy of the Bible at the time. And why would this be significant? When the Dead Sea Scrolls were compared with the Bible we use today, they were found to be the same, except for a few spelling variations. This goes to show that after all of those years, the Bible was still being copied accurately."

Jeff wrote notes as fast as he could. "So are you saying the Bible hasn't been altered and it's been correctly translated and copied?"

"It's true," Jordyn said. "And now with everything being on the Internet, you can find copies of the texts in the original Hebrew and Greek languages, and if you could read those languages, you would be able to test the Bible's accuracy that way as well."

Jeff remembered how he had thrown the Bible across the room just a few days ago. "Why am I just now hearing this? What is the point of going to church all these years but not ever learning this important information? Everyone needs to know this!"

"The hamburgers are ready!" Kate yelled from the kitchen. Jeff and Jordyn went to the table to join Kate.

"You know what?" Jeff asked Kate. "We've never prayed before a meal. What kind of Christians are we? Let's thank God for this meal."

Without hesitation, they all bowed their heads. "Dear Jesus," Jeff prayed, "thank you for saving me from Hell, healing me, and saving my life. You have given me a second chance that I don't deserve. Thank you for my wonderful wife, Kate, who has been by my side this whole time. Thank you for Jordyn and the wisdom you have given her. Thank you for this meal, and please bless it as you have already blessed me. In Jesus' name, amen."

They all said "amen" together, and then Jordyn continued where they had left off. "You're right, everyone needs to know these basics about the faith," Jordyn agreed. "But most churches these days just teach the same old things without getting into the heavy theology, or even worse, they teach something contrary to the gospel."

"Like what?" Kate asked.

"There are a lot of churches out there—some good, some bad. The good churches present the gospel, offer its members the lifesaving power of Jesus' sacrifice, and then equip people to evangelize to the lost. Those churches are becoming few and far between. The bad churches, though, are growing. The pastors there are more interested in being politically correct and not offending anyone. They are more concerned with getting people to come and give an offering, and the best way to get people into their church is to tell them things that tickle their ears. No one wants to be called a sinner or be told they are going to Hell, so these pastors instead act more like motivational speakers. It's rare they use the Bible or confront sin. Instead, they make the congregation feel good about themselves, but this does nothing for their eternal salvation. It is a very dangerous problem."

Jeff paused before speaking as he thought about Pastor Bill. "I think my church might be like that."

"What church do you go to?" Jordyn asked.

"The Experience."

Jordyn's eyes opened wide. "Yes, that is definitely one of those churches! Both of my parents have tried several times to confront Pastor Bill and his father, Larry, about their heretical teachings. Neither of them would listen; instead, they just shunned my parents away. We still pray for them, though."

Jeff felt himself getting angry, not because of Jordyn's comment, but because Pastor Bill was a catalyst in Jeff doubting his faith. "The last time I went to church, Pastor Bill said Genesis was all allegorical and just a story from which we could get a moral lesson."

Jordyn waited to swallow her bite and replied, "You're right. A lot of change needs to be made. There are so many out there who claim to be Christian, but they have no idea what they believe or why they believe it. Some of them are false converts, walking a well-worn path to the gates of Hell."

"Let's change topics because I have another question," Jeff said. "Some of the evidence used to support evolution is the common traits found in a wide range of species. How does creation account for that?"

Jordyn began, "I agree that there are common traits found in living things. Generally speaking, most mammals have two arms, two legs, one head, two eyes, two nostrils, and one mouth. One would think we are all descendants because of these similarities. Even at the genetic level, there are commonalities in the DNA.

"If there was not a special creation, then we have a common ancestor and descended from simple organisms to more complex. But if one thinks we have a common designer, then we would expect our designer to use common features in his design. It's similar to how an artist will use the same paint, brushes, and canvas, but each of his paintings look different. Our Common Designer made a variety of living things but presented them in different, creative ways. That's why many mammals have similar physical characteristics. The proteins coded in the DNA are used in different living things for common features like eye color, hair texture, and so on, but that doesn't mean all life forms are related. Humans are made in the image of God, and no other creation has that claim."

Jeff asked, "Then why is there so much debate?"

"It all boils down to a person's worldview, or starting point. Everyone has a worldview. We all believe that either there is a creative force or there isn't. Either things happen for a purpose or they happen due to natural causes. Evidence does not speak for itself—it requires an interpretation. Creationists and evolutionists have the same evidence. Whether you are a scientist or a theologian, when you look at evidence, you automatically interpret it based on your worldview. At Grogan University, the worldview is that everything has happened naturally and there has never been a divine intervention.

"For example, if you were to find a dinosaur bone, your only evidence would just be that—a bone. Maybe you could identify the type of bone and what kind of dinosaur it belonged to, but you would not be able to tell how old it was just by looking at it. In evolution, scientists claim that dinosaurs died out sixty-five million years ago. They base that on the age of the sedimentary rock layer in which the bone was found. That is the secular worldview, but from a Biblical worldview, we know that the earth is not millions of years old, and this comes from counting back through historical events in the Bible and the genealogies in Genesis. We also believe in a literal, six-day creation because of the Hebrew word '*yom*,' which was used to mean a literal, twenty-four hour day in the context of Genesis. Based on these facts, the age of the earth is less than ten-thousand years old. We do know there was a worldwide flood, and all of the sedimentary rocks that we see were formed during that flood. All of the land-dwelling animals that weren't on Noah's ark died and were buried in the loose sediment. Over time, the sediments hardened into stratified rock layers and the bones fossilized. The catastrophic flood caused many of the geological formations we see today, making the earth look very old while in fact it is very young."

Jeff interrupted. "But what about radiometric dating? Haven't these bones and rocks been tested for their estimated age?"

"Radiometric dating is heavily relied on, and there are different measurements that scientists use for dating, but the problem is that there are assumptions in place that cannot be proven. Scientists assume the bones they test have always had the same rate of chemical decay; that the specimen has never been contaminated with other chemicals or lost chemicals through other processes; and finally, they assume to know the initial conditions of the specimen when it was first formed. Because of these assumptions in place, we cannot conclude that the old ages are accurate.

"Actually, when rocks have been tested with radiometric dating, and the ages of the rocks are known, like lava rocks from recent volcanoes, the radiometric dating was completely incorrect. But when the tests are performed on rocks that have unknown ages, the test results are just assumed to be correct. No questions asked."

"Okay," Jeff said. "I've got one more question, and then we will need to call it a night before my brain overloads. How did Noah fit all the animals on the ark?"

"That is also a commonly asked question," Jordyn replied. "The simple answer is: he didn't. God commanded Noah to build the ark to house two of each kind of animal, not each species. He also brought a few other animals that would be used for a sacrifice after the flood. The kind represents a family of animals, like the canine, feline, equine, and so forth. The species, well, there are thousands of species of dog, and no boat could ever be big enough to hold two of each species!"

Jeff had never been taught this before. *Why didn't my Sunday School teachers know about this?* "You are telling me things I have never, ever heard," Jeff said with a deep sigh.

"You have answered so many questions I had as a child in a matter of minutes. After all those years in church, I didn't learn anything outside of the same old Bible stories. You have so much to teach me, but I need to take a break so I can absorb this stuff first."

"I look forward to talking to you more. It excites me to see people hungry for God's Word," Jordyn said with a bright smile.

"We can set up a time to talk again. I'm interested in learning more about the Bible, God, creation—all of it. This is all so new to me."

"You are not alone," Jordyn replied. "I was fortunate to have two loving parents who taught me all of these things, even when I was still in diapers. It's a lifelong journey, and I'm still learning."

How nice it would have been to have Dad around teaching me instead of abandoning the family. "I can't wait to learn more," Jeff replied. "Have a safe trip home!"

"Okay, good night."

CHAPTER THIRTY-THREE

JEFF WOKE up bright and early Monday morning, full of new life and insight into who his Creator is. No one at the university knew he had been healed from his wreck, so he decided to pay them a surprise visit even though he wasn't scheduled to teach today. He couldn't wait to see the looks on their faces, especially Robert Farris. Jeff quickly showered, got dressed, and headed to the university.

He opened the door to the faculty offices in the Farris Science Building. Robert and several others were gathered together near the receptionist's desk drinking coffee and talking about current events. When he walked in, everyone looked at Jeff in astonishment.

"What are you doing here? We thought you...almost died," Rhonda Matheson exclaimed.

"Yeah, I thought you were in the hospital!" exclaimed William James, one of the physics professors.

Jeff smiled with confidence, "You are both right. I was in the hospital, and I almost died, but Jesus healed me, and now I'm better than ever!"

His colleagues looked at each other. At first they didn't say anything, but then a few of them snickered amongst themselves.

"Jesus healed you? What are you talking about?" William asked mockingly. Some of the others laughed.

Jeff gave them a blank look. *Should I have expected them to understand?* "You don't believe me? You knew I was in a bad accident just last week, yet here I am standing in front of you, completely healed."

There was no response except for the growing sound of laughter and mockery. The crowd started to disperse as they walked to their offices to avoid further dialogue with Jeff. He was mad about their reaction and refused to be their source of entertainment. He walked past the dwindling crowd and down the hall toward his office. Just as he was beginning to open the door, Robert called out to him.

"Dr. Duncan, can I have a word with you?"

"Yes, sir," Jeff replied. He didn't have a good feeling about this, but he knew he couldn't refuse talking to his boss.

Robert left the receptionist's desk, came down the hallway, opened his office door, and motioned for Jeff to come inside. Jeff approached the same chair where he was last chastised and took a seat. Robert closed the door and sat on the edge of his desk.

"I'm…glad to see you are doing well. You must be in good shape to be able to heal as quickly as you did," Robert said nervously.

"It's like I said: Jesus healed me," Jeff replied casually.

"Healed? Yeah, whatever," he cleared his throat. "They showed the picture of your wrecked car on the news. I'm shocked that you even survived."

Jeff recalled his ambulance ride and how he ascended through the ceiling while watching the paramedic shock his heart. "I was barely hanging on."

"Dr. Duncan, because of your severe accident, I did not anticipate you coming back to work anytime soon. Actually, I thought you were dead. Others here thought the same thing."

"I'm not though. I'm healed and ready to work again," Jeff replied with an upbeat voice.

255

Steven Wright

"I'm glad to hear that, Jeff. I really am. But there's sort of a problem." Robert's voice became more serious. He slid off the desk and went to sit in his chair. "Since I thought you were going to be on long-term medical leave, I hired someone else to take your place."

Jeff's eyes opened wide as his mouth dropped open. His heart pounded hard in his chest, causing his shirt to vibrate from the intense palpitations. "What!?"

"I called in one of our retirees. Great professor, very well educated. He's going to take your place for the semester. He came in and signed the contract on Friday." Robert looked away from Jeff and stroked his beard. The tension grew thick.

"But what about me?" Jeff asked. "I can't teach anymore?"

"I'm sorry, but what's done is done. The contract has been signed. But I still haven't gotten to the bad news."

Jeff's face turned red with anger, and his heart pounded harder. "What are you saying?"

"You just started here, Dr. Duncan. You are young; you're a rookie compared to my tenured faculty. You were aware that you had a six month probationary period when I hired you. Well, because of our little talk the other day, and your health, I've decided that we no longer need your services here."

"But...I'm healthy! I'm walking and talking again. Can't you see that? And I changed! I taught evolution just as you told me to do!" Jeff had not been this angry since his last encounter with his mother.

"The decision has been made. There is some good news, though," Robert smiled slightly. "Since our contract worker will only be here for the rest of the semester, that leaves an opening for his position next semester in the spring. Feel free to reapply for that position. And now that we already know you, there will be a better chance of getting hired again, that is, if you continue with the changes we had discussed in our little talk."

"But you can't do this!" Jeff's voice was now loud enough that other faculty could hear him. "You are firing me because you thought I would die or be on medical leave, but I'm not! I'm alive and well!"

"Jeff, I cannot go back on my decision now that the contract is signed. And frankly, you cannot tell me what I can and cannot do. My parents paid for this very building, and I've got authority at the state level to make these executive decisions."

"Why didn't you just call me first to see if I was okay before hiring someone else? You can't fire me! I have medical bills to pay; how do you expect me to pay them now, much less put food on the table?"

"This conversation is over. Pack up your things and leave." Robert's faux-friendly expression transformed to anger. "You and your 'Jesus' aren't allowed here in the science department anymore. I don't tolerate these fairy tales too well. I've got a half-brother who is a pastor, and I've told him the same thing."

Deep inside, Jeff felt his hands wrapping around Robert's thick, wrinkled neck and strangling his boss to the point of him passing out. *If he died now, he'd go to Hell. Just walk away.* Jeff stood up and walked to the door. Before he left, he turned around and said as calmly as possible, "You will not get away with this, Robert Farris."

"I've done it many times before. I've got connections like you wouldn't believe. Take your Jesus out of here or I'll call security."

Jeff forced his tongue into his jaw and bit down. His eyes watered as his teeth dug into the muscle, causing blood to trickle out. He left and went into his office. He surveyed his room, searching for his personal belongings. There were none, for he still hadn't brought in his personal effects from home or even hung up his diplomas. He turned the light out, closed the door, and left the building in silence.

He arrived back home just as Kate got out of bed. She had needed the extra rest because sleep had been so difficult to come by at the hospital due to the constant flow of nurses and doctors entering the room to check on her husband.

"Where have you been?"

"I made a surprise visit to the university," Jeff said.

"Were they happy to see you again?" she asked groggily as she wiped her eyes.

"No. I was fired," Jeff replied bluntly.

"Why? What now?" Kate asked, now fully awake. Jeff went on to explain the reasons he was terminated. "That is stupid!" Kate yelled. "How could he make such a hasty decision? Can't he let you work now that you are healed?"

"No, he said that the other person signed a contract and policy doesn't allow them to cancel any contracts prematurely. He already sent in my termination paperwork. It's too late." Tears of rage and hopelessness filled his eyes. "What are we going to do?"

"I don't know," Kate said solemnly. "Maybe the church could help?"

"That reminds me," Jeff replied. "We aren't going to attend The Experience anymore unless Pastor Bill makes some changes. He has been leading others astray, and it has to stop."

"But I like the church, and the people there are so nice. I'm not ready to leave and start looking for another church," Kate said.

"Pastor Bill only tells us what we want to hear. He has distorted the truth, watered down the gospel, and I know he is keeping more than his share of the offering. I'm going to confront him right now!" Jeff grabbed his Bible and abruptly left the house.

CHAPTER THIRTY-FOUR

AS JEFF pulled into the church parking lot, he saw construction crews working on the west end of the church excavating the ground and preparing to lay a concrete pad for the multi-purpose building. The parking lot was vacant except for the work trucks and Pastor Bill's metallic blue luxury car. He sneered as he looked at the car, knowing that ill-gotten money had purchased it. Before getting out of his car, Jeff opened the Bible his mother had given him.

Not knowing where to read, he let the Bible fall open on his lap. It landed open to the book of James. He read the first few verses of chapter one out loud: "Count it all joy, my brothers, when you meet trials of various kinds, for you know that the testing of your faith produces steadfastness. And let steadfastness have its full effect, that you may be perfect and complete, lacking in nothing. If any of you lacks wisdom, let him ask God, who gives generously to all without reproach, and it will be given him. But let him ask in faith, with no doubting, for the one who doubts is like a wave of the sea that is driven and tossed by the wind. For that person must not suppose that he will receive anything from the Lord; he is a double-minded man, unstable in all his ways." (James 1:2-8, ESV)

Wow. "God is speaking directly to me," Jeff said aloud to himself. He clasped his hands together and prayed, "Lord,

I am about to speak with Pastor Bill. Give me wisdom in doing this, because I don't know what is going to happen. I only want to do Your will. Allow Bill to see the error of his ways, and call him to repentance."

Jeff got out of his car and went to the front door, but it was locked. He knocked several times. After a few minutes, Bill came out of his office, recognized Jeff through the glass door, and then approached.

"Well, I'm shocked to see you here! I was just on my way to come see you at the hospital," Bill said, smiling through his thick mustache as he opened the door.

"It's good I caught you before you left, Pastor," Jeff said, shaking hands with Bill.

"How…I thought you were in critical condition. How come you are out of the hospital already?" Bill opened the door to let Jeff come inside. While walking to Bill's office, and for several minutes after they both sat down, Jeff explained the turn of events that had taken place up until now.

"So although I'm healed, I'm now unemployed," Jeff concluded.

"That's quite a story," Bill said cautiously. "I guess the Lord works in mysterious ways."

I visit Hell and have an amazing encounter with Jesus, and all you can offer is a cliché? "Do you think I'm making this up?" Jeff inquired while forcing himself to be respectful.

"Not that you are making it up, but, you know, you've never been one of the spiritual elite here at the church. I never see you dancing and clapping like the others or getting slain in the Spirit. I'd expect a vision from one of them, but for someone like you, your experience was probably caused by the trauma from the accident."

"What I experienced was very real," Jeff proclaimed, ignoring the subtle insult, "and that is why I have come here to talk to you." He had now gotten Bill's attention.

"If you've come here for money to help with your medical bills, I'm afraid the church is not able to help you.

We just sank all of our money into this new building," Bill said.

"I'll address the money issue later. Pastor, I mean this with all due respect, but you have not been preaching the real truth of the gospel. I have heard many of your sermons, and frankly, I believe you are afraid of upsetting people, so you tell them what they want to hear instead of what they need to hear. I don't remember the last time you addressed people's sin and need for repentance."

Bill's face began to redden with anger. While gathering his thoughts, he looked out the office window to watch the contractors working and then turned back to Jeff. "I admire your honesty, I guess, but I think you are out of line. My father taught me everything I know up until I went to seminary, and there I studied under the brightest theologians. I know how to run a church. You are a scholar, but your expertise is in science. Mine is in theology. We do not need to be mixing science with God."

An uncomfortable tension was forming, but Jeff didn't let it interfere. "That's another thing I wanted to talk to you about. Science and God can go together. That sermon you gave last Sunday goes against the entire Bible. You made it sound like Genesis could not be relied on and that it was just a bunch of stories handed down from other cultures. Pastor, Genesis is the foundation for every doctrine we follow. If the foundations are destroyed, then the rest of the Bible comes into question."

Bill grew angrier. "I am not a scientist; I'm a theologian. I have a half-brother who is a scientist, you may know him. Robert Farris?"

"You are related to Dr. Farris at Grogan University?"

"Yes. We have the same mother, different fathers. We don't talk much or agree on hardly anything. He thinks I'm foolish for being a pastor. I think he is foolish for rejecting Jesus. Although we don't see eye to eye, there is one thing he said to me, and I'll never forget it: 'You can't mix fairy tales in a test tube.' I myself disagree with Genesis being true history. Those stories were most likely derived from other cultures. I'm here to bring people to Jesus, not make them scientists. We don't need Genesis to get in the way of the gospel."

"But Pastor, how do you know these stories came from other cultures. How do you know that other cultures didn't borrow from the Israelites? Have you ever compared the different creation legends or flood legends? Honestly, which ones make the most sense?"

"It doesn't matter, Jeff. That is all Old Testament stuff. It happened so long ago and has no effect on teaching the gospel today. All that matters is what Jesus did for us on the cross."

Jeff looked sternly at Bill. "You are destroying the foundations. Without Genesis, how would we even know we were born into sin and needed a savior? How many people in this church are actually studying the Bible on their own? I'll tell you that if they read the Bible and really put some thought into it, they would be confronting you about this as I am. You teach that we need Jesus, but you never give the foundational reasons why."

"Come to think of it, no one has ever questioned me. Could it be that they respect me and my seminary training?" Bill said with a hint of sarcasm.

"Pastor, this has nothing to do with respect. I do respect you, but the time has come for me to show you the problems. I used to be in full agreement with your interpretation of Scripture. I never questioned it. But ever since I had my encounter with Jesus, everything is different now. I've been reading the Bible for several hours a day ever since I came back, and from what I've seen you are not teaching according to the doctrines in the Bible. I have seen the errors in your teaching, and you need to change or you'll be held accountable before God, and believe me, you do not want His wrath! I am asking you to teach the church about creation and the foundations of our doctrine."

"Jeff, the people don't want to hear about Genesis. Maybe long ago they did, but these days I get about twenty minutes with them once a week, and they want to come here and feel good, not go away with their heads hung in shame or feeling like they had just left an advanced seminary class. Do you think people would keep coming back if they got a history lesson each week? No, they wouldn't come back, and we would lose money and have to close the doors!"

Jeff's hands started to shake from the anxiety. "Pastor, which is more important: Saving souls or earning a paycheck?"

Bill responded without hesitation, "Saving souls, of course!"

"Where does all of the offering money go? I've seen the offering plate when it is passed around, and it is full of large checks and big bills. This church is bound to have more than enough."

"Well, we get by. We have a lot of overhead with the missions and daily lunch program. Add that to the staff salaries and there isn't much leftover. I've even had to make some pay cuts. Some of the staff members are working for free now."

"But, I've seen your large house, your luxury car, your clothes…how can you afford these things?" Jeff asked.

Bill stammered, "They are…gifts. We have some very generous donors here at the church and in the community. Why are you asking all these questions? This should not concern you."

"Pastor, I am asking these questions because there is something very important on my mind. I'm going to say something that will get you mad, but I would be in error to not tell you this. During my experience, Jesus showed me something very unsettling. There was a certain man in Hell who was a charlatan preacher. He deceived thousands of people who put their faith in him instead of Jesus. That man conned people out of their money, and he lived a wealthy lifestyle until he died. Now he is suffering an eternity in Hell.

"Jesus showed me some type of video—like I was watching a movie—of what you have been doing with the church's money. You just said the church didn't have enough, but I know that isn't true. Instead of giving the money to the church and community, you have been falsifying records and hiding the offerings in a safe behind that picture." Jeff's heart pounded as he raised his hand and pointed his finger at the picture on the wall behind Bill. The painting was of Jesus hanging on the cross in-between two criminals. Jesus' face hung down, looking mournfully to the ground. From Jeff's angle, it looked as though Jesus was staring directly at Bill.

Bill stared blankly at Jeff. His jaw quivered as he tried to form words. He turned his head around and looked at the picture, and then turned back at Jeff. In an angry, hushed voice, he warned, "You will keep your mouth shut about this! This is no one's business, especially not yours. That money is mine! I earned it. Do you realize how hard it is to make a living on a common pastor's wages? Do you!"

"I don't, but I do know that stealing is a sin in the eyes of God. It is time you stop, repent, and make a confession to the church about what you have done. I have confronted you about this the Biblical way. The next step is for me to bring a group in here to confront you."

Bill jumped up. "I've done nothing wrong! I work every day at this church, prepare sermons, and do everything I can to please the congregation. I've earned every penny, and you better not say anything! Get out of my sight!"

Jeff thought back to the charlatan he saw in Hell and how he was constantly in torment. "Please stop what you are doing and repent."

"Get out!" Bill yelled as he threw a stone paperweight in Jeff's direction. Jeff casually watched the stone fly by and crash into the wall behind him. He stood up and quietly showed himself to the door.

CHAPTER THIRTY-FIVE

As JEFF got in the car to drive away, the Holy Spirit convicted him. *I am a thief also.* He remembered his selfish goal of trying to take his mother's money, and then stealing some from her before his fateful accident.

Jeff called Kate as he hurried out of the parking lot. "He didn't take it too well," he said.

"What do you mean? What did you say to him?" Kate asked, having never known what Jeff's intentions were in the first place. Jeff retold the events that took place. "He's been embezzling money? How did you know that?"

Jeff had told Kate off and on what he had seen in Hell ever since they came home from the hospital. He didn't like talking about it too much because it was so unpleasant. He had yet to tell her about Jesus' revelation of Bill's wrongdoing.

"I'm surprised at you for confronting him," Kate said. "Apparently it is true; otherwise he wouldn't have gotten so mad."

"He admitted to it," Jeff said. "There's no denying it. I don't want to cause any more problems in the church, but if he doesn't confess then something more will have to be done."

"Yes, something definitely needs to be done about it," she replied with a sigh.

"Kate," Jeff said with a change of tone. "I've been through a lot today. I got fired from my job, and I rebuked my pastor. But there is one more thing I must do."

Kate didn't know where Jeff was going with this. "What is it?"

He sighed. "I broke the law. I did that awful thing to my mother, and nothing has been done about it. I'm going to the police right now to turn myself in."

"Are you crazy!" Kate screamed. "You can't go to jail! What about me? I need you here with me! Don't do this!" Her voice quivered, and he knew that soon a crocodile tear would poke out from her right eye as it always had when she got upset.

"Please don't do this," Jeff said calmly. "I know it's a crazy thing to do, but I'm a new man. Jesus has changed me, and I know that if I have done something wrong, I need to confess and make amends."

"Jeff, please don't!" Kate screamed again as she cried.

"I have to do this. I'm going there now. I'll call and let you know what happens."

"I can't believe you!" Kate yelled as she slammed the phone down on the receiver. Her lack of understanding frustrated Jeff, but he knew he had to do the right thing. He felt God leading him to do what was right regardless of the absurdity. *Is it the right thing to do at a time like this?*

Jeff drove downtown to the Grogan City Police Department. He hid his cell phone, watch, and wallet in the glove compartment and then locked the door, not knowing when he would return. He then walked inside and was greeted by a tinted security window.

"Can I help you," said an impatient woman's voice from behind the glass.

Jeff fumbled for words. "Yes, uh, I'm here to turn myself in."

"Excuse me?" asked the woman.

"I committed a crime and I'm here to turn myself in."

"Um, just a minute. I'll send someone out to talk to you."

Jeff waited in the lobby. *This is just awkward. I wonder how many people actually come here to turn themselves in.* He sat down and looked at the nearby bulletin board full of mug shots. *At least my face isn't up there yet.*

A door across the hallway opened a few minutes later, and Officer Tom Baker approached Jeff. "You wanted to report something?" he asked.

"Yes, sir. I'm here to turn myself in for a crime," said Jeff, still fumbling to get his words out.

Tom hesitated and then said "Okay, please come with me."

Jeff got up and walked through the door the officer held open for him. He stopped as he waited for the officer to lock the door behind him. They then entered a room labeled "Interrogation" where Tom offered him a seat.

"So, what are you turning yourself in for?" asked Tom.

"A few days ago, I got frustrated with my mother. I forced her to take too much medication, and she was sent to the hospital because of it. Afterwards, I stole five-hundred dollars. Also," he sighed, "I lied to you about my mother's money. I did plan on keeping it and spending it on myself."

Tom squinted his eyes as he studied Jeff's face. "I recognize you now…but I thought you were dead!"

"You could say that," Jeff said. *Dead in my sins.* "I was in pretty bad shape."

"But I responded to the scene of the accident. I pulled your tattered body out of the car! How come you are alive?"

Tom was genuinely shocked at seeing the dead man walking. Jeff went on to explain his out of body experience, meeting Jesus, visiting Hell, and then being miraculously healed by his savior in the hospital. "And today, I lost my job because my boss thought I was dead, or would at least be spending a long time in the hospital. But I am fully recovered, and I'm here to confess what I did to my mother. It was the wrong thing to do, and I should be punished."

"I was called to the scene when the paramedics came to help your mother at her home. They thought it looked suspicious, and I did too," Tom paused. "But it's over now. You've been through a lot it sounds like and your mother is back home. Jail is the last thing you need."

"I have a guilty conscious and need to get this taken care of. Will you please help me, officer?"

"I'll have to call the county attorney. Are you sure you want me to do this?"

"Yes, please."

"Okay," he sighed. "I'll be back in a few minutes." Tom left the room to call the attorney. Jeff waited behind in the interrogation room. The room was quite a boring place. There were no posters or anything to keep his interest…just a tan, windowless concrete wall. Jeff started to wonder if this was the right thing to do after all. *What will jail be like?* Butterflies fluttered about in his stomach.

Thirty minutes later, Tom returned to the room. "I'm sorry it took so long. The attorney was unsure about this, so he called the judge. We had a three-way call and the judge decided that because of the high population in our jail right now, there just isn't any room for you. He said he respects your honesty, and he understands you have some guilt you want to take care of. For that reason, he assigned you one-hundred hours of community service."

Having had to wait for so long, pondering what jail would be like and then second guessing himself, Jeff was relieved he didn't have to be put in jail but would still get to pay for his crime. "I think I would like that better than being stuck behind bars," Jeff said reluctantly. "What kind of service work will I be doing?"

"Most of our service inmates have been picking up trash along the roadside so the highway department can mow. It's getting late in the season, but I'm sure you can still get your hours in just by picking up trash. You will start at eight o'clock tomorrow morning." Tom stuck his hand out to Jeff. "Sir, I admire your honesty. I know you have been through a lot lately with your mother, and we all get stressed out at times, but you made the right decision to confess. I wish more people had your integrity. It would sure make my job a lot easier."

"Thank you, sir," Jeff said as he shook the officer's hand. "My mother taught me to take responsibility for everything I do."

"Speaking of which, have you figured out what you are going to do with her yet?"

"I think we found someone to help her," Jeff said.

"Okay, call us if you need our help or the social worker's help."

"Will do," Jeff said as he smiled at the officer and walked out a free man.

CHAPTER THIRTY-SIX

"I ALMOST lost you once! I don't want to lose you again!" Kate yelled. "What if they had kept you for a long time? What would I do without you?"

"I know you're mad at me for turning myself in, but this is who I am now. I'm a changed man, and I have to take responsibility," Jeff said calmly to Kate as she sat crying on the couch. During the drive home, he had tried to plan for the conversation, but this time he couldn't anticipate how she would react.

Jeff sat down next to her and sighed. "You're right, honey. I should have come home and talked this over with you first. I thought I was doing the right thing, but looking back, I should have at least come home to say goodbye. Will you forgive me?"

Kate sniffed and wiped away the tears of betrayal. "Yes, I do." She leaned onto his shoulder as Jeff hugged her side. "You are definitely a changed person ever since this accident. Even though you lost your job, we probably lost the church, and now you have to do community service, you still have your integrity. I'll never understand how that brain of yours works."

Jeff chuckled. "You don't have to understand it. When Jesus takes hold of you, nothing else matters because you know the Creator of the universe is in charge. He holds the future in His hands, and He has good things in store for those who love Him. As long as He is on my side, I've got nothing to worry about."

Kate smiled, and they sat silently on the couch for several minutes. "Oh, yeah," Jeff said. "On the way home, Jordyn called and asked about going to meet Mom this afternoon. I asked her to come over after class."

"I hope it works out," Kate said. "I went over there this morning after you called me, and she was just as bad as before. She was talking to her ceiling folks and confused as always."

"Alzheimer's disease is very complex, but you have to remember that her brain is being overtaken by plaque and that is making her decline so much. She is still the same, wonderful woman deep down, and we can't forget what she has done for us. Remember how she made all that food at our wedding?"

"Yes, it was wonderful," Kate said. "She took the place of my mother since mine died long ago. It's just so sad to see people decline. So when do you start community service?"

"Eight o'clock tomorrow morning. I have to meet at the police station, and they will take a bus load of inmates to a section of highway. I can only work eight hours each day, so it will take a few weeks to get my time completed."

"I'm very proud of you for doing this."

"It has helped me with my guilt, but still, I wish Mom would forgive me. The problem is, though, she has no memory of what I did to her and wouldn't even know why I wanted her forgiveness. Not to mention she doesn't even know who I am."

"I'm sure she forgives you, Jeff. You're her son."

"I know, but it's this thing I developed when I was a child. Whenever I upset her, she would give me the cold shoulder. I had so much guilt from that, and I would follow her around the house all day asking her to forgive me. But she would always reply, 'Not until you say you are sorry.'" Jeff

271

paused. "I was such a stubborn child, but the guilt would weigh me down so long that finally I forced myself to apologize and immediately she would say, 'I forgive you.' And just like that, all of my guilt would be gone, and we would be back to normal. Mom taught me so much about humility." Jeff began to cry as he reminisced about his mother while also acknowledging that she was living on borrowed time. "I hate to see her decline. It really hurts. She was such a good woman; she doesn't deserve to suffer like this."

Kate positioned herself in front of Jeff so he was forced to look into her eyes. "You know why she suffers. It's from nothing she did. Just like what Jesus showed you, it is part of the curse of Adam."

Jeff recalled his time with Jesus in the Garden of Eden. "I know. The effects of Adam's sin have spread throughout all creation. We all suffer and die because of sin. This is what must happen, but it doesn't mean I have to like it."

"No one likes suffering and death, but think of the glory that awaits us on the other side."

Jeff smiled. "There will be nothing like it. That's the hope I hold onto. I know when my mom is called away from here, she will be healthy again, and she won't have to suffer anymore."

Jeff dried his eyes and stood up. He never liked for anyone to see him cry, but after all he had been through, he just had to let it go, and it was a huge relief. "Jordyn should be here in a few minutes. I guess I should look online for a job. I have to put food on the table somehow."

Jeff had paid for his Internet service prior to losing his job, so he had a month left before it would get disconnected. He busied himself looking through different employment websites. He found a few unskilled labor jobs, some part-time positions at restaurants, and only one teaching position, but it was for mathematics. Jeff filled out applications for some of the labor jobs.

Jordyn arrived at the house while Jeff worked at his computer. "Hi, Kate! Hi Jeff! How's your day going?" she asked in a cheerful tone.

"Oh, I've had better," Jeff said dryly. "I'm applying for jobs right now."

Jordyn came over to the computer to see what he was doing. "What are you talking about?"

"I got fired today," he replied casually, trying to add some humor to his financial worries.

"You did? Why?" she exclaimed. Jeff told her about the unpleasant encounter he had with his boss.

"That is wrong in so many ways!" Jordyn said angrily. Jeff had not seen her angry side ever since he insulted her in class. "I'm calling my dad to report this. Dr. Farris cannot get away with it."

"I'm not going to stop you," Jeff said with a laugh. "Something needs to be done to him. He has become enslaved to his own power."

Jordyn sat down on the couch, took out her cell phone, and called her father. Jeff was surprised she was calling him right then. "You're calling him now?" he asked. "We need to go see my mother."

"It will just take a minute," Jordyn said as she listened for her father to answer the phone.

Jeff listened in on the conversation, and although he could only hear Jordyn's voice, he could follow the dialogue based on her statements and responses. Jordyn told her father about Jeff's situation and how Robert had fired and demoted countless employees in the past just because they taught about alternatives to the theories on life's origins. The phone call did not last long, and from the way it sounded, Jeff felt as if something would be done about it very soon.

"I think Dr. Farris will get in trouble for it this time," Jordyn said. "Dad said he has violated employee discrimination laws and that is a federal offense."

"What do you think will happen?" Jeff asked, happy to hear something good might come of this.

"He will be investigated by the Department of Education. It's closing time at my dad's office, but he said he will begin the paperwork first thing Tuesday morning and then an investigator will be sent to the university."

"But he's been investigated before and got away with it. Why do you think something will happen now?"

"If a professor is investigated multiple times, it looks really bad on his records, regardless of the findings. Just because they don't find the evidence doesn't mean they don't think he is guilty. They will also want to interview you and past faculty members."

"I will happily let them interview me," Jeff said. "Are you ready to go meet my mother?"

"Sure," she replied. The three got into the car and drove over to Evelyn's house. While in route, Jeff informed Jordyn about Evelyn's symptoms and her "attic people."

"I hope you can do something to help her," Jeff said. "She's got a very progressive form of Alzheimer's disease."

"I have a knack for the elderly, Jeff. Let's just see what happens."

When they arrived, Jordyn got out of the car first. "You all stay here. I have an idea."

Jeff turned to Kate and then back to Jordyn. "Go ahead. We are open to anything at this point."

Jordyn went to Evelyn's door and knocked. Shortly after, Evelyn came to the door with her friendly smile. "Hello, Ms. Duncan. I understand you have people in your attic. I've come to talk to them about leaving. May I come in?"

Evelyn looked more fragile than ever before. Jeff had not seen his mother since the day of the accident. "Yes, please come in. They are making such a racket today." Evelyn opened the door and Jordyn entered. Jeff and Kate were shocked at Jordyn's quick ability to reason on Evelyn's level. They both got out of the car and stood to the side of the front door to listen in on the conversation while being careful to make sure Evelyn didn't see them.

Jordyn asked Evelyn, "Where is your attic door? I need to go up there and talk to them."

"It's down the hallway."

Jordyn walked a few feet down the hall, pulled the attic door string down, and extended the attic ladder. She carefully climbed up the old steps and entered the attic. Jordyn walked around on the ceiling joists back toward the living room where Evelyn had poked the holes in the sheet rock. She purposely made a racket as she crawled across the boards.

When she got close to the holes, Jordyn yelled, "You people are trespassing. You are not supposed to be here. This is Evelyn's house and she wants you to leave now!" Jordyn had always been soft spoken, but she even surprised herself with how loud her voice had gotten.

After a few moments of her charade, Jordyn crawled back across the boards and exited the attic. Evelyn waited at the foot of the ladder for her. "Well, what happened?" She asked.

"They are gone," Jordyn replied, knowing that people could never survive in that hot attic to begin with.

"Oh, thank you!" Evelyn exclaimed, clapping her hands together.

Outside, Jeff looked at his wife and whispered, "That was ingenious! Why didn't we ever think of that? We didn't even bother to look in her attic. That's probably all she wanted anyway."

Kate whispered back, "I think we have found the right person for the job."

Jeff agreed. They put their ears against the window to continue listening.

"I would love to visit with you again," Jordyn said in a sweet voice. "You are such a nice lady, and I'd like to get to know you."

"Well, hardly anyone comes to see me. You are welcome to come by anytime!" Evelyn said. Jeff could tell from Evelyn's voice that she was being authentic and truly appreciative of Jordyn's kindness.

"May I come over tomorrow?" Jordyn asked.

"Of course you can! I'm always here," Evelyn replied cheerfully.

"Okay, I will see you tomorrow!" Jordyn replied as they embraced. Evelyn closed her eyes as tears of joy streamed down her tired face.

"You are so nice. Thank you," Evelyn said as she wiped the tears away.

Jeff and Kate hurried back to the car as Jordyn came out the front door. "You are amazing," Jeff said to Jordyn as she hopped in the back seat. "You really do have a knack for the elderly."

"I just try to treat them like human beings created in the image of God," Jordyn replied. "Just because they are older or don't function like they used to doesn't mean they still don't have basic human needs. She's just lonely. Jeff, I would love to work for her. You don't have to pay me until you can get a job, okay?"

Both surprised and elated, Jeff asked, "Are you sure? She can be a handful."

"Yes, I'm sure. I trust that when you get a job you will pay me a fair wage," Jordyn replied. She was so young, but her maturity exceeded that of most adults. "I anticipate that she might hear the attic people talking again. If so, I'll just climb back up there and tell 'them' to leave. That seems to work for now."

Arriving home after the busy day, Jeff requested that they postpone their creation discussion because he had to wake up early on Tuesday to begin his community service

CHAPTER THIRTY-SEVEN

JEFF ARRIVED at the police station a few minutes before eight o'clock to find Tom in the lobby. "I'm glad to see you are following through. Of course, if you didn't, then I'd have to come take you to jail."

"I think I'd rather pick up trash than the alternative. I could use some fresh air anyway," Jeff said.

An old school bus soon rolled up in the parking lot. "There's your ride, Mr. Duncan," Tom said. Jeff went outside and boarded, but he immediately felt out of place. The bus had about thirty seats, and each seat had one or two orange-clad inmates. Their expressions were hopeless; he saw no joy in their faces. He found a seat in the middle of the bus and sat next to one of the men but was too intimidated to make conversation. This was the first time Jeff had ever been around a criminal. He now second guessed his decision on whether or not he should have ever turned himself in at all.

The bus pulled out of the parking lot and drove for twenty minutes. Jeff looked out the window but was careful not to make eye contact with anyone for fear of their getting angry at him. *Stop stereotyping, Jeff. They are human beings made in the image of God.* Not much conversation took place in the bus as the inmates awaited arrival to their destination.

Jeff was familiar with all of the roads they travelled on—he had lived here his entire life. The bus turned North onto Route 401. The beauty of the Appalachians to the east and the rolling foothills to the west calmed his anxiety. He then realized that they were on the road on which he had had his wreck. *God is up to something today.*

The bus pulled over to the shoulder, and without being told, all of the inmates stood up and marched outside. One of them went to the side of the bus and opened a storage compartment. He returned with a box full of black garbage bags, and then walked to each of the inmates and gave them a few bags each. The men grabbed the bags, opened one up, and stuffed the others in their back pockets. Jeff followed suit.

"You must be new here," a man said to him.

Jeff turned to his right and saw a tall, middle-aged man wearing a mop of curly gray hair and a grizzled beard."

"Uh, yes. It's my first day."

"The name is Henry—Henry Jennings. The guys here call me Doc." He stuck his hand out.

"I'm Jeff," he replied, offering a friendly smile while shaking his hand.

"Nice to meet you. How many days did you get?"

"One-hundred hours. How about you?"

"Thirty days of jail with community service. Well, twenty eight days now. I served two already," Henry replied.

"That's...a long time," he replied, not knowing exactly how to respond.

"That's nothing," Henry replied while nodding his head toward a group of men standing near the bus. "That tall one there—he's been doing this for about a year. The one next to him is just under ten months now. They go to jail at night and work these streets during the day."

"What did they do?"

Henry paused. "Most of the guys don't like to talk about their crime. They will tell you they are innocent or blame a lawyer for their problems. Me, I'm different. I want people to know why I'm here."

The bus driver ordered everyone to start working. Without hesitation, the men paired off, and half of them crossed the highway. The bus driver gave Jeff a reflective vest since he was not wearing the trademark orange jumpsuit. Jeff put it on, and then he and Henry walked along the right hand side of the road. They continued their conversation as they picked up pieces of paper, empty cans, bottles, and everything else people had carelessly discarded along the road.

"Well, if you don't mind me asking, why are you here?" Jeff inquired, hoping to not offend his new acquaintance.

"I'm here because I'm a thief," Henry said as he reached over to pick up a broken bottle. "I stole from a grocery store not far from here. My family was hungry and I was unemployed, so I had to do something. Of course, this is neither my first nor second offense. You'd think I learn my lesson by now, but my family has to eat."

Jeff waited for Henry to continue talking, but he didn't. "Why do you want people to know why you are here? You just stole food for your family. Why is that so significant?"

"I want people to know that I used to have a high paying job at a university over in Titusville. I have a doctorate in chemistry and a master's degree in physics. I was working on my doctorate of physics until I got fired."

Jeff was surprised to see someone else of high education on trash patrol with him. "So that's why they call you 'doc.' Can I ask why you were fired?"

Henry grunted as he reached down for another bottle. "I was fired because McGregor University over in Titusville did not allow for academic freedom. I taught at that school for four years. I was a great professor and all of my students passed. I never had one complaint from them. But one day out of the blue, one of the other professors, who I thought was a friend, came up to me and asked about my opinion on evolution.

"It turns out that this so-called 'friend' had a hidden agenda. I told him I thought there were a lot of gaps in the evolution theory; that evolution in and of itself was a collection of non-falsifiable 'just-so' stories. Although I do reject evolution, I never outright told him that. I see more evidence of there being an intelligent designer. When you look at things at the microscopic level and see the complex arrangements of molecules, especially in DNA, you have to be intellectually honest with yourself and conclude that this could not have happened through unguided evolutionary processes.

"Anyway," Henry continued, "My friend reported this to the dean. One thing led to another and I was terminated. They told me the school had to cut back on their budget and lay people off, but I know they were lying because they hired someone else in my place a week after I left.

"I was discriminated against because I challenged their dogma. I disagreed with the mainstream, but apparently that wasn't allowed. After I got fired, I had trouble finding a new job—no one over in Titusville was hiring. My family—I have two teenagers and a wife—was struggling also. We had already depleted our savings and used up our vouchers at the local food bank. A couple weeks ago, I drove over here to Grayson where no one would recognize me. I went into Barnett's Grocery and stole some food so my family could eat. Yeah, it was wrong, but I had no other choice.

"I miss my family," Henry said. "I hope I can get out of here soon and go see them. They haven't had any gas money to come visit me."

Henry had a loud voice and he spoke with confidence, but when talking about his family, Jeff could hear his tone sadden. "That is terrible. It sounds like you really got cheated."

"You can say that again," Henry replied.

Jeff told Henry about his similar experience which brightened Henry's day. He was happy to meet someone else in the same predicament.

"You and I can do something about this, you know," Henry suggested. "Here are two doctoral level scientists picking up trash. How many more like us are out there?"

"You're right. There are bound to be thousands of others just like us across the nation."

"When we get out of here, let's get this taken care of," Henry said. "If they can't discriminate on race or creed, then they definitely can't discriminate on a person's worldview."

The two men carried on a long conversation throughout the rest of the day, and the eight hour shift flew by. They picked up trash for several miles and ended at the intersection where Jeff had his wreck. He could not remember anything about the accident except that, prior to the wreck, he was being chased by the police. After that, everything was a blur. Jeff pointed to some skid marks on the highway and a large section of scorched pavement. Highway crews had already replaced the torn down utility poles and street signs.

"That's where I nearly died," Jeff said to Henry.

"What are you talking about?"

"I was in a serious car accident a few days ago right over there, but Jesus saved me from death. I owe everything to Him."

The bus pulled up behind them. Men on the other side of the road crossed over and climbed on board, happy to have their shift come to an end. Jeff and Henry put their filled trash bags on the side of the road where a truck would later come by to pick them up. They boarded the bus, tired, sweaty, and dirty.

"I don't know much about Jesus," Henry said after they collapsed in the seat. "I was never raised in church, and the church people I met never impressed me. But you...you're different. I wouldn't mind hearing more about this Jesus."

"Jesus is wonderful. Because of His ultimate sacrifice, I've been forgiven and guaranteed a home in Heaven when my time on earth is done," Jeff said, smiling.

"I've heard people talking about that, but I never really understood it," Henry commented.

Knowing they had established a good rapport with each other, Jeff asked point-blank, "If you were to die right now, do you think you would go to Heaven or to Hell?"

"Heaven, I guess. I've lived a good life."

"You may have lived a good life by man's standards, but let's see how well you do compared to God's standards."

"What do you mean?" Henry asked.

"Let me ask you some questions. Have you ever told a lie?"

"Sure, I've told quite a few lies in my life, especially when I was a kid," Henry laughed.

"What would you call a person who told lies?"

"I'd call him a liar."

"That's right," Jeff replied. "Have you ever lusted after another woman?"

"Well, I've seen quite a few attractive women back at the college. I guess you could say I lusted after a few of them, but I've never cheated on my wife."

"Jesus tells us that if we even look at another woman lustfully then we have committed adultery in our hearts."

"Guilty as charged," Henry replied with a chuckle.

"And no offense meant, but you already admitted to stealing. Our crimes of theft brought us together today."

"I stole many times just to feed my family."

"Regardless of the reason, what would you call a person who steals?"

"A thief," Henry replied, now casting his eyes down. "I'm a lying, adulterous thief."

"I am too, Henry," Jeff said. "I've committed all of those sins myself."

Henry turned to Jeff and looked astonished. "But, I thought you were a Christian?"

"I am. Christians sin, but we are forgiven, and the Holy Spirit convicts us of our sin so we know when we have gone astray."

"Hmmm. I always thought Christians were self-righteous and perfect."

Jeff chuckled. "Not perfect—just forgiven. And you, too, can be forgiven. See, God tells us that if we break just one of his commandments, we are in violation of all his commandments."

"I don't know of anyone who hasn't told a lie," Henry said.

"You're right. Everyone has sinned against God. And just as there is a penalty for committing a crime of theft, there is also a penalty we have to pay for breaking the laws of our infinitely holy Creator."

"If God is perfect, who could ever pay the penalty for a sin against Him?" Henry asked, showing more interest.

"Well, no created human could ever pay the penalty for sin," Jeff replied. "Long ago, when the world was only six days old, God created the first two human beings—Adam and Eve. They were created with the ability to obey God or disobey Him. Adam chose to disobey God, and because of that, he and the entire creation were brought under the curse of sin. Just like we inherit different traits from our parents, we also inherited the sinful nature from our first father, Adam. We are all descendants of Adam and Eve. The entire earth was put under a curse. But God loves the world and His creation. He knew that since humans have fallen, they would never be able to fully pay the debt owed for sin.

"During ancient Bible times, animals had to be sacrificed to atone for sins. Families couldn't sacrifice just any animal—it had to be spotless and without blemish. Death and blood shed were required to atone for the sins committed by people. This practice went on for thousands of years, but it was never fully sufficient because people had to continually sacrifice animals at different times of the year to make atonement.

"When Jesus was born," Jeff continued, "He was both fully God and fully human. Jesus never sinned—He was perfect. In fact, since He is God, it is impossible for Him to ever sin. Just like the spotless animals, Jesus was without blemish. He would be the sufficient, perfect sacrifice needed to atone for the sins of all mankind. Jesus willingly chose to be that sacrifice that would end all animal sacrifices and sufficiently atone for our sins, even still today. God loves us so much that He sent His son, the perfect sacrifice, to pay the penalty for our sins. Only Jesus could fulfill that debt and redeem us."

The bus came to a stop in front of the police station. "You gave me a lot to think about, Jeff," Henry said. "Can we talk about this more tomorrow?"

"I'd love to," Jeff replied as he shook Henry's hand and exited the bus. He knew they would have a long lasting friendship, and he looked forward to seeing him again tomorrow. The bus drove away, and Kate pulled into the parking lot as Jeff walked over to his car. He met her as she got out and handed him a bag from his favorite fast food restaurant.

"You are a delight," Jeff said to Kate as he approached her and tried to greet her with a kiss.

"Not so fast," she said as she leaned away from his pursed lips. "You smell terrible and there is not one inch of dry clothing on you. You get home and take a shower, and then I have some surprising news that will definitely make your day."

Jeff laughed at Kate's comment about his poor hygiene. "C'mon, give me a kiss."

"No, you are nasty," Kate said with a look of disgust, but Jeff knew she was teasing him. "Here, I brought you some supper. It's your favorite."

Jeff grabbed the bag and found a cheeseburger. With his dirty hands, he opened up the wrapping and took a huge bite. The small lunch he had earlier in the afternoon wasn't enough to equal the calories he had burned off. He gobbled up the burger and downed his drink.

"That was wonderful," he said as he finished.

"Follow me home. You won't believe the news," Kate said as she got into her car and drove away. Jeff hurried to start his car and get home. He was ready for a hot shower, and even more, he wanted to hear some good news for a change.

When Kate got home, she went inside and started Jeff's shower so the water would be warm. He jumped in the shower, eager to get the filth off his body. The hot water flowed through his greasy hair, washing away the sweat, dirt, and grime. *Just like Jesus' blood washing away our sins.* Once out of the shower, he put on a fresh set of clothes Kate had brought him. Quickly, he dressed and exited the bathroom, still drying off his hair as he went into the living room.

Jeff came up from behind Kate and grabbed her waist. He gave her a long kiss on the cheek. "There, that's much better." They both laughed. "Now, what is this big news?"

"While you were out today, the church called here asking for you. You know the deacon, Donald Stiller, right?"

Jeff nodded. He had not talked to the man much, but he had seen him at church.

"Donald told us Pastor Bill called an emergency meeting of the elders and deacons last night, and he announced his resignation. Bill confessed he had been stealing funds from the church, and the only way to come clean was to tell the truth and resign from his position."

"I don't know if that is good news or not, Kate," Jeff replied. "I'm glad he was honest, but did he have to go to the extreme of actually resigning?"

"Let me finish," Kate replied. "Bill told the elders that the only reason he wanted the church to grow was so he could get more money for himself. Bill admitted to being an 'ear-tickler' instead of telling people the truth. You must have had a big impact on this man."

"It's the Holy Spirit that convicts people—I just do what God tells me to do," Jeff said humbly.

"Well, I still haven't told you the best part of all," Kate continued. "Bill requested that you specifically give your testimony about Hell this Sunday in church, and in the coming weeks, he requested that you teach the church the truth about Genesis."

His heart stopped for a full second. "What?!" *You have a mission.*

"Donald said Bill was convicted by what you had told him regarding the foundation of Genesis and what would happen to him in Hell if he didn't repent. He realized he had destroyed the foundation of the gospel, and you were the best man available to start rebuilding it."

"Sunday? He wants me to do it this Sunday!" Jeff said, his eyes wide open and heart pounding through his chest.

"Yes. Sunday. Ten o'clock," Kate said. "And then continue indefinitely in the coming weeks. Oh yeah, they are also going to put you on the payroll!"

Jeff fell to the couch as he tried to collect his thoughts. Overcome with both joy and shock, he said, "I was so worried how I was going to pay the bills, but God had something in store for me all along." *You have a mission.* "So you're telling me that in just a few days, I'm going to start teaching at church and earning an income for us again?" Kate nodded. "Our Creator is so awesome!"

After Jeff calmed down, Kate asked, "After you give your testimony, do you have a title picked out for your sermon series?"

Jeff thought back to the last sermon title Pastor Bill shown upon the screen at church, and the perfect heading came to him. "How about this: Creation or Evolution: It really *does* matter!"

EPILOGUE

JEFF GAVE his testimony about his experience in Hell that Sunday morning to a packed house. Many were shocked to hear such authenticity from Jeff, who had beforehand been quiet and reserved. In the following weeks, he continued to learn from Jordyn about creation and how to logically defend the Bible. He also spent many hours each day studying the Bible. Jeff preached on topics from Genesis each Sunday at the church, and although many held onto every word he said, some, especially those dubbed as the "spiritually elite," decided to leave because they no longer heard the ear-tickling, feel-good sermons. Those that remained, though, heard the true gospel each week as Jeff tied the teachings from Genesis to the Cross. He also gave subsequent sermons about the reality of Hell, which was something that hardly anyone in the church had ever heard about before. Even Bill and his father Larry attended the sermons, and both repented of their erroneous teachings. Having heard of his miraculous recovery in the hospital, Linda, the doubting nurse, started coming to The Experience, where she eventually began a new life in Christ.

The Holy Spirit worked through him to lead others to Christ, and a true revival spread at The Experience like never before. Jeff continued with the food pantry and community involvement at the church, but he also fed the gospel to the needy instead of just filling their stomachs. The construction of the new, hi-tech building was put on hold as Jeff and others on the leadership team at the church reorganized the project to make it a more affordable educational complex where apologetics would be taught. Never again would people come to that church and not know how to defend their beliefs.

Jordyn continued to stay with Evelyn at her home, and she had to make the occasional trip up into the attic to appease Evelyn's hallucinations. Jeff was able to pay her a decent wage after he started preaching at The Experience. Evelyn's mind and body rapidly deteriorated, and both Jeff and Kate, along with some trusted church members, spent a lot of time trying to help her enjoy her last days on earth before she entered into glory. She had declined so much that she spent most of her time sleeping. She lost her ability to talk and swallow, resulting in her losing weight and having a decreased appetite. Despite Jeff's feeling fully forgiven by his Lord, he still yearned to hear those three magical words from his mother. Until then, he could not feel fully forgiven.

Jeff fulfilled his one-hundred hours of community service, and during that time he had many discussions with Henry about Jesus. Their friendship grew strong, and although Jeff's time was served, he still went back to the jail to visit Henry. Jeff also saved up money and sent it to Henry's family so they could purchase groceries and afford gas to come visit their devoted father and husband while he served his time. Through Jeff's kindness, Henry and his entire family came to know Jesus as their personal Lord and Savior.

An intense investigation at Grogan University resulted in the termination of Robert Farris. Due to the nature of the gross discriminatory acts he had committed over the years, Robert was arrested. After the arrest, Dr. Rhonda Matheson, the one colleague at the university who Jeff had a trusted relationship with, called Jeff to inform him that she was promoted to Dean of the Science Department, and that his biology position would be available in the upcoming spring semester. Jeff applied for the job and was quickly rehired. Dr.

Matheson allowed for both sides of the origins issue to be taught without fear of discrimination, denial of tenure, demotion, or termination. Jeff talked to Dr. Matheson about hiring Henry. Although there was not a position open at the time, she was able to hire Henry as a part-time faculty member, and he started his career during the spring semester alongside Jeff. Henry and his family moved to Grayson so they could be closer to the college, and their families became close friends. Later, Jeff and Henry located many other professors who, just like them, had been discriminated against because of academic censorship. Through the help of Jordyn's father and local legislators, Jeff and the other "dissidents" were able to pass a bill allowing teachers to have true academic freedom and never again fear discrimination.

Although he had much dislike for Robert, Jeff knew his former boss was a lost soul and made in the image of God. He was housed in a federal prison several counties away, and Jeff felt God calling him to pay him a visit. It took several visits before Robert would open up and talk to Jeff because he harbored a lot of bitterness and guilt toward himself. Over time, Jeff was able to form a friendly relationship with Robert, and this allowed him the opportunity to present the gospel to the lost man. Being broken down and full of hurt, bitterness, and rejection, Robert gave his life over to Christ, and he has never been the same since.

*　*　*

On a cold January morning, Jeff delivered a sermon on Noah's Ark. He taught the church that it was not only an actual historical event, but also a theological lesson on how God does not tolerate sin. Jeff preached to the growing church that in the near future, God would come back and destroy the earth again by fire because of the pandemic sin in the world. Jeff never watered down the gospel or the message of eternal damnation, and this resulted in continuous church growth not only numerically, but also spiritually. Many had come to know Jesus for the first time, while twice as many came to rededicate their lives.

After that sermon, Jeff felt exhausted. His life had become so busy that he felt like he deserved his Sunday afternoon nap as opposed to the past when he took his nap just because he was bored. Jeff curled up on the couch with his beloved Samson perched up on the cushion above him. He quickly entered into a deep sleep and began to dream.

Jeff found himself walking in the same field as before where the tree had fallen and the weeds had strangled the roots. Parts of the ground were still missing, and the fire deep in the earth raged on. He had to watch his step so as to not fall into the holes. He approached the tree and a tear formed in his eyes as he put his hand on the exposed roots broken near the trunk. *Why did it have to fall?* Jeff looked toward the end of the tree where the once magnificent branches full of leaves now withered away into a pitiful decay.

A strong wind suddenly blew from all four compass points. The force of the wind knocked him off balance, but he was able to keep standing as he held onto the crumbling tree. The ground started to shake. He looked up at the tree branches, and they, along with the rest of the tree, began to rise up into the air. The mighty tree elevated several feet until it was fully upright. Jeff stood in awe of the spectacle before him. The tree slowly hovered back to the place where it had originally grown, and then lowered down into the ground, firmly planting its roots back into the rich soil.

More shaking occurred below him. He looked down and saw long, sinuous roots growing from the base of the tree and extending far out into the field around him. He could not see it, but he knew the roots were growing far into the earth also, forming a strong foundation for the mighty tree. He looked up at the tree and saw the dead leaves falling off the branches and landing on the ground near his feet. Out of the bare branches burst forth vibrant, green leaves with a healthy glow. The colossal tree thrived once again. The wind stopped blowing as a light in the distance distracted Jeff from the tree.

He looked to his left and saw Jesus walking through the field toward him.

Jesus approached Jeff and stood next to him as they both admired the tall, healthy tree. Jesus raised his hands and spread them out across the field. A fire came from the horizon, spreading over the ground and destroying all the weeds both far away and around the base of the tree. The impact of the destruction restored the ground, filling in all the holes. A northern wind came and blew away the fire, and out of the ashes, right before Jeff's eyes, small blades of bright green grass started to grow.

"I gave you a mission and you have obeyed me, my son," Jesus said as He put His arm on Jeff's shoulder, similar to how a proud father would give affirmation to his son. "I am well pleased, my good and faithful servant. You have restored the foundations of My Word. The many lost people at The Experience are now coming to repentance, and the angels rejoice."

"Thank you, my Lord," Jeff replied humbly, not really sure how to speak to the King of Kings.

Jeff then heard singing. It was not just one or two voices, but a choir of several hundred thousand voices creating the most beautiful sound he had ever heard. All around, a countless multitude of angels hovered in the sky as they sang praises to Jesus. Jeff could not keep himself from crying as the incredible music penetrated his soul.

"These angels rejoice when people are added to my kingdom. Jeff, they are here to help you. There is still more work to be done. There will be times when you don't know what to do or you will feel lost. When the thunder roars and lightning strikes, remember you have me and all of these angels on your side. They are fighting spiritual battles every day to protect you. Attacks will come, but just remember this angelic army is always on guard for you."

Jeff fell to his knees as he was overcome with unending gratitude for his savior. "I'm not worthy of this," Jeff said, as he continued to bow before his King.

"You are worthy because you are mine," Jesus replied, and He reached out and lifted Jeff up to his feet.

Jeff wiped away his tears. Jesus said, "I have someone I want you to see."

Jeff looked up at Jesus, and just a few feet behind him he saw his beloved mother, Evelyn, approaching, but she appeared much different. She was younger, and her hair was thick and black as it had been when she was in her prime. There was no trace of wrinkles on her face or body, and overall she looked healthier than ever before.

"Mom?" Jeff said through a quivering voice.

"It's me, son," Evelyn said as she stretched out her arms to hug him. Jeff walked toward her and they embraced. He had never felt so close to his mother as he did now, and he was happy to see her in such better condition. There was even a blue glow around her body.

"Mom, I am so sorry for what I did to you," Jeff said through painful sobs.

Evelyn continued to hug him in silence. She patted his back reassuringly like she did when he was a child in need of encouragement. "I have to go now, Jeffrey," Evelyn said as she eased up on the hug. "But first, I need to let you know one thing."

Jeff wasn't sure what she was talking about. "What is it, Mom?"

"I forgive you, Jeffrey," Evelyn said with her warm, affirming smile.

Jeff broke down again in tears. He had so longed to hear those words, and finally they came out. Jesus walked over to Evelyn and grabbed onto her hand.

Jesus said in a firm voice, "I know you will do well, Jeff. There is much to be done, so continue to fight the good fight. Tell them all that I am coming back very, very soon."

Then, Jesus and Evelyn turned their backs to Jeff and walked away from him on the fresh grass. As they walked, their bodies ascended into the sky. Far above, the sky split open, and a brilliant light shined through. Jeff watched as his

292

Lord and his mother entered into the glorious eternal kingdom above.

Jeff was awakened by his cell phone ringing. "Hello," he muttered, not fully awake yet or even aware that he had been asleep.

"Jeff, this is Jordyn. I have some bad news." He could hear the sadness in her voice.

"I already know," Jeff said. "I'll be there in a few minutes."

* * *

A large crowd filled The Experience on the day of Evelyn's funeral. God had allowed it to snow on that day, which was just right because Evelyn always liked to watch the snow fall. Old friends, many of whom knew Evelyn back in her younger days and had watched Jeff grow up, came to the podium and shared fond memories about her. The grief shared by many was often mixed with laughter as people recalled both the funny things she did and the numerous acts of kindness she had done throughout her life. The funeral was long, but no one was in a hurry to bring an end to this wonderful life.

Evelyn had long ago picked out a burial plot in an old cemetery next to a mountain stream. The snow had stopped falling as the funeral procession arrived at the final resting place. The stream, blanketed by fresh snow along the banks, could be heard running fast over the smooth rocks, offering a relaxing sound for those nearby. *Mom picked the best place to be buried.*

Henry offered the benediction at the burial as people huddled together to stay warm under the funeral home's canopy. Evelyn's body, riddled with age and the effects of Alzheimer's disease, lay in the ornate casket before them, but Jeff knew her glorified body was in Heaven with Jesus, and one day they would meet again.

The funeral was especially hard for Jeff. Losing his mother meant he had no other blood relatives. His dad had abandoned the family before he and Evelyn ever had another child, and Jeff had no knowledge of cousins or distant family. It left him with a unique loneliness, but still, he had Kate and many newly formed friends to keep him company.

At the end of the ceremony, Jordyn came up to Jeff and gave him a hug. "I'm sorry about your loss. She was truly a wonderful person."

"And you lost a dear friend too, Jordyn. I know Mom was very fond of you. She may not have been able to form the words, but I know she loved you like a daughter," Jeff said, wiping tears away from his reddened eyes.

"Thank you," Jordyn replied. "I'm really going to miss her."

"That reminds me," Jeff said. "Come to my car. There's something there I know she would have wanted you to have."

Curious, Jordyn followed Jeff to his car. He opened the trunk and reached inside for a paper grocery bag. He carefully picked it up with both hands, closed the trunk, and walked over to the side of the car where Jordyn waited.

"Here, this is for you," Jeff said as he gave her the bag.

Jordyn had a puzzled look on her face. She wasn't expecting anything today; she just wanted to pay her respects to Evelyn. Jordyn grabbed the heavy bag with both gloved hands. Before she opened it, Jeff said, "I know all too well how expensive college is. You have a bright future ahead of you; I want to see you succeed, and I know Mom would want to see that, too. I wish I could have paid you more for taking care of her, so maybe this will help."

Jeff went back toward the funeral tent, leaving Jordyn behind at the car. The bag had become too heavy for her, so she walked to the back of the car and sat it on top of the trunk. She looked inside, and before her sat two old and tattered Feagan Brand shoe boxes.

When Jeff arrived at the tent, he saw an elderly man standing there, sobbing as he caressed the smooth oak casket. Jeff didn't recognize the man as someone from the church or as one of Evelyn's friends. He wore a long, black overcoat with a matching hat. A disheveled beard covered his aged and wrinkled face, and thin gray hair poked out from below his hat. Jeff stood next to him, admiring the assortment of flowers that had been placed on and around his mother's casket.

"She was a good woman," Jeff said, trying to make light conversation. "But she is in a much better place now."

The man fumbled for a response. He stifled his tears as he remorsefully replied, "I know she was a good woman, son." He took a handkerchief out of his back pocket and wiped away his tears. "I was her husband."

"…Daddy?"

You have a new mission.

www.ingramcontent.com/pod-product-compliance
Lightning Source LLC
Chambersburg PA
CBHW060537180626
46817CB00002B/609